Chaotic Karma

For Christopher,
My six a.m. wake up call

Foresight

It was the sound of the sirens that I heard off in the distance that made me want to know what was causing so much havoc. The rain poured down on the streets. The wind was howling, and the leaves from the trees were rustling off in the distance. My arms shivered from the drops of rain. They seemed to pierce their way through to the bones. Although, It was a bit more refreshing than the constant tears that occupied them before. Hard incessant rain, caused goose bumps from the impact. Like tiny serrated knives. There was a loud yell around me, although I couldn't seem to detect from which direction it was coming from.

I was alarmed to hear the sound of my name in the short distance. I seemed to have caused the commotion, which was currently taking up everyone's time.

"Were losing her!"

"Let's just try and get her stabilized first then move her."

"No we need to get going or she won't make it."

"I'm going with her."

I heard this and tried desperately to remember who belonged to that voice.

"What is your relationship?"

"She's my wife."

Wife? Were they talking about me? What was going on? Why are they in the background talking? Who was my husband? I was exhausted from the thoughts pumping through my head at the moment. Maybe it was just the throbbing and pounding of my lingering headache. Either way it was too much for me to try and concentrate on.

I had shifted focus on just moving one part of my body. Finally, the eyes fluttered. They were met by the bright, blinding light from inside the ambulance glaring down at me. It made me squint under its stare. There was a clouded haze over my sight, now the voices were speaking quickly, yet now it seemed a bit further away.

Like a dream unfolding, right before me. I think I am having one of mine. I have no control over this one though. I lay here motionless as they shuffle me around. Sirens screaming in the distance and I could barely make out the red lights flashing. My arms strapped in with hard belts permanently preventing me from breaking free.

This wasn't the kind of red sky I saw so long ago. This was the wrong shade. This red and white were the wrong colors and they certainly weren't supposed to be mixed together. No, no, no, this was all wrong.

This had to be a bad dream. Eyes now closed again. My head was still pounding like a thousand drums out of unison. The medics were being a bit too intrusive by pricking me with all types of needles, and fluids. I just wanted to wake up from the nightmare I was currently having.

The voices started fading. They were going away. Were they finished with me? Were they giving up? Is this not actually a dream?

The dark started to immerse me; I thought back to when the first red sky entered my world. What was I thinking? I wanted to go back to where I first remembered it. That was when my possibilities were endless.

Red Sky

What's that old saying about the sunset all pretty and red? "Red sky at night, a sailor's delight, red sky in the morning, a sailor's warning." Well here it is dawn, and it is a vibrating yellow, with just a hint of red following in behind. There doesn't seem to be anything warning me about that one. I took a moment to absorb the landscape around just to make sure.

Although in reality, the landscape consisted of a road in front of me. A carbon copy that made its way to a dead end, right in front of my parents' driveway. The houses that fell in line down the block, being the cookie cutter suburbia that they were, didn't look too hateful with the rays of the sun gleaming down on them. The road was completely absent from traffic for now.

This was one of three plats that were somewhat of a new development, and ours was named Treetop Terrace. It was aptly named because every street in this typical suburbia compound was named after trees. Our street happened to be named, 'Royal Oak,' although, there was nothing royal about where we lived.

A loud sigh escaped as I watched the non-traffic happen. I knew it would pick up at some point though, as people would be getting ready for work. I contemplated the humiliation of all the prying eyes as they drove by, while I was sitting outside at the edge of the driveway. Hopefully none of the kids I graduated with would see me. I wouldn't have been able to live this one down. This was an uppity neighborhood and the kids were all extremely snobby.

When our family moved here from the city, we tried our best to fit in. However, families with nine kids vs. the one or two kid household here, well let's just say we couldn't compete. The 'in' outfits alone would have killed my parents' wallet if they had to provide that, for all nine of us.

It also didn't help that my dad was not a white collar, tie back corporate person that fit the norm here. There were your average blue collar workers here too, but, they only had one child. My parents had nine. Nine kids to feed and clothe. Who does that? We shared clothes. We shared everything and because we did, I was forever marked as a less than fortunate geek.

It's been almost an hour since my dad and mom decided to kick me out to the wind. Since then I have been sitting here waiting for my friend to show up and take me away. The problem with that though, is that it might be a while. Mom and Dad woke me up, and in my sluggish state, I saw the clock said five thirty in the morning. Who throws their kid out that damn early? Yet another loud exhale escaped. Well I might as well enjoy the quiet view. It seemed to be the only thing in pleasant mode today.

I closed my eyes and let the gentle wind brush across my face. I could hear the birds sing their songs off in the distance. I inhaled every bit of fresh air I could manage to fill the lungs with. This particular morning, everyone in the household was filled with nothing but hot air, so I wanted to fill up with fresh, clean air.

It was exhilarating, except it made me remember I had to pee. My eyes opened to see the red sky finally starting to peak out its eye. Now the brightness of the sun was taking its secondary place to a bright vibrant red. It reminded me more of a poinsettia with amazing white clouds dancing around as leaves. Then it dawned on me that the red was a sailors warning in the morning. I started a slight panic, then laughed and reassured myself that, thankfully I wasn't a pirate.

Still somewhat lethargic, I laid back down to doze back off. I positioned myself between the driveway and sidewalk, making sure I touched none of their property. I refused to touch any of it, not even the grass. My luck, my parents would have the cops come arrest me for trespassing.

Immersing myself in deep thoughts, I fell back asleep, hoping I would dream of what was to come. Instead I just passed out, nothing but darkness that time. Usually I was always a dreamer, especially when I had issues on my mind. I would always inevitably have a dream about possible outcomes. But translating them was a whole different talent that I was still learning.

The bright yellow sun awakened me while roasting me like a turkey. I sat up, rubbed my eyes while I noticed the sun's position to be somewhat close to noon or shortly after. I took a moment to appreciate its warmth. If I could have only had something to quench the thirst, how amazing that would be.

There was a loud angry grumble from down in the pit of my stomach. It must have wanted me to realize that I was really hungry. I told it to pipe down. I considered trying to think of a game plan so I could get some food. Who was I kidding though? I had ten dollars and I was famished. Did I really want to battle the sun for a dollar drink and ho's ho's at the local store a mile away?

I opted instead to conserve my energy, besides I may end up having to pee on the side of the road, and we didn't want that in this small town. Anything made it on the front page here, and that was not how I was going to leave my name.

Then again, maybe that was the way I should have left it. A going away gift for the town that seemed to suck back in every life it ever created here. This small town was a big mush pit of depression. No jobs, nor any hope for a future. Yet, I was always bewildered by the fact that everyone kept coming back here. It was like there was some vicious virus in the water, and no one was aware of it. The more water they drank the more mindless lemmings they became. Thank goodness I always bought bottled water.

I was somewhat comforted that my parents weren't truly heartless in all their ways. They did allow me one phone call to make, thank my lucky stars for that one. So when I was packed, I made the call to the only friend that I had a number for. Karen said that she would gladly come to pick me up; however, she didn't get off work until about eight-thirty pm. She ended up scoring a director's position for a play that was about an hour and a half away. So because my parents decided to wake me up from my deep sleep, and ask if I had chosen a worthwhile job that didn't involve theater, I naturally said no. Well, that was all she wrote. So I was going to be here a while.

I was told to get dressed, get my belongings and hit the curb. So this was where I sat. On the curb with one plastic garbage bag, and my favorite stuffed animal in the world. One well used koala bear with no face, named Iggy. I didn't quite appreciate the rude wake up. Iggy said he knew it was coming though, and that I shouldn't have been too surprised. Apparently he was telling me for weeks now. Iggy was my main man for sure. Even though he was just a stuffed animal, he knew everything about me both good and bad.

I received this little guy, scuffed up that he is, at the ripe old age of six. He and I connected from the moment I unwrapped him under the Christmas tree. He was my 'Velveteen Rabbit.' He had his rough encounters though. His face was mauled off by our dog named Roadkill.

Don't get me wrong, I understood our puppy was just teething, but of all the stuffed animals that he chose, it was poor Iggy. He had to have his face sewn together, just to have Roadkill do it all over again. This time though I made Iggy's buttons colorful. Now even with his mismatched buttons and all, he was still absolutely perfect!

"Well damn!" I let out a rather depressing Sigh.

I would have at least appreciated, some water to take with me, but then again, I would have had to pee worse than I do now. Maybe they were doing me a favor, but right now, it sure seemed like they conspired against me. What a lame plan, and how embarrassing to have been sitting here, while the neighborhood drove by. On the other hand, my being out here, surely would get some looks and questions from the nosy neighbors. I'm sure the excuses would be creative.

I took out my pen and notebook, and wrote for most of the hours I endured sitting there. I had an idea for a screenplay about how people randomly met in a restaurant. The play however would be narrated by an emcee that would sprinkle a little twist of fate at his discretion. It would be called 'Coffee Stains.' Most of it now composed with a painfully numb bottom. Out of the corner of my eye, I saw the sun finally settling back to its bed for the evening. The sun was now a deep red with a hint of yellow, almost the color of blood.
"Hey!"

A loud horn accompanied a shout. Someone yelled from a car that I didn't recognize until they pulled directly up in front of me.
"Oh hey Scott, What's up?" I replied standing up to lean in his car.

Scott was the father of a high school friend that I didn't care for. Thankfully, my theater skills that my parents despised so badly, managed to have everyone convinced otherwise. So I believed my choice in acting was a no brainer. The amazing red sky above confirmed it for me, unless it was supposed to be a warning. I was confused momentarily when the horn beeped again.
"You good?" Scott asked interrupting my train of thought.
"Yeah, yeah…I'm fine, just waiting for my ride to show."

"Does that make two or three now, that they've kicked out? "
He laughed

I had to chuckle at that as well, because it seemed like the whole neighborhood knew my parents.

"Something like that." I smiled back at him

"What did you do?"

"Well for starters, I was born."

He chuckled back at me. Before he could interject with a witty sarcasm I finished my explanation.

"My career choice didn't have a conveyor belt with a weekly paycheck attached." I couldn't help but laugh.

I stood up from peering into his car. He smiled and simply stated.

"Then put your best foot forward and move onward and upward."

Why my parents couldn't be that supportive, I'll never know. Nevertheless, I'll do just what Scott suggested. Right now though, it seemed like the pause button had been pressed. Soon enough, I'll press play and see what happens. As soon as I get off this damn curb.

Scott drove off and I could see my Dad standing in the huge bay window just staring down at me. Beyond him my mom sat crying, like suddenly now I mattered. Maybe she wasn't even shedding tears for me, but rather for my father...to see him in pain like that must have bothered her. She was, in my defense though, the one that caused the whole fiasco. So there were no sympathies on my end for her tears.

I plopped back down and continued where I had left off in my screenplay. I wrote until I could hardly see the paper. It had to be getting close to Karen's arrival. I packed my notebook in my bag with pen alongside. Then I took a casual stroll down half the block, and snuck behind a bush to relieve myself. If I hadn't, I might have taken a trip with soiled pants. Returning from my little excursion I stretched my bones one last time for the trip.

It wasn't very much later my ride finally appeared. The time must've been close to ten at night, as that is when Karen said she would be here. She pulled up like lightning squealing to a halt. She jumped out to give me a hug, then grabbed my bag and threw it in the back of her car while screaming to the figures in the window.

"SCREW YOU!"

She laughed the whole time.

"Get in the car girl….lets hit the road."

I complied. Karen peeled out like she was in the Daytona 500. I felt exactly like that movie 'Thelma and Louise.' She swerved out and flipped my parents' one last bird. It was a climactic way to leave I suppose. Not really the theater drama I wanted to end on. But then again, who cared?

I was starting my life. Not a new life either. Just simply my start down the rabbit hole everyone called life. I had ten dollars to my name and not a clue where I was going. Whatever doubts I was having, or fears that may be within, were quickly subsided with Karen talking nonstop and wanting answers quickly in response to her questions.

"So what the hell happened?"

"My parents want me to go work at city plant for the next thirty years….I need to choose a real job in life. That's what they said, anyways."

"Bullshit! Theater is more work than standing at a conveyor belt for eight hours; tell them to get a real job! What next?"

"What do you mean?" I was puzzled.

"Well what do you want to do now?"

"Honestly I am starving but I only have ten bucks to my name

"I got you!"

Whipping the car around, she pulled into a Jimmy Jack drive through. She ordered me the largest combo meal. Karen handed the cashier money, received our order, tossed it gently towards my way then zoomed back off onto the road to my new temporary home.

"Thanks Karen I freaking owe you big time for this, I just want you to know this."

"No problem, we have about an hour and half for the drive and for now you stay with me. Since I am off the weekend, we will take you back to the city to see what we can find for you there. You are going to need a job, for sure; do you have any friends down there?"

"Yeah I do, I am just not sure I can stay with them."

"Well we will make it happen for you, you don't have a choice."

All I could do was nod in agreement as I was more focused on getting ready to take the biggest bite of cheeseburger in my life, and eat tons of fries to go with it. The food was so amazing that being homeless right now meant nothing.

Exhausted after the food and stress of the day, I dozed off rather quickly.

"Rise and Shine, girl."

Karen was in the driver's seat shaking me gently. I sat up to look around and could see nothing but a dense smoke in front of me. A cough replied back to her.

"What is that smell?" I said rubbing my eyes, shaking the smell from my head and nose to clear the haze that was around me

"Here, have some."

"No thanks... I don't smoke Cigarettes."

She laughed then handed me her hand rolled item.

"It's not cigarettes, although you just reminded me I am out....damn."

Karen put the car back in gear, backed out of her spot that was in front of some town homes, and then sped off again.

Karen explained what I was holding, and for me to take a hit or two. I was to keep the smoke in for a minute then exhale.

She was emphatic in her statements to me, that it was better than a nerve pill. Her thought was; since I hadn't had either before,

"…logically I would advise the natural relaxant for you over the man-made one." She smiled at me

Who was I to argue with nature, and its relaxants?

Well… I'm an adult, sort of, and on my own. At this point, since my nerves were shot, I justified the adult decision I was currently in the process of making. I lifted the cigarette to my mouth and followed her every order.

After the first inhale and almost gagging from the cough that followed, I stayed with the regiment and followed through once more. Karen was absolutely correct on her theory. It was from this experience, I learned that natural remedies were the best, but of course being fresh from my parents' basement that wasn't saying much. However, I can say it was definitely better than the wine cooler I had at my graduation party.

"Where did you say we were? What city? "I was a bit confused at the moment.

She laughed. "Blue River. That's also the name of the play."

"Oh, got it now."

I leaned back in the seat and repeated the name over and over for a moment, as I was a bit off in wanting to remember anything currently.

We arrived at the gas station and proceeded inside. Karen went to the counter and purchased her cigarettes. I could only stare at the section of chocolate candy bars, and the huge slushy machine, conveniently located right next to them. Karen grabbed some items to add on to the bill. I considered grabbing one of everything, but Karen tugged me by the arm and said;

"Let's go, I got you a Snickers".

I was elated that she thought of me like that. It was like, she was reading my mind. I was sure glad she was too, because I wouldn't have had any closure leaving that store without something in hand.

Finally, we pulled back in to her assigned temporary home. Nothing but lined up town houses that looked like a bunch of cabins out in the woods for camping. There was a crowd already there listening to music, smoking and conversing somewhat rather loud for my ears. A thick haze of smoke filled the air, smelling similar to the 'cigarette' now known to me as weed. Karen announced her arrival with a very boisterous voice.

"Listen up folks! We got a guest that will be staying with us for a little bit so treat her kindly! Everyone this is Skye. Skye this is everyone!"

They all applauded like theater people would. They welcomed me with open arms and hands by passing those lovely cigarettes that just seemed to never end. I managed to hang for about an hour or so, and then it put me down rather fiercely. Karen gave me the spare room to go in to sleep, so after saying my polite goodbyes, I vanished behind the door and heard nothing for the remainder of the evening.

The next morning I laid in the bed for a moment to soak up the new day and contemplate yesterday's memories. No parents, no judgments, no decisions being made in advance for me. What a great feeling to experience. I was a bit groggy after the evening's festivities, eventually though I managed to pull myself up, making my way into the kitchen where Karen was already awake, and reading the morning newspaper.

"Morning, did you sleep OK?" She asked not even looking up from the page.

"Yeah I slept great. Thanks." I mumbled.

"Great." She responded back.

"Well make yourself at home and if you want to go with us to town later to pick up some groceries you are more than welcome to come, otherwise just chill out and relax I will take care of the groceries."

"Thanks Karen, do you by chance have coffee?"

"Oh of course, that is the one thing I don't run out of." She smiled and pointed to the cabinet.

Opening the cabinet I saw a stockpile of coffee and creamer as though she was preparing for a third world war. I shook my head and laughed, then proceeded to make more coffee for both of us.

"Here is a cell phone that you can have. I don't need it anymore. My husband always gets me the latest when it comes out. Seeing as I have fifteen of these lying around you can have your pick, I will have him add minutes for you so you have a way to stay in contact with everyone."

"Karen, I really don't know what to say."

"Then just say thanks and get me some more coffee."

She smiled at me and I smiled back with a nod.

Sitting in her housing unit waiting for her arrival back from the store I wasted no time getting back to the screenplay. I started to write, yet for some reason, my mental ink wasn't flowing for me as it was the day before. I finally conceded to the defeat. I laid the pen down on top of the paper. I stared out the window for a while lost in deep thought.

My parents were more on my mind then the story. Had they regretted telling me to leave? Had they even told my brothers and sisters about it? Did anyone even question them? I was sure the neighbors would do what they were skilled at, and just gossip, whisper and talk. Well at this point it didn't seem to matter. I needed to focus on trying to survive. Maybe writing the screenplay will bring a couple of dollars my way to help the cause.

I shifted back to the concentration of the story. Twenty minutes later though, still nothing creative was flowing, in fact it wasn't even trying, which was extremely disappointing. After staring out the window for a while, my thoughts lost in the storm that was pouring down, I strolled back to the room and placed the manuscript back in my bag. I noticed my tarot cards lying there in the black box I customized for them. It dawned on me that now would be a perfect time to do one of those. So snatching the box up, I headed for the back porch grabbing my cup of coffee.

Like My Nanny, I inherited a gift for reading leaves, palms, and tarot cards. When she found out I had it, she wasted no time in helping me understand the gift. My gift was stronger though in dreams than on a physical level, as she later explained, and Nanny was always interested in hearing about them ever since.

When I was about seven; she was down visiting for a month. I woke up and asked for my mom. Nanny had replied that she went to the store, so I asked if she would listen to the dream I had. She made us tea that morning and we talked about my secrets from the previous evening.

At the end of drinking the tea and my story, she simply smiled, and told me what to do with the dream. Then she read my leaves for me from that cup. Nanny showed me how to interpret their secrets every time she came down.

Mom was always pleading for Nanny to stop, but Nanny would always say right back to her;
"She has the gift Laurie. She needs to understand that gift."

Mom would sigh and ask that it not be flaunted in front of my father. My father was a devout Catholic, mom converted when they married. Ironic though, they never went to church...ever.

The kids on the other hand, were involved in every part of the church, including baptisms, communion, confirmation, retreats, to ritualistic weekly masses. Saturday evening confessions were always an absolute must. Otherwise we would burn in hell, and we wouldn't be able to eat that damn wafer on Sunday's.

The nuns loved us too, because Mom and Dad volunteered us for the summer months to help them clean out their classrooms; and with nine of us in tow, they had a field day using us to scrub lockers and floors. But we didn't mind so much, we got to take home all the left over school stuff they were going to throw away.

Maybe the torture wouldn't have been so bad if we didn't have to always trudge the mile and a half long walk to and from. I believed it was just so my parents could get rid of us, so they could have some alone time. I mean with nine kids, who could blame them?

I believed there was something more to us than just kneeling, and praying. I believed my mom did as well, but seeing as she was in love with my dad, I would never really be able to speak of this amazing gift with her.

Unfortunately, I was the only one out of the nine kids that ever really spoke out loud about the curious nature of that realm. I was always hushed, and then laughed at. I wasn't really allowed to bring it up either and that really bothered me. Nonetheless, I followed my Nanny, and her teachings. With her insights and lessons, I could sense the energies now. I understood my gift was stronger in dreams, and that I would have to practice other divination ways to become skilled at interpreting them.

Now, because of the current family situation I wouldn't be able to see Nanny anymore. I wished I could at least write to her though. Unfortunately I had no idea what her address was to write anything. There was only one logical conclusion I could derive from this. I must have learned all I could from her; if the universe saw fit that this was the end of 'family' as it were for me. I wouldn't allow that feeling to get me down though. If Nanny was that in tune, she would still chat with me other ways.

I finished a small reading on myself, and it spoke of change, and telling me to slow down. The slowing down, disturbed me as I felt at the current moment I had no time right now to honor that request. So surely the reading must be wrong. Now was the time, to not be slow. I sat reflecting while I finished the warm beverage now ice cold to the lips. Karen waltzed in the back room to make her appearance known.

"Hey."

"Hey back to you." I smiled and took the last swig.

"What are you doing? Is that a tarot reading?"

"Why? Would you like one?"

"Hell yeah!" she exclaimed right back.

She made me laugh at that comment, so I gathered the cards for her shuffle. She of course, had her bowl with her, so we exchanged hands. Taking the first couple of hits while she shuffled, I sat back to enjoy the continuous rain outside the window. Her reading was a pleasant one to say the least.

After that reading, Karen hooked me up. She was so impressed that she told everyone in the play about it. The cast, the staff, she even told the gas station attendant about the reading. Within twenty minutes of her next rehearsal, I was receiving text requests for appointment times.

The next thing I knew, by the end of the week I had nine hundred sixty dollars simply from doing readings. Nanny would be proud of me for sure. That brought a smile to my face. I had readings scheduled from morning to night. What an absolute relief, she was a great help in relieving the stress of my money woes.

That weekend we took a ride down to the city just like she said. It was nice to stay with her but I was somewhat happy to leave. Every night there was a party in her house after the play. I supposed though when one had nothing to do night after night but a mundane and monotonous play, the only logical thing one can do is party. It wasn't that I minded, but it was rather difficult to keep goal oriented if I couldn't even hear my own thoughts.

Riding the interstate with her top down the entire way, it was a refreshing drive without any incidences. We stopped for lunch at some dive of a restaurant before finally making it in to town. I was eager, ready, nervous, and terrified to start this adventure. I didn't really have any another choice but to figure it out and move forward though.

So that's how it all started. The great thing about this was that the sky seemed a bit clearer today. Not a hint of red to be found.

Roomies

Karen made some calls during the week to get things set up for me ahead of time. She made it all magically happen. On the ride down we chatted about how the housing unit was set up, and what expectations were. She informed the roommates about my situation and they were all extremely accommodating towards me, which was a huge relief. I even knew one of the roommates, from the previous quarter in a class we had together.

Apparently, how housing worked off campus, was that there were usually seven people to a four bedroom house. They made bedrooms in the basement, garage, and even from spare bathrooms. I was told it was so people could afford to live while away at school. I met some great people in that house, which were now my new house mates.

So I moved in, all one bag and Iggy. I was given a space a little larger than a walk in closet. I was told the rent was fifty dollars a month. When I was on my feet I was to start throwing the money towards Kasey, the girl I knew, because she was in charge of the bills. I politely nodded and agreed.

They already had most of my housing needs furnished, so that was even a bigger help. I didn't have to worry about anything except my own food and bills. This would work out well.

First order of business was to find a job. Since I had no car, I had to travel by foot. I had an option for the bus, but I had never been on one, so I chose to foot it down the hill. I stopped in the local gas station, and filled out the application. I had an immediate interview, and was hired on the spot. They had me starting the next day.

"Awesome." I thought to myself walking back up the hill towards the house.

"That was the easiest job interview ever. Man if I continue like this, I'll be rich and famous in no time."

I grinned at that point. If only my destiny would reveal some clues for me. Too bad, gazing into my future was harder to accomplish without being biased. That would be amazing. Or maybe it wouldn't be, but it was definitely worth contemplating over.

I did just that too while I made my way closer to the hangout pad. By the time I reached the porch, I had concluded that I indeed, would not want my future to be seen, at least at the current moment. However, that may change again later down the line. For now, this job would suffice nicely, because I was hired on for third shift cashier. My work schedule wouldn't interfere with school, which was just perfect.

I worked every day, was always told I did an outstanding job, but the situation with the house mates seemed much like Karen's house at times. Although for fifty bucks a month, one could hardly be too frustrated with it. That's where I learned that saying 'One gets what they pay for.' For now this was still better than being homeless.

Different people usually came in and about; there were almost always parties, and always people I never knew. I'd come home and usually try to go straight to my space. Sometimes I socialized taking part in the smoke fests, but for the most part I pretty much stayed to my own. There was never a day though, that there wasn't some random person on the couch to greet me when I came through.

I was off on Thursdays and Fridays. It happened to be a Thursday morning when I entered the house to be greeted with some random guy chilling on the couch. He was smoking and wanting to make conversation with me.

"Hey" He said real monotone.

"Hey" I reply back.

"You live here?" He was dressed in dark green pantaloons with a well-worn t shirt that stated,

'A friend with weed is a friend indeed.'

He had dreads to the bottom of his back. While he sat there holding a bong full of green, He scratched his head moving his Rasta hat from side to side.

"Do you?" I snap back Not in the mood for any type of conversation he may be wanting.

"No I am here for the party."

"What party?"

He took a hit and passed it to me; I stared down at him for a moment, sighed, sat and joined him.

"There is a dishwashing party tonight."

"What?" I responded by coughing almost directly in his face.

"Yeah it's gonna be great. All you have to do is show up ready to wash a dish and then you get a beer. The more dishes you wash the more beer you get. Cool huh?"

"I suppose."

Seeing as I never ate there, nor really used the kitchen, I was obviously curious to know just how many dishes were there. I casually strolled into the kitchen to see the mountain of plates and cups in the sink greeting me as I entered. However, that amount paled in comparison to the skyscrapers that took up every bit of counter space.

Shocked that there could be this many dishes in one house, all I could do was stare in disbelief. The Rasta man, whose name I found out was Mouse, followed closely behind, all the while smiling, and smoking. I was in a state of awe and bewilderment, when Mouse laughed under his breath right into my ear.

He simply stated that when the guys ran out of dishes, instead of cleaning them, they would just buy new ones. Now, however, the kitchen was so full, they were being forced to have to scrub and wash them. He was not exaggerating in the least.

I had learned that people who are in theater love to play the dramatics on any situation. It was not to be the case now, though. Every ounce of space was taken up with used dishes, pots, pans and utensils. All I could do was shake my head, and pick my mouth up off the floor. After all, who knew when the floor was actually mopped last?

I also found out later, that Mouse was one of those guys that were just always there. No matter what was going on, or even if there wasn't, he would just be around. He never really said much, I'm not even sure he really attended the school either. No one ever paid him much attention, and when I eventually asked around later about him, everyone just sort of scratched their heads and stated they didn't really know. He was a chill guy, so no one minded his presence to much.

"What time does the party start?" I asked now inquisitively.

"Tonight around fourish" He stated.

"Oh. Well then…wait. Why are you here then at seven in the morning?" I was completely perplexed at this point and was curious on what the response would be.

"Well I wanted to be ahead of the game you know."

He fussed around his pockets looking for something of importance. He was searching frantically and feverishly. He had what seemed to be three thousand pockets too! Who has that many items to carry, that a pair of pants constituted this madness? He finally found his item, it was a lighter. All that fuss over a lighter! Just to hand it back for me to take a toke. I was not about to shatter his accomplishment by telling him I had one in my hand already.

"Oh, well then I guess you are to be commended for preparation."

"I know right? Want to meet my friend? I dragged him here to party with me, but once he found out the party didn't start till later, he cursed me out then went to pass out in the corner."

He pointed to a gentleman who was napping in the corner and didn't at all resemble a person that would hang out with a guy named Mouse. But yet there he was, curled up in the corner, trying to get comfortable.

I approached him and told him he could sleep on the couch if it would be better on his bones. He smiled and thanked me. In the course of helping him to one of the many we had, he introduced himself as Kyle. He seemed extremely conservative and opposite of Mouse which shocked me as to how these two were even remotely friends.

"So what is your name?" He asked as he moved to the couch, pulling out a joint to light up on his way. I had found the connection between the two.

"Skye." I responded back.

"Nice to meet you, here...."

He tried to pass a newly lit joint to me but I declined stating I was going to get some rest before the festivities began. Mouse thought that by me stating that, I invited them up, but I advised him that it meant 'female alone time.' He grinned from ear to ear and added a simple comment.

"Let me know if you need any help I am pretty good at that stuff."

I rolled my eyes and simply nodded back. Reaching the top of the stairs I turned the corner and entered my room; I threw off my clothes and laid on the mattresses that were on the floor for me to settle in. I had closed the eyes and was thankful to just be alone at that moment.

At some point there was a loud bang which startled me from my deep slumber. I listened for a moment to hear the music.

"Great."

I fumbled for my phone and saw the time, a bit taken back to see that I had been sleeping for exactly seven hours. I could have sworn it felt like two. Gathering the senses, I grabbed some jeans and a shirt and made my way for the shower.

Afterwards I could hear the crowd downstairs becoming a bit louder, and after getting dressed I made my way down the stairs. I saw Mouse again, still smoking, this time though with a hazmat suit on. He was struggling with the joint he held in his hand that was occupied by the oversized gloves. He stood with a welders' mask on, and seemed to be having issues trying to hit it before passing it off, as it was his turn at the sink. He was thoroughly enjoying himself, which made it amusing to watch the seriousness of his face as he washed.

There was an extremely long line of people patiently waiting for their turn at the sink, there seemed to be no end. All these people here, waiting their turn to scour through dishes. All dressed up, as though they were preparing to deal with Armageddon. The attendees wore masks, some carried surgical utensils, and there was a guy with a blowtorch, one with a fishing pole with a bleach bottle attached to the hook. There were those who even brought their dogs to lick the plates. I guess when you don't specify how the dishes had to be cleaned I guess a dog is as good as a human. For every dish you scrubbed you got a beer, so there were a lot of people, and even more beer.

Kasey slapped a beer in my hand and said the housemates got free beer, well that was a plus. Once the people were done with their dish, they could go into the party. I watched the lovely imaginations of people who interpreted what a dishwashing party was about in their minds. Completely humored by all the ways they could come up with to just simply wash a dish. Chainsaws, pressure washers, and one guy even brought a midget with a monkey. Where do these people find this stuff? I loved the life of theater and their creative ways of interpretation.

The night continued even when there were no more dishes to be had. People now were rewashing dishes just to get a free beer. When the free beer finally ended and they had their fill, they eventually went home. I asked Kasey how much was invested in beer and she said too much for her taste, but since it was the guys that bought the beer she wasn't complaining.

Everything was pretty much gone except Kasey's private stash upstairs. She invited me to help myself and since I had nothing else to do I did just that. I made my way past the number of theater people who were deep into a conversation on analyzing Hitchcock's "The Birds."

They discussed the subtle hints and symbolism the normal audience would always miss. They were deep in their thoughts and views upon dissecting every scene and every line. I laughed and thought that, only a film major could take an hour movie and turn it into three.

At the top of the stairs I hit Kasey's room to grab a beer before heading back to my space. Kasey yelled my name from the bottom of the stairs,

"Did you get my message I left for you on your bed?"

"No when did you leave me a message? And you mean the mattress on the floor I lay upon? I smiled at her responding back.

"Crap no I didn't read it, I didn't even see it! What does it say?"

"Donnie moved out and so I thought you might want his room, but the rent is sixty-five a month."

Sixty-five dollars a month? Hell, I would pay three hundred at this rate for my own room and not just a closet space.

"Sold!" I said eager to make it mine now.

"He left the stuff he didn't want to take. So you can either have it or throw it out OK?"

"Perfect!!!" I was so happy. I never really realized how important someone's personal space was until I had to live in a closet.

Opening his door, it was like a tornado hit. Ironically just that room too. There was hardly anything that was even salvageable to keep. He chose not to take anything, and I could see why. Maybe I should throw a space saving party and see where that got me for a clean-up crew. I snagged some garbage bags from the bathroom and started throwing everything away. While preparing my new room, Kyle managed to make his way up to peep his head in.

"What are you doing?" He asked

"Well I got promoted to a bedroom, so I am cleaning out what the other guy left for me as a housewarming gift."

"Looks like fun. It also looks like you will be here a while. Want some help?"

"No I wouldn't ask my worst enemy to help with this mess."

"Well good thing were neither friends nor enemies, as I would have to walk away, but with that said...." He snagged one of the garbage bags and stood there for direction.

"Can you do me a favor then, and take off the sheets? Just throw them deep into the garbage bag please."

"Maybe I should go get Mouse's hazmat suit first" We both laughed at that one, and as he ripped the sheets off he stated in his best Queen of hearts voice.

"Off with the sheets!"

I was quite impressed with his cleaning skills, so I paid him a compliment about it. He replied though that when you live in a house full of guys, as he did, one had to be somewhat organized and clean. So we scrubbed while we drank, laughed and made some sly remarks about the previous housekeeper of the room.

At the end of the evening I could tell Kyle was exhausted. I offered him the bed. I would go back to my little room for one last rendezvous; he gladly took me up on it, so about four in the morning we both crashed out calling it a night.

The rest of the month I worked extremely long arduous hours. In theory, it was so I could back off work in the winter months. Not sure why, but that was always my least favorite time of the year. During the times I wasn't working at the gas station, I would be in the coffee house's doing readings for twenty dollars. That kept me busy and out of trouble, and I loved the extra money. I finally managed to work enough hours that I could purchase a small car. I had my eye on it since I started work at the station. One of my coworkers was selling his and I jumped at the chance to purchase it. He had no problem with pre-arraigned payments, so that was a benefit.

The car was a God send to me. I now knew what freedom was about. This was going to be perfect, and it was just in time for school. After a couple of weeks passing by I had started to grow accustomed to my new space around me. The communication between house mates was very open. I had also become accustomed to having Kyle around now on a daily basis. We became good friends, after about a month and enjoyed having each other around.

One day after work he surprised me, when I entered from work to see the entire living room was filled with roses and balloons that said 'Happy Birthday.' I was stunned to see it and thought odd of him to remember, seeing as I had only said my birthday once, and in passing at that. Kasey greeted me with a cup of coffee when I got in the door.

"I wish I had a man would be this attentive when it came to my birthday." Then she let out a sneeze.

"Are you catching a cold?" I asked

"Oh no, I am allergic to roses." Kasey said between sneezes.

"Well shit Kasey!" I dropped my purse to the ground then started taking all the roses out front to the porch.

"No, no it's OK, no worries that is what they made allergy medicine for."

She smiled but I started to quickly gather the pesky flowers and stash them in on the porch outside. There was message waiting for me on my phone when that task was completed. It was from Kyle. So when I was done with my coffee and rose dashing, I listened to the voicemail. He simply stated "Happy Birthday I will be over to get you in an hour."

It brought a smile to my face, although it was a bit frustrating because it was a bit overwhelming. I wasn't used to having such a big deal...wait, make that any deal over me. So it was all pretty alarming, and I felt uncomfortable about the whole essence of it.

Kasey could see that I was a bit frustrated, so she hugged me and said not to worry, he was being a nice guy. She told me to relax and let someone spoil me for a change. There was a slight nod back in agreement.

Well forget any sleep at this point now. I jumped into the shower and took a moment to relax from the steam. It was nice to ponder on the moment at hand and I was excited about the prospect of going out. I hadn't been out actually on a date so Kasey and I took some time to make myself up for the first time since…well ever.

Right on schedule, Kyle pranced through the front door like he owned the place singing at the top of his lungs "Happy Birthday" from the bottom of the stairs. I came down to the landing and Kasey from the kitchen. We watched his performance which actually, was entertaining.

Afterwards, she asked for the band leader to come talk with her, and he obliged. I retreated back to my room, gathered my belongings then headed downstairs to where they were finishing up their talk. He nodded and then took my hand and whisked me out the door.

We had a great time going around town. We stopped for a bite to eat before heading back to his place to grab some things he wanted to bring back to Kasey. He had three roommates and not surprisingly, they were all in the theater program. One was a stage tech; the other two were film majors.

With evening approaching we headed back to my place. He held the door open for me and to my surprise I entered the house to a completely filled room with everyone shouting "HAPPY BIRTHDAY." I didn't even know most of these people, but yet here they were gathering on my day to wish me a good one.

In the corner sat Kasey with her current male friend Brian, they were both smiling at me. I made my way through and hugged her tightly to which she responded.
"Don't thank me, thank your boyfriend he was the one to arrange it all."

I looked at her somewhat confused because I never really considered Kyle my boyfriend. We never ever really officially started dating. So imagine my surprise when I glanced back meeting Kyle's eyes, seeing the smile he showed just for me.

The first time

Having realized Kyle started carrying feelings for me other than the friendship, I spent limited time with him after the birthday. I would find myself purposely ignoring his texts or calls. He was either a great sport at rejection, or completely oblivious to it.

I had done a tea reading on the matter to gain some insight. However, unlike my Nanny, who used her leaves, I preferred to use my coffee grounds. I grabbed my wide mouth coffee cup specific for this occasion. It was a sloping sided cup, which was completely plain with no decorations anywhere.

I brewed the Greek coffee that I had as my secondary choice. I was always told to use Turkish, as it was stronger. But in times of a pinch, like right now, Greek coffee would suffice. I added a pinch or two of dry coffee grounds to the brewed coffee so that there would be enough grounds to read when they settled. I sat and pondered or as Nanny would say, "opened the heart..." The grounds finally sunk to their bottom. I could hear Nanny in my ear whispering.
"Like any other tool of foresight, it would require skill to be able to see into our own future with clear objection."

Before even starting the reading, there were some messages for me, which made me smile. I saw the thin bubbles floating on the surface. I was elated because that told me money was on the way. There were some grinds that chose to stick it out on the sides, and not sink with their counterparts. That told me I would have some visitors. That made me chuckle, because every day I had visitors.

I had finished the coffee sip by sip. Pondering on the whole silly situation, I left a small amount of liquid in the bottom. While holding the cup in my left hand, I swirled the grounds around three times in a clockwise direction. I poured the remains across a plate, and interpreted the patterns that were left there for me.

Then I closed my eyes and placed my thumb at the bottom of the inside of my cup. I twisted clockwise, ever so slightly. That would be for after the reading. It was considered to be my inner thoughts or emotions of the situation.

My gut was telling me what the grounds confirmed. It was rather a mundane reading in itself. But there was a position from some of the grounds that showed their revelation and quite demandingly. It was a warning. It was trying to tell me something, but I was not skilled enough to understand the warning in its entirety. The reading showed a negative dilemma but I couldn't quite make it out...this was where it was frustrating because my Nanny would have known what this meant.

A deep unsettling breath came from the bottom of my lungs. I jotted the positions down, and then pondered on the rest and their whispers to me. I shuddered when I felt a bit of a cold energy. I brushed it off as intuition. Or maybe it was a loved one trying to reach out. I will have to gather some moments of clarity on that one later. But for now, I would wait a bit before trying to communicate with Kyle. Best let things just settle for the moment. I went upstairs to catch up on some sleep.

"Hey...man wake up! What the heck...you good?"

Kasey was shaking the hell out of me. I was drenched in sweat. I was in a whole different world, trying desperately not to lose the dream that just occurred...

I mumbled back quite shaken.

"Yeah sorry, just had a bad dream."

"I guess," she stated and said on her way out the door.

"Okay well then I'm off to work, I'm late or otherwise we would chat."

"OK." I quickly tried to recall the dream.

Was the dream telling me not to approach the subject? I desperately sat back to recall. I remembered I was on a country road; it was around ten in the morning, the number ten was dominant throughout. I watched a younger version of myself from a distance. The birds were singing while the sun peeked its' way down to the winding road below.

The younger version of me, maybe seven, stood at a mailbox as if ready for school. The road with its never-ending turns seemed so serene with the morning sun glistening down between the trees. It was early spring or summer. I remember I had the feeling of waiting for something. There down the road, was a bus that moved forward in slow motion towards me. As it approached, I aged at the same speed.

Once in front of me, the bus stopped to open its doors. I did not move, I said not a word. I stared at this 'person' or whatever it was that stared right back at me… not moving, nor speaking. It waited for a long moment as we inspected each other. The doors finally closed and the bus continued on.

Staring into the back of the bus, there were horrible scenes of murders, torment, despair, lost souls, and evil energy. Some trying to escape, others just laughed, and one set of eyes, eerily looked at me directly with a smile.

In my journal that I had since I was nine, I wrote this dream down like I did all the others for later contemplation. Funny part about that was, I was never really good at going back to contemplate.

Well I guess now was the time to hash it out with Kyle. This would be a first for me. I never really had to break up with anyone before. Hell, no one even asked me out, for it to get that far. How does one 'break-up' with someone when you didn't even know you were really dating them in the first place?

Well, that settled it. This had to be done. I would send him a text after breakfast to see if we could hook up to discuss matters at hand, or in his case heart. His response came back suggesting dinner at his place the next evening. Of course I didn't turn that down; I mean it was a free meal after all.

The next evening turned out to be difficult one. I had seen the remnants of the slaved labor of love that turned into a great and delicious meal. Dishes were everywhere. The kitchen appeared as if the Tasmanian devil were hosting the dinner himself. It was a delicious meal though, no complaints from the peanut gallery, otherwise known as me.

Kyle chose an eccentric dish, which was chicken asparagus roll ups. I never thought that vegetables could look so sexy. But there they were, killing it. The taste itself was divine, they were cooked to perfection. The crisp was so incredibly juicy and it left me wanting more. But I was lady like so I fought my inner fat kid and only ate three.

Afterwards, we sat on the sofa and talked on how it would be more beneficial if we just kept hanging to the minimum for now. I wanted to remain friends and nothing more. He had insisted we were only just friends. I disagreed and told him a few examples where I felt things were not.

Things started to get a bit louder for just a moment but then he just kind of stopped....took a breath and looked down at the floor, almost in defeat. I wasn't sure if this was a theater move or not. But I could see the hurt in his eyes and the disappointment that I had just delivered to him. Nonchalantly he agreed and then leaned over, and kissed me. It was as though this was some sort of last dramatic stage kiss. I originally thought he was kissing my cheek, till he came in for a deeper one from my lips. I allowed him a little one, and then an uncomfortable smile followed.

He eventually confided his feelings of how he had hoped there would have been more, but he was OK with just hanging out being platonic with each other. So that evening, we both decided to call whatever it was we had to a halt. We never really did hang out with each other after that.

Presents

School had started up and things were finally falling into place. One brisk Saturday, around Halloween Kasey invited me to a poker game that the theater people played normally on a weekly basis.

"Come on just go with me...it'll be fun, I promise." She was rather persistent.

"Why do you want to go so bad?"

"Cameron will be there, which means there will be presents for us."

"What type of presents?" She had my attention.

What possible presents could have my roomy all up in excitement?

"Acid." She smiled from ear to ear.

"Acid? Like LSD?"

She giggled "Yes LSD."

She told me about the past two times she had tripped, and how magical it was, to feel so enlightened. She was more ecstatic because Cameron's acid seemed to be the cleanest around, meaning there were less cramps later after the come down. I was silent all the while. She wanted me to go because she wanted to trip with me as her new best friend and roommate.

Not quite sure about it, so for a moment I sat in hesitation. There had to be a decision to make soon though, I was informed she had to know immediately, we were leaving in an hour. By her referring to the 'we,' I assumed she wasn't going to take no for an answer. So I guess that was settled then.

Kasey got all dressed up for this poker party. I threw on my favorite jeans with a simple spaghetti style crocheted crop top. It was a dark teal in color, and matched the jeans nicely. It was perfect for tonight, the season was unseasonably warm. Just in case it got colder though, I brought my chunky knit gray sweater. It was a great fall back. Kasey suggested I put some makeup on, but I opted to decline. It was more of a hassle to me, and always made me look like a hooker.

"You just haven't had it done correctly, that's all. You can't put blues and pinks on every skin tone Skye."

I shrugged my shoulders in response then settled across her bed to watch her finish getting ready. We were going on a quest to meet up with Cameron to get some acid for our Saturday evening entertainment. Kasey told me to look at this night as nothing more than looking on the inside of a journey here in this mundane world.

That reminded me, I should have pulled a card to do a quick reading. Kasey told me not to do that, until I started to trip later. It was then, she suggested would be the better time to do the reading. Kasey explained how the LSD would help the enlightened state by having a heightened awareness to the senses. So I opted to wait to see if she would be correct, I had no idea just how correct her statement would be.

We reached the poker game at last. She was in no hurry to get there, while I worried that we were extremely late showing at around ten thirty. She assured me we were fine. Things of course were already in full sway upon our arrival. Kasey made her way through to the fridge to see if there was room for a couple more beers. Afterwards, she doubled back and handed me one, as we watched the way the numbers unfolded for the players at the table.

There was Ken, and some others I hadn't recognized from the film department. I skimmed the room and caught the gaze of Kyle, who was currently playing at the table. I wasn't sure if I felt at ease or uncomfortable at that moment. It was the first time I had seen him since that sexy vegetable night. I shrugged it off and continued to glance around. The rest of the room seemed rather relaxed and laid back.

The table was full at the moment so Kasey and I stood back. Kasey would occasionally flutter around the house socializing in search of Cameron, her knight and shining armor tonight. I preferred to study the game, which is what I did after finding a spot to plant myself. I grabbed a chair, sat behind the lady of the house while she scooted over to allow me to watch and learn.

The topic at hand at the table, in between hands was the current production on the main stage. I kept quiet because I wanted to be in a mainstage production but normally juniors and seniors got the parts. Occasionally though, once in a blue moon, you would hear about some second year college talent getting a part, but mostly that was unheard of. Every second year and up student was required to try out in at least one main stage production. This year I was already content in knowing I would not be one of those privileged few that would be fondled over.

They called break at the table after a large hand that took most of the people's money. This was my chance to jump in at the table as some were already calling it for the night. After buying in, I stretched the legs then strolled out to the porch to find Kasey. Sure enough, there she was talking to another film guy smoking his cigarette. They were conversing about Cameron and the evening's events. She invited him to join us and he jumped at the opportunity to do so. When I joined them she informed me that Todd would be joining the evening's festivities later on with us. I nodded, and then followed the others starting to pour back into the game.

My first hand was rather a simple one. It was nothing more than a simple five card stud. Of course, I lost that hand but not by much, this game could become addicting. Ken was pretty good at always going back over the instructions for everyone at the table. In the middle of one of his explanations for the next hand, the front door flung open so hard that it slammed taking most of us off guard. Our jumps made it obvious to him.

In walked a man who stood about five foot eight inches high. He had shoulder length sandy blonde hair, perfectly blended with even lighter shaded accents. Included with that were blue eyes to match. He sported a well-worn wrinkled brown leather jacket, with just as equally worn brown boots. He carried two cases of beer and a fifth of rum like a professional bartender getting ready for his shift.

"I am here! You may now start the party." He arrogantly stated.

I turned to Kasey, mumbling to her

"I think your man is here."

She turned right back around gleefully expressing her joy.

"Oh Yeah he is." She giggled.

She left to help him with his beer. I wasn't sure what she saw in that man. He was obviously very arrogant and used to being the center of attention. He was handsome, which is exactly what made him unattractive. It seemed he'd have no problem letting one know, how better off they were, now that he entered their life. I was sure a conversation with him would be a one way street. He was definitely not my type. How some could even humor it, I'll never understand.

Cameron sat next to the dealer, across from me. He peered around as he threw his disheveled twenty dollar bill on the table to buy in for the next round. Ken stopped to exchange it, while doing so Cameron caught my glance watching him as he made himself at home.

"Hi, I'm Cameron." He put his hand forward for me to shake. Kasey approached from behind him grabbing another fold out chair to place directly close next to his. She finished the introduction.

"Cam, this is Skye, she's my roomie."

"Hi Skye, pleasure to meet you."

I was completely taken off guard at his polite, courteous tone, opposite of what just walked through the door a minute ago.

"Hi." We stayed in the moment briefly before Ken interrupted.

"Alright, you two get a room later, this is time for cards. We will start fresh so Cam your call."

Ken handed the cards over to Cameron, and while he shuffled I could see his small glances my way as he called the title of the next round, so appropriately named 'between the sheets.'

The poker party had been hopping for most the evening, people left when their money ran out, but the diehard weekly players were in it till the end. Kasey looked like nothing more than arm candy when she sat next to him.

Cameron chose to play exactly how he arrived, loud and in charge. He turned out to be a very skilled player. I could see why the moans came around the table when one mentioned he may show up this evening. He was a master manipulator at the table but he showed up every week and always brought beer and 'presents.'

The cast of characters at the table though were all completely opposite of his personality. I found out later that he dated a girl in the tech department for very long time, so by default I suppose he just became finally part of the department. Cameron was one of those regulars that never missed a week if he could help it.

With antes in, he started the round. He cleaned the table and everybody started back with their moans. The players were just pathetic at their best attempt, trying to read his face, when they thought he was bluffing. Frankly I was amused....because for a bunch of theater and film buffs, surely by now, somebody would have been able to read his micro expressions. But apparently when you drink enough beer there are no micro expressions.

Kasey and he flirted back and forth, although as he conversed with her, he would look at me and smile. This was enough for me to get up to go get my own beer.

"Hey!" He yelled as opened the refrigerator door.

"Help yourself to some of mine, there's plenty in there."

I thanked him and grabbed ours instead. He caught that and snickered. He was flirting with me, even while Kasey sat there. Yet another reason I would never date him. The cards played through the evening and eventually Cameron took what was left. As everyone moaned, whined and complained how he always did that, Kasey and he spoke in the corner amongst themselves. I had been helping clean up when I noticed her heading back my way.

"OK were ready to go."

I was a little shocked and turned to ask "Wait, aren't you two going home tonight?"

She laughed and said she had no plans on leaving with anybody tonight but me.

"Although, He may also join us later, and wont that be fun."

She took my hand and we started to pass him on the way out the door. I met his eyes, and the whole time, He smiled and as I was taken past him, he whispered to me

"Enjoy your trip tonight. I might stop by."

"I'll hold my breath in anticipation." I could sense he felt the sarcasm.

My new best friend

Back at the house an ecstatic Kasey couldn't wait to eat the sugar drops. She was hardly inside the door before discarding her coat tossing it to the nearest chair. She was like a child getting her first big sundae. She un-wrapped the foil and exposed the three drops.

After Todd's arrival we ate the sugar. We started conversing on things in the theater department at school, and then it shifted to discussing poker. At one point I had heard them starting to discuss politics. Half an hour later or so, nothing was happening except for some weird feeling in my hands.

Then ten minutes or so later, I started noticing things about our house that I hadn't noticed before (or at least I didn't think I noticed). I had to turn off all the lights because it was getting to be dawn, and they were a bit too orange for me. They reminded me of the color of the lights in city parking lots. This was really exciting because I could feel the effects were starting.

I made my way over to look in my mirror and I got really startled, not really scared, but surprised. My pupils were about the size of my irises. Kasey laughed at me from the other room and told me to get out of the mirror. She told me I would be there the whole trip if I didn't. She was right too; I didn't want to leave seeing my skin melt in the mirror. It was weird to see my eyes as wide as a puppy dog with circles enhanced underneath in black. I had to close my eyes, and leave the reflection for a later moment.

In the other room Kasey and Todd started to explore the beginnings of their trip. I could see red and green patterns of curvy checkers on the wall. These checker shapes would spin and change color frequently. I started seeing actual pictures around the house, in waves, and swirls.

Then about ten to fifteen minutes later I could see, such vivid and unimaginable blends of colors decorating the walls with their brilliance. Lucid colors with images of anything, from the silhouettes of people to cars to vivid trees and plants. I had to lie down as it was a bit much. So I found my way to the couch and laid there with my eyes closed for what seemed like an hour. Opening them back up, now almost every object in the room was a different color. The furniture would be a dull red, and the gray carpet looked pure white; I was looking at the wall for what seemed to be forever, because the wallpaper, (that had been there since probably the invention of it) was telling me its story and dancing for me at the same time. I loved the visuals. I would see such picturesque patterns all throughout it. The trails were refreshing and breathtaking, all at the same time. They would be like fractals sort of, but with actual depth into the wall.

We had a pretty cool painting of a perfectly smooth and sandy beach with a diving cliff off in it to one side. I allowed myself to be lost in that for a while. The waves actually moved, and if I was quiet enough, I could hear them crashing on the sand. It was fascinating honestly. If I closed my eyes with that image in my head, I had sworn I could feel the breeze on my face. Surely it wasn't the fan on low, which was next to me. That would not have explained the smell the ocean I was enjoying.

Kasey walked around the room chatting as she normally did. I had made a comment how wonderful this was, and we should do this more often. She laughed.
"No seriously….We should do this again."
"Of course we will silly."
"Cameron has some good stuff, how do you know him?" I was a bit puzzled or maybe just nosy.

"He's the dealer for the theater department and he's got a great package."

"And you know this how?" I laughed.

Of course she knew this. Not that she slept around at all, but she was a free person, who loved to experience people in all their glory and did not discriminate against anyone. If you were an interesting character, then Kasey would seek you out. She was a magnet for charismatic characters in one's life.

She laughed informing me that he was a player and she enjoyed him whenever she could get the chance. Wow, so now he deals *and* does delivery service. I just smiled and continued mentally on my way.

A little while later feeling a bit lethargic from all the visuals and the length of the previous evening's game, I opted to go up to my room to try and catch up on some sleep. They both laughed. Todd, who stood in the corner, fascinated with the patterns he was seeing on a reprint of Van Gogh's 'Peach tree in blossom" joked with a response.

"Good luck with that one. We'll see you in about an hour." They laughed again.

"You just focus on Van Gogh's message to you, and I'll worry about the shut eye factory."

As I passed by to go up the stairs I saw the messages he was seeing from the trees and the petals in their dance. He was in a good spot to take advantage of the hallucinations. Leave it to theater people to have such great visuals for occasions like this.

When I reached my room I hit the sheets, I must have passed out, because when I came to, I felt rested enough. Now everything was in a haze and still moving, and I was a bit off in my head. I figured I'd go back down to Kasey and see if they were still hanging out still feeling its effects. I was honestly surprised that I still was, and that I was able to fall asleep on it.

There was a knock on the door though. It was Kasey, she had beaten me to it, and not waiting for a response she peeked in.

"How long have I been sleeping?" I asked lethargically.

"About fifty minutes or so..."

"Wow it actually feels like I've been sleeping for eight hours. However I don't feel so right."

"That is why I came up. I wanted to check on you. Do you want to come downstairs with us?" Kasey was looking around my room for something as she replied back.

"Not sure."

"What are you not sure about?" She was curious now in her response.

"Things are kind of feeling a bit weird. And everything is moving is still moving pretty hard."

"That is normal, Come on...we're hungry. We are going to go get some food. You should go as well, get something on the stomach."

"Wait...you mean outside?"

"Yes...." she giggled. "Outside, to a restaurant, come on, it will be fun."

"Well you may have to give me a minute; things are pretty off right now."

She laughed explaining that was understandable. While helping me get ready she managed to talk me into a very calm state. One that I didn't panic at the visuals moving past me everywhere I turned. She told me to look at all the visuals as an outsider looking through glasses at the world. That helped put things in perspective a bit. I didn't get lost in the moment or distracted by small visuals that took away from the bigger picture of the trip itself. The pep talk worked long enough to get me out of the hallway down the stairs. She was a professional in dealing with acid trips, she could calm anyone down. Now I was actually quite thrilled to go to the restaurant.

We climbed into her car and off we went. I was impressed by her ability to drive so well, and awe struck at the fact that she could operate a car, while tripping.

Finally arriving at the restaurant we went inside. I was trying hard not to look like I was experiencing any type of hallucinating visuals currently, but I was sure my distorted face screamed something was off. Every color at that moment was a great big giant fluorescent light bulb. Conversations were blurred with amplification into a background that echoed. All I could do was follow the host when she sat us down.

The waitress had asked if we wanted something to drink. I couldn't meet her eyes when she came around to me for my response. Her face was appalling to me. I was sure I wouldn't be able to hide the fact that I saw her face melting off at the door. Kasey answered for me though.
"She'll have coffee."

With that she whisked herself away to get our beverages. She left some trails for me to watch. I was left to the blur of the conversation in the background, and the overwhelming amount of confusion with loud colors being amplified, in waves. It seemed like forever for the coffee to arrive. I started to panic but Kasey assured me it had only been two minutes since she left to fetch the beverages. It felt more like an hour, but finally it arrived.

A bus that was tagged with some religious church sign pulled up and opened its doors for a group to come in. One lady with the church group, probably not more than sixty-five, had blush or rouge that was so painstakingly prevalent; it was standing on its own. When someone's on acid, sixty-five instantly becomes ninety-five years, and all I could see was wrinkles and bright pink rouge. It was so neon pink on her pale face...it petrified me. Then I happened to make the mistake of looking into her eyes. Those made me lose it, because the bright blue shadow on her pale eyes just screamed Easter outing gone awry!

I started to freak out a bit when Kasey tried to calm me down. It worked enough just in time for when the food arrived. I didn't even remember ordering food, but apparently when the waitress asked five times I was in a zone, so Kasey and Todd ordered for me.

I couldn't even begin to think about food. The coffee alone was even disturbing to my taste pallet, once it let me sip on it. Kasey and Todd continued to converse while I continued to just stare at all the swirled colored people around me. They ate their meals while I watched mine. My food wanted no part of the human ritual of destruction. For me the food communicated via its own method at that point, as it danced around my plate for me. In the background I heard Kasey at one point ask for a box for my food. I said not a word, but in my head I was thinking the exact same thing.

"Great idea!"

Any longer on this and I am pretty sure I would be dancing with my food...in sync nonetheless"

Kasey and Todd thought it would be a good time to go since I was lost in the food and staring blatantly at all the people I was visually amazed at. Todd went to get the check. They then realized that no one brought any money with them to pay. I certainly had no money so I was out for helping. Kasey had a great idea though, she told Todd she would go back and get money, while we sat there and drank coffee so as not to alarm management to the situation.

After she had left, I was ok for a bit till my mind raced ahead of me and started to panic at her being gone so long. Todd kept reassuring me it was only five minutes since she had gone. However, I wasn't buying it. I started to lose my bearings a bit, and could feel the slight build of panic in my chest. Todd was able to calm me somewhat but then suggested I go wander outside, I agreed.

I went for that breath of fresh air. I could take no more wrinkles and rouge. I didn't even care I was like a sitting duck outside on the bench. I watched all the people pouring in to come have a bite to eat after their Sunday mass services. They were all exactly the same. It was overwhelming to see just how much Rouge could be caked on pale skins. Dresses and skirts adorned lots of seniors with bright red lips and even brighter eyes and cheeks. They were not making the trip any better.

Todd stayed seated and would remain there till she returned. I inhaled the fresh air, then after a bit I noticed Kasey's car pulling into the lot. I felt so relieved. She exited her car, and the passenger door opened, it was Cameron.

"Great." I mumbled. I brought my hands to rub them across my eyes, as though I needed to verify I wasn't seeing things.

"Just what I need right now." I mumbled.

Cameron indeed stepped out of the car, with his well-worn brown leather jacket, standing just as tall as I remembered. He seemed to have a tendency to want to blend in, by his slumped shoulders in the way he carried himself. He always had those well-worn boots on and hair back in a ponytail. He had a stride that he definitely owned, one that was extremely bold and confidant in its mannerism.

As they approached, Kasey went in to complete our transaction fiasco, while Cameron stood in front of me stating very calmly.

"You look wrecked."

He laughed and moved the hair out of my face so he could peer into my eyes. This was humiliating. I was flushed beat red from the grilling stare he was giving me.

"I'm a little off...I have never done this before so I'm not sure how to feel, but right now, yes I probably do look wrecked."

I just continued staring at the ground. He lifted my chin with his hand and gazed into my eyes for a moment. I pulled back reengaging my inspection of the cemented sidewalk we were on.

Once more he laughed.

"Are you new to the theater department?"

"Kind of."

"I figured, because I haven't seen you around."

Todd greeted us when he came out the double doors.

"Hey you...come to join the fun?" He asked eagerly.

"Of course." Cameron smiled as we caught each other's eyes now.

Todd had asked if I was alright, I stated that I was fine but I just really wanted to get back to a more comfortable place at the moment. He was two steps ahead of me on that one though as he nodded in agreement as they sauntered back to the car.

Back home, there sat Cameron's truck in the driveway. I just wanted to go back to my room, but of course none of them would have it. Instead they told me to smoke out with them, as it would lessen the intensity. I listened, but they lied. It only enhanced the trip and made me peak a bit more after the many waves already still in progress.

Kasey was too busy enjoying her trip to sense Cameron's stares in my direction every couple of minutes, and I sat feeling somewhat uncomfortable by his glares. I wasn't sure if he was tripping or if he was sober. Kasey was alive and dancing in the room when she came up with a brilliant idea, at least according to her words. She thought it would be great if everyone went and played at the park. They agreed with her and rose to the occasion.

I however, wanted a more relaxed time by myself. I was going to hang back on that adventure for the time being to chill at the house. Kasey appeared worried, but I reassured her I was better than she originally thought. With that, they left to go play. Cameron's presence was throwing me off and I couldn't figure out if it was a bad feeling or good one. Consciously though, I was willing to bet it was a bad vibe flashing in front of me.

Upstairs I attempted to lie back down and rest the mind along with the visuals I was still experiencing. About an hour or so later on LSD time, Kasey came back to check on me. I yawned as I was coming back from the somewhat surreal nap I just took. Once more assuring her I was even better than the last time she had asked. I insisted she go back downstairs with the company, but she said the guys had decided to go shoot some pool at the bar. She was pretty much exhausted from all the festivities herself, and chose to sit out on the pool game this time.

I was never so happy to hear that they finally left. She sat with me on the bed and we started to chat a bit about everything. It seemed we talked for hours on anything we could think of, and we probably did. We spoke of her trips and experiences with people and what she still craved from a partner. I let her speak, because I was curious to hear her stories of people, and what led her to believe they were ones she wanted to "experience."

I had absolutely no clue in this field, so I was always the quiet one when people in a group would start discussing times of joy. She was in mid-sentence talking about her time with Cameron, when she abruptly stopped and shot a glance my way. She was quiet for a moment and then she asked me if I thought Cameron was cute.

For a brief moment I pondered the thought of him and me in a relationship. The flash I had, on the situation from an earlier dream showed that he and I would not even remotely be compatible. I thought the dream was referring to him anyways, because the guy that appeared in it stood naked with pink cowboy boots on trying to tell me something. Seeing as he was the only one I knew that wore boots I guess I assumed. Never did figure out what the pink was about though. But my luck I was probably wrong on that one too. But for now, I shrugged with a half response for her that he was handsome in his own way but he wouldn't be worth a relationship.

Kasey informed me that when Cameron is actually with someone he is a very dedicated individual. If I hadn't of known any better it was like she was trying to be an advocate for his character. Did they discuss me at their adventure in the park? Why was she trying to defend him in his arrogant ways? It was just not like her to do so, but I was able to find out the story on them. Turned out he dated her friend for about seven years. His ex-girlfriend left for a job in a different state then she cheated on him. Thus the player effect from the bruise she left on his soul.

I had inquired whether it bothered her that she was sleeping with her friends ex, but she simply stated no, it was just sex. There were no feelings involved. That statement was always mind blowing when I would hear someone say it. I never really understood the "it's just sex" game.

She confessed at one point she thought she did want a relationship with him, but he was the one that didn't want one after he was hurt. He made that abundantly clear with all the ladies, she had informed me.

I was curious on what she thought made him a decent enough person to want to "hook up" with on that level so I inquired. She responded with a smile from ear to ear.
"Well I never had someone who could get me off each and every time like he can."
"Really? What's that like?"
"What...?" She asked "Getting off or getting off every time?"
"Getting off."

Her mouth hit the floor when that statement was made.

"What do you mean? Have you never gotten off?"

"No, I don't think so. I would know something like that right?"

"Yeah you would know that feeling." There was a slight pause. "When you are by yourself, have you ever thought about it? Like have you even tried?"

Her voice rose with an excitement of intrigue, wanting to know more about my body, then finishing her story about Cameron. I answered what I thought she was trying to ask.

"I guess I thought about it. But then again, it didn't really ever become an issue for me." Now I was deep in thought.

Kasey just sat there again with her mouth to the floor. I had to slap her on the arm to snap out of it.

"Wow."

That was all she could say. Then she jumped off the bed ran into her room and then came back with some contraption in her hands.

"Have you ever seen this?"

"It looks like a back massager."

"It is. It is also a favorite toy. It should be for all females really, if you ask my personal opinion. Want to know why?"

She didn't even wait for my reply. She made her way over to the outlet by my bed where my alarm was and plugged in. While she sat facing opposite of me, she turned it on low. Kasey took my hand and placed it on the tip, I hesitated. But she held it there, as we allowed the feeling to run up our arms. It sent a tingle down my body; I wasn't sure what to make of it. I wanted to know how this was supposed to help a woman out, yet afraid to ask because the tingling I was feeling was answering that.

I had questions and was working up the courage to ask, but instead, my friend put her finger to my lips, and quietly stopped me from saying a word. She leaned towards me then lightly kissed my lips, both still having our hands on the massager. She climbed on top of me, pushing me back on the bed. I was now resting on the pillows as she unbuttoned my shirt. It was like I was having an out of body experience. This was a bad idea, it was wrong on all levels. At the same time, while thoughts of guilt plagued my mind; all I could do was close my eyes and feel how amazing her touch was feeling on my body.

Her lips kissing with small bites in between, and all over my neck and breasts. Her small nibbles sent goose bumps all up and down my body. She moved her hand from cupping my breast, to caressing my body gently down my stomach and thighs. With the massager still in her other hand she took her free hand and slid it right between my legs. She tugged with a soft gesture for them to part, and they did with ease. I was surprised to see just how wet I was, when she slid her finger just barely inside of me. Her stroke was so gentle. I laid back, closed my eyes in anticipation of what she would do next.

This was such a huge sin in Catholic teachings. This would be a reason that if it were not confessed on a Saturday, I would go straight to hell over. I had to find a way to justify what was happening in my head because something was happening and I wasn't interested in wanting to stop it.

I let a small laugh escape me, Kasey was turned on by it, I could tell. I only let it slip because my pathetic reasoning was that since my parents decided to disown me, I assumed I was disowned from the religion as well. That was my justification anyways, so I went with it. I washed the thought away when Kasey came back up for a moment to move her hands back up to cup my breasts as if they were just some delicate flowers being arranged for a surprise. I returned with a moan and that is when she stood up and kissed me feverishly on the lips again, only this time parting my lips with her tongue.

Kasey was quite skilled in pleasing herself as well as others. I never for a moment thought I would ever find myself in a situation like this, let alone enjoy it just the same. She placed the 'back massager' down there then rocked it gently back and forth. I could feel something building and was confused at this "new" surge of emotion I was experiencing. Completely immersed in the tingling down there to try to even want to stop her now, I let her continue.

Her finger slid around ever so barely inside me, Kasey moved them in such a way that every ounce of my body was craving more. No matter where she touched me, or licked I was holding back my shivers. Just when I thought I couldn't handle it another any longer, she stopped. She turned off the massager and came up to place her lips on mine.

I told her not to stop because something was happening. She took me by my hand, both of us now completely naked, and showed me the way to the bathroom. I followed. She didn't have to say a word; I knew where she was leading me. I stepped inside the empty bathtub and she instructed me exactly what she wanted me to do. I lay how she positioned me by the faucet. She had the warm water running and told me to close my eyes.

There I was tripping on acid with my legs up the side of the wall in the bathtub with a female no less. I started to think about that as the warm water rushed down on my womanhood, then as I started to wander, all of a sudden I was whisked right back to the current situation when suddenly my body tensed up and I felt such a rush of emotion and tingling, the only thing I could do was let a soft cry of a pleasured moan. When she caressed my body I had to let another cry out. I was paralyzed with such a tingling and light headed euphoria, I could only look into her eyes as she smiled and continued to help me through this new and amazing moment in my life.

New experiences

Next morning I awoke, a bit groggy from the night before, I was in her bed. I glanced around with my eyes squinting from the morning sun, but didn't see Kasey. I had to roll back over to shield my face from the blinding rays screaming at me.

Thoughts about what happened last night came rushing back in. I wasn't sure how to even feel from it all. The whole evening was weird, but kind of erotic at the same time. So confused, but basking just for a moment at the taboo of it. Last night really opened my eyes to some things. Be it as it was, I had to come back to reality. Slowly, I made my way out of the bed, stumbled just a bit in to the hallway. Now the feeling of being hung over decided to creep in, and I was feeling every bit of it too.

"Kasey?"

I called for her but realized I was standing there naked, so I ran into my room to grab a robe. A quick peek made me realize we had more of an evening than I remembered. Grabbing the shirt I saw on the floor I threw it over me, when I turned around there she stood. Kasey was really good at sneaking up of people. This time though she stood with a cup of coffee to greet me.

"Good Morning."

"Listen, I'm sorry I didn't return the favor last night..."

"What are you talking about? We both had the same amount of fun." She smiled and continued her thought.

"It was amazing, especially since you have never experienced another woman before."

"How did you know that?"

"You told me last night. Do you not remember?" She continued to laugh.

"Not currently."

I made a mental note to sit and reflect on the evening after the bathroom incident. Kasey asked if I was hungry, and now I was the one that was smiling. She made us breakfast, while we figured out schedules for the upcoming exams.

The library was my home for the next couple of weeks, so coordinating calendars' was a must for us because we were sharing the car for now. I was becoming pretty stressed about it all mid-way through, but Kasey took it in stride. She said not to worry, do my job. If I studied well and rehearsed, than everything would pay off in the end. Her smile made me return one back. Guess people eventually get used to chaos.

The weeks flew by and we were like two ships passing in the night. Kasey flew in to say hello sometimes when she was on her way out the door, or sometimes returning from her all-nighters. My door was always unlocked for her, and she loved to peek in to see how I was doing with the stress of things.

It seemed Kasey even managed to have found her a new guy to start hanging out with during all of this. She was spending most of her time now with some guy that no one in the group even heard about. Where she learned time management skills I wanted to know, so I could sign up.

From what little she had disclosed about him, He sounded like an interesting guy. I had seen him come and go or pick her up as she would fly through on her daily schedules. One morning he was at the bottom of the stairs when I came down for coffee. He introduced himself, and said his name was Matt. He was quite tall about six feet or so, just as tall as Kasey, only where her hair was blonde, his matched with auburn.

He and I chatted a bit but briefly, and then had to say our polite goodbyes when she came to whisk him out the door for their rendezvous. He seemed nice enough, and it seemed like they were becoming serious, that was quite obvious.

Exam week was grueling. There was never so much caffeine consumed in my entire existence, than in that week. It finally halted to its painful stop after my last class that Friday evening. Tests were done. We were all beyond exhausted from the non-usable knowledge, they had forced us to regurgitate after hours of memorization.

There was going to be a poker party tomorrow evening to start the break in an 'official' capacity. Now I was a regular with the others, almost as if it were like a ritual to go and hang with the group. They became the weekly vent sessions about the department at school. I had not been able to attend for a week or two because of the exams, so when the text came through, I texted the group back to confirm my attendance. I had already lost my mind that week in tests, so I figured losing money at a card game was just what the doctor would order.

Upon my arrival the following evening, there were people hanging out in the living room, of course discussing the tests they felt they passed or failed.

Wandering into the kitchen I could see just a few of the regulars at the table. I placed my drinks in the fridge, sat at the table making small talk with the guys until the game started. My wallet was ok to lose tonight at a total of twenty dollars, but definitely not any more than forty.

Cameron made his normal late entry, and everyone knew he would have gifts. Seeing as I wanted to be done with the quarter mentally, I took his presence as a sign to partake in the festivities of the evening. Maybe it was just a lame way to justify my wanting to party.

Cameron waltzed in,taking immediate notice of my appearance.

"Have a beer." he tossed before I even answered.

"I have one, thanks'"

"Have another one, the night is young."

He placed the rest in the fridge, and then joined us at the table to start the game. Now there was a full table.

"Missed you the past couple of weeks Skye, hope you're ready to lose tonight."

"It's what happens when people have responsibility." The guys laughed as he took off his coat.

"It's a full table and you know what that means?" Not waiting for an answer he continued.

"Full table, means it's time to whoop some ass!"

Of course he was met right back with the sarcasm from the rest of the players. Cameron of course, said he had something to curb the boredom. With that he pulled out a bag with what appeared to be dirt inside, at least from the point of view I had.

"Is that acid?" I asked completely perplexed.

He cocked his head to the side and smiled at me. Inspecting my curious look staring back at him, he seemed somewhat amused at my response.

"This isn't acid." He shook his head at me.

"Deal me out this hand. I'm gonna brew some tea for everyone." He said.

"Tea?" I couldn't help but respond back.

Cameron could tell I was lost in thought. I was now beside myself with questions, but not wanting to show my complete lack of experience, I chose to keep my mouth shut and go with the flow. Seemed the room had a positive attitude about this 'tea' thing so it couldn't be all that bad. I wondered if it was like acid with its visuals and time warped version of its own reality.

The game continued on. By the time the tea was ready I ended up winning three dollars from the pot. Cameron passed out the tea but handed mine last. They all lifted in unison while saying;

"Bottoms up."

I couldn't get past the smell when he answered my confused look and halting moment with the cup.

"Don't think about it, you just have to guzzle it. Now drink!"

He raised the mug to my mouth with his hand underneath the cup, to help force it back in my throat. He almost choked me on the taste and smell by doing that. He guzzled his then said;

"Here's to your first mushroom trip"

"What makes you think it's my first?

That assumption somewhat embarrassed me. I could feel the heat rise to my face. Cameron just smiled back, cocked his head to the side, leaned in to my ear then whispered softly.

"Call it a hunch." he finished his cheer by tapping my cup.

"Cheers to your first time."

The game moved on and as the mushrooms started to take their effect on everyone, I had opted to sit out for a couple of rounds. I wanted to explore more of what this tea was about to offer up for me. Cameron decided to as well. Our seats were eagerly filled by the standing room regulars in the room and we headed outside, for the breeze.

We rocked on the porch swing while he explained exactly what shrooms were. Surprisingly, it was in great depth and detail. He understood all types of mushrooms and their properties. He could even tell you the Latin name of them. He explained how amazing these were, because unlike acid with the trailers, shrooms just enhanced colors. He certainly knew what he was talking about, and if he didn't he sure could talk a good game. It was believable.

"Well, are you going to be the one responsible for me if I freak out?"

"You won't, I promise. But if you need someone to look out for you I got your back."

They were exactly like he had described. The next eight hours flew by like a whirlwind. After the game finally ended which was about two in the morning, the people that were there for the duration of the trip migrated into the living room. We joined them and as I lay on the floor, looking up at the ceiling I watched the third dimension holographic waves flowing around the room, and through me. There was so much laughter from this tea.

At one point it was as if we were at a comedy show. No one knew why the other was hysterical with giggles, but it was definitely contagious. I randomly brushed my hair, and for some odd reason, just the stroke of the brush caused me to grin and laugh. For the next three hours it seemed everything brought smiles and laughs from the room no matter what we did. Conversations would start, and maybe some were actually having quality ones, but it seemed as though everyone was amused with just the laughter. It was definitely a new experience. Cameron watched the whole time, making sure to have my back, and see that it was a wonderful time for me.

I was asked if I wanted another dose as Cameron went around, topping off those who wanted to continue until the sun came home. I hesitated briefly, then politely declined the invite the second time around. After filling up their cups, he joined me on the couch that I had managed to make for my final seat of the evening.

"See I told you that you wouldn't freak out. This stuff is natural."

"I rather enjoyed it for sure. I liked it better than acid." I replied. Resting my head back on the sofa we stared at each other while the room continued on. It seemed like everything about this guy was sexual, so my guard stayed up around him. He smiled and then opened my hand to give me some weed.

"What is this for?"

"You'll want it for the end of the trip when you get back home. It will help you sleep."

With that he took his beer and waltzed out the door. I stayed a bit longer until I was sure I could drive back to my place. After the long evening and the start of break, I was thankful to know I could just go back to my place, kick off the shoes, smoke some herb and nod off without having to set an alarm for anything. I felt like this was going to be a great break. I must have finally nodded off, because I awoke to a gentle tug on my arm. It was Kasey staring at me in my bed.

"Hey you, I thought I would wake you before you slept the day away.”

“What time is it?” I asked a bit confused because it seemed as though I had just closed my eyes five minutes ago.

“Two in the afternoon, I noticed your car coming home early this morning, so I figured I would let you sleep, then we could go get a bite to eat and chat it up for a bit.”

"Sure, just give me a moment."

I started gathering the senses while she was hopping around looking for some clothes to put together for me. She was going to drive so that was a plus. We went to the same restaurant where I dropped the sugar with her. I wasn't sure what her obsession was with this run down dive, but I wasn't going to complain either, since she loved to pay.

This time as we ate, we recapped the past evening's events, I told her all about Cameron and what presents he brought this week. She smiled and told me he was always like that. She filled me in on her evening with Matt. I could tell she was falling for this guy pretty hard. I was hoping it was going to work out for her.

Matt was becoming more and more a fixed character in her daily life. He was more serious than any of the theater people were, so no one knew quite how to take him. His mannerisms were polite, with a touch of dry witted humor. They seemed fitting for the type of man that he projected.

His clothes were always very neat and tidy, never a wrinkle in anything, and always dressed as if he had somewhere to go. They met in accounting class, one of her per-requisites and one of his for his major. Of course it was business that would be his major, which is why he seemed to stand out amongst the rest of our group.

She honestly felt as if he was the one for her. Her 'soulmate' as she stated. That news somewhat alarmed me to hear. They had only just met, but she was convinced that he was the one who 'rocked her world' as she worded it.

I was astonished when she revealed she loved him and just that quick, I was actually left quite speechless. I wanted to express my concern, but hearing how elated she was when speaking about him, and seeing the love she genuinely held for him when she would say his name, forced me to just remain silent.

I would just be able to watch this love from afar and be there if it didn't work for her. Her voice sounded like she was determined to make this happen though. She tried to explain.
"When one knows it's the real deal, time means nothing in how long someone knows the other."

Her shrugging off my concern of it just made me a skeptic, if only a silent one.

Christmas break had officially started. I had no plans for anything or anyone. Seeing as I had no family obligations to worry about, I was free to come and go as I wanted. Although in my current financial state, I couldn't really hold up the latter statement. So I was pretty much free to sit, and watch movies and enjoy some much needed alone time.

With Kasey spending her time now with Matt, and everyone gone home for the break shopping for their loved ones, it appeared it might be a lonely Christmas for me. However, I was ok with that. For once I didn't have to worry about time schedules, obligations, or spending money I knew I didn't have. For that day though, I needed to get some much needed groceries. So it was off to the store with my list and budget reminder in hand.

After the first couple of days I actually started to miss socializing with my friends. I had become so used to the roommates always in or out that having the house to myself was lonelier than I had anticipated. Kasey was meeting Matt's family and the school was completely emptied for the winter break. I was thankful I had chosen to do a film project with a second year film student named Bart.

Bart and I met the previous year in acting class. He had a script he wanted to try and film for some competition they were having. Since he and I were the only ones pretty much staying behind we decided to film and see what happened with it.

So over the break that second week, I filmed a short film, with yours truly as the starring character. I found out on the day we actually met for the first round that Cameron was also going to be assisting with the film crew. So I took comfort knowing that I was at least going to spend some time with at least one person I knew from school over break. We bribed some locals to be extras in the film, and they were all more than willing to do so. So after spending half the day collecting the signatures for the release rights we finally started an independent film.

I learned right before Christmas break, I didn't make the spring musical for the main stage, and since I wasn't expecting anything less, I wasn't as devastated as some of the second year students. They had melt downs at the creative arts center around the casting board the last day before break. I wasn't sure why they always posted these things before a break and never right after. The psychology behind that should be looked into I had thought.

I was fortunate enough to be close to the director from one of my previous classes, to know who was already casted for the upcoming performance. Truth was, there were only twelve parts and like a hundred people trying out for the slots, so it was no news to me that I would not be amongst the chosen ones.

One night watching the history channel after settling back in from one of the last days of shooting, a text came through on my phone. I was surprised to see it was Cameron

"Hey." I answered his text back with the same

"What are you doing?" His response back was simple enough.

"Nothing, U?"

"Bored. Did u leave town today too for Christmas dinner with family tomorrow?"

"No. U?"

"No I'm from here." He replied

"Well that's convenient. LOL" I sent back.

"Want to hang out?"

"Sure, I'm just watching TV though. I'm going to stay in for the evening."

"Great I'll bring some take out and meet you at your place in about an hour or so."

"OK C U then."

We watched some movie and ate some fast food. He invited me to his mom's house for Christmas dinner the following day. I went because there was nothing better going on anyways.

His mom was a very high strung character, so I saw where Cameron received most his genes. But on the other hand, his Dad seemed normal. Cameron inherited nothing from his father. That was evident after spending time getting to know the family. All in all though, he managed to make the lonely winter break a nice relaxed vacation for me.

Break came to its close after the New Year celebrations. It no longer bothered me when I would come home to see random people chilling on a couch or two. Schedules were back in place and roommates once more came and went. The film crew had finished the last of the retakes the day before school started, and Cameron and I actually started to become good friends.

Mythology

After the break, most of my classes appeared to be an easy course load. By this point I had decided to get a job on campus to be closer to my studies. My time traveling to and from everywhere was wasting more time than I wanted. I applied for a job at the information booth, and received the offer before I left the interview. I was pretty sure the fact that I listed theatre as my major was a bonus for this service field.

My counselor convinced me to knock out most of the general education classes in the beginning. I agreed, but along with that decision was a class that I signed up for that was not my forte. It was Mythology. I was interested enough that I thought it would be an easy A for my GPA. I couldn't be further from the truth.

Sometimes my theories are far skewed; I found this out the hard way via mythology. The first day of class, I sat in the last row. I knew it was a cliché, but my repetitive nature usually worked in my favor any other time. Sitting in the cold hard unforgivable plastic seat, I had assumed I was a couple of minutes early. There was no sight of a professor around, so I had a chance to study my notes from my previous class. I broke out my notebook to study while waiting on the current instructor. Glancing at my watch I noticed I wasn't early at all. It was the professor that was late. Well this was going to be annoying if this was his forte. But seeing as it was out of my control, all I could do was sit back and be thankful, the interruption was on his time and not mine.

About ten minutes into the class, in walked a man that seemed as tall as the sky above me. He was trimmed in black from head to toe. His frame was but skin and bones, and just as overly lanky. He came with a stride just as reaching as he was, but perfect for his build. He wore a black belt to match the rest of his ensemble. I found myself wondering if his underwear was black as well.

Peering at his waist he must have been maybe a total of a hundred and thirty pounds. There was something so thrilling and baffling about this guy. He came in like a storm. Like a chaotic cluster of clouds, in complete turmoil with itself.

I didn't know what to make of this Avant-grade want to be artist, so I thought just be quiet and take notes then. I couldn't take my eyes off of him, though. His blond hair effortlessly hung around his shoulders, flowing every time the wind offered air circulation in the room.

His cheekbones were to die for. They were as high as I was currently, in a baffled state of euphoria from his presence. The pit of my stomach crawling into my throat, he was maybe forty years old, if I had to guess. I was pretty sure I had just fallen in love.

He was the Matt in Kasey's world to me right now. What was it about this guy that just snatched me up in a whirlwind of emotion? It was crazy, to have all that sensation running through my veins within one minute of his late arrival.

After throwing his disheveled items down on the desk, Dr. Davidson stood at the front of class. He turned to the board behind him, chaotically scribbling a bunch of notes. The entire class got down to business, and repeated the exact same motion, only in their self-supplied notebooks. When he was finally done with the notes, he stepped back and pondered the words on the board. Only after he was pleased with the end result, he placed the marker down, and turned to face the class. He stared at all of us intently, and slowly. Moving closer in my direction, he stopped when his eyes met mine. He stared for what seemed like an eternity.

He had a puzzled look to him as did I. He cocked his head to one side, and matched my curiosity. He inspected me from head to toe, somewhat amused it seemed at the dress I was wearing. What was wrong with my dress? It was just a simple one piece v neck dress that hung just below knees, but he seemed intrigued with it.

I knew one wasn't supposed to wear white in the winter time, but Kasey said; off white was the 'in' thing for the winter wardrobes this year. It was on sale so we both grabbed one for our own. Whatever the case, the dress seemed to either mesmerize, or confuse him.

He shook his head. What was that about? What was I supposed to make of that? Could he tell that I thought he was hot? Crap- I always messed these things up. I was horrible at this stuff. I have got to stop being so obvious with my emotion and visuals. Obviously I needed to work on my acting skills more. This was going to be a very difficult class!

His first name was Robert, and after the deadly stare down contest he had with the class, he then told us a little about himself and where he was from. Turns out he graduated from University of Cali but had traveled extensively all over. He was offered a position to teach here at the university.

Listening to him ramble about anything but Mythology for the first ten minutes intrigued me. He had a reasonable excuse as to why he was late, but then made it a point to have everyone understand that he; himself did not tolerate lateness of any kind. After five minutes the door would close and there would be no entries to class at that point.

He then passed out the syllabus, and instructed us on the rules he expected from all his classes as a whole. As he went row by row, he finally approached where I had been sitting. While passing it to me, he held the paper in his grasp rather tightly so I had to tug at it. I looked up at him with a questionable look; he met my eyes with his hard gaze. He paused momentarily with a dissecting or maybe undressing look. Suddenly he let loose and continued exactly where he left off in his conversation with the class.

What was he *thinking*? Why was he making a point to be over dramatic on his stares with me? Did I have something hanging from my nose? How embarrassing if that was the case. While he sauntered back to the front of the class, I quickly took a sneak into my compact mirror. I had to verify that I didn't ignore my hygiene. His glare was almost uncomfortable really. I took a deep sigh and thought this class was going to be extremely brutal.

"What the hell was that?" I asked myself.

Then it dawned on me, Oh hell, the moment he looked at me, I swore he knew I was a dripping hot mess. What was with me lately? First with a female, now my teacher? Seemed I was knocking the taboo fantasizes out of the park for sure. That question though immediately answered itself, with an automatic response: Blame Catholicism. So I did, and felt much better.

This was crazy. How in the world was I supposed to take this class and not only pass, but go the whole quarter without trying to let on, that I wanted to jump this man's bones? I'm tormented this time around, and especially since his lectures were completely opposite of him, dry and uninteresting.

The first half of the class, I implored my weakened acting abilities to appear as though I were listening to him. Meanwhile, all I could really do was trail off to my fantasy place and undress him secretly under the hidden gaze of learning. I justified the daydream, with it only being the first day of class.

How much could one possibly miss by fantasizing for ten minutes or so? His mysteriousness bewildered me. I was more interested in finding out why a charge of electricity surged through me when he so candidly, walked into the room. That same feeling that was on my body when Kasey and I were together came back.

Unfortunately, it seemed his teaching style was all over the place. It was rather difficult to keep up on the many tangents he veered off into. By the time whatever topic he was on, came back around to being tied to the lesson, everyone had more questions than answers. I peered around the room and was hopeful in the comfort of knowing, I wasn't the only one who was having issues keeping up with this man in front of us. Two nights a week? Yeah this class was going to be the death of me.

Nothing was said on the way out, because I ran, wet panties and all. I couldn't even bare to look at him, although from the corner of my eye I could feel his stare on me. I wasn't sure if I felt elated or devastated. Either way it was really exciting.

I had no idea what to make of that class. Nor could I wait to make it home, to talk Kasey's ear off about it. I sent a text to see if she had plans that night, and she did. She was free the following night though, so I told her to pencil me in. I was dying to tell someone about this crazy encounter.

I drove home, threw something together to inhale for dinner. I was not at all skilled in the kitchen, so I was happy to be able to walk out with something edible each time. That was always a confidence booster. I snuggled back into the somewhat contemporary well used brown couch, and tried to watch a movie.

I was not even remotely paying attention due to obvious reasons. I had my own movie playing out in my head, and it was definitely going to be a chic flick.

My internal movie stopped me in the middle, by flashing one of my cards in front of me. It briefly appeared, then was gone. I couldn't make out what it was, but it seemed urgent in its message that I should do a reading. I had stashed my bag in my room, so I ran up the steps to grab them. In the brown satchel, there were different gemstones to accompany my cards. There were runes brilliantly crafted with such intent; it was hard to not feel the energy radiating from them. The runes wanted me to use them this evening.

Grabbing my juice and bowl I placed the items on the end table next to my bed. I sat Indian style and took a couple of hits while I lit some incense. I pulled down the tapestries that hung around the room on the windows. Staring at them and their symbols, especially when the Sun was up, made them come to life with their radiant energies, and visuals. After the candles were all a flame, I wandered off into thoughts of this amazing human being that just dropped into my life for a minute.

I focused on my question about him. I had asked if there was a connection that should be addressed. While holding the stones in my left hand, then with the fingers of my right hand, I mixed them up. I read the symbol written on the stone that I pulled. That answered my question. I wanted to be sure on this one, so I opted to ask them one more question for a bit further clarification. It came back with pretty much the same answer.

"Inevitable."

Was that even allowed in College? I mean technically it should be OK. I wanted Kasey to be here right now, and then it dawned on me, who in their right mind would want someone like me? I was a short plain Jane chic that had not a lick of sense about her. I had no clue on anything in the world, especially about issues that mattered of importance to Dr. Davidson. He was way out of my league.

I kept coming back to his stares; I was confused on the looks he sent my way. The whole thing was just so frustrating, yet alluring. I was becoming rather upset about my incessant thoughts now, because the whole damn situation, was taking up too much of my time, currently. I could hear Kasey now.

"Just go with the flow, enjoy the individual completely and see what happens."

"How does one tell the butterflies to take a hike for a minute?"

I smiled at that, and then dropped the runes back in the bag to their rightful place.

I figured a warm shower would help get my mind off of things so grabbing my robe I made my way towards the bathroom. I needed to wash up and rinse away the thoughts I was having. The hot water felt like a gentle massage down on my back. I stood under the steam pretending I was under some waterfall. Opening my eyes I let my neck enjoy its massage. I glanced at the faucet and flash backed to Kasey and me. So I closed my eyes again to relive the experience while gently caressing my body with the soap.

There were no intentions of rushing the shower, because the hot water and wicked thoughts of Dr. Davidson were turning me on currently. I was okay being lost for a minute. At least until I heard one of the roommates coming up the stairs. That popped the fantasy balloon, and any delicious thoughts I may have had. I grumbled and forced the fantasies to stop, at least just long enough to get to my room. I opened my eyes, turned the water off and said goodbye to the waterfall.
"Till next time my love."

I stepped out of the shower, careful not to slip like most every other time. I wrapped my overly plush robe around my soaked body. This wonderful piece of magic was like an immediate liquid hug, knowing how to melt every ounce of worry away into the universe. I loved this robe, and it loved me right back. I gathered my items and with a towel on my head, the robe loosely tied around me, I made my way back into the bedroom to think about my dreamy professor.

On the bed I laid with the robe still around me. Not bothering to dry off I closed my eyes and once more thought of my teacher. I imagined what it would be like if he and I had a chance encounter that resulted in a physical relief for each other.

I must have passed out because I awoke to a blaring alarm going off. My towel was on the floor and I was upside down in the bed. I stumbled to turn the noise off. I sat for a moment to actually wake up, and then realized that I had passed out for like ten hours straight. Well there went any plans I may have had the previous evening. Then I realized, no wait it was me. I never made plans, so I was free and clear. Nice, score one for me.

Recalling the dream I had last night, I quickly jotted some key words I could remember. I kept a notebook about the bed for just such occasions.

I stretched on my way up to get dressed for the day, but realized while rubbing my eyes, that I was just as wet as I was the night before. I contemplated for a moment, to see if I had time to take care of the problem. With as wet as I was currently, I didn't really have a choice, but then I heard a knock at the door, so that thought was quickly shot down.

From then on though, I paid better attention to my wardrobe for his classes. I found myself now starting to want to dress rather a bit more revealing than the plane old Jane, who was used to hand me downs and ragged seconds.

For his next class, I ended up raiding Kasey's closet. She always had really cool clothes. Since I didn't really ever dress for anything, I thought Kasey would have some better clothes than dollar store, and thrift items that currently occupied my closet space.

I made my way past the mound of clothes on the floor that greeted me as soon as I entered the door. I pushed the pile with the door, sweeping them to the first closet right behind. There was a small path to the other closet, so I opted for the easiest plan of attack. I was careful not to step on her plates, or jewelry she loved so much to take off in the middle of the night.

I scrambled through some tops and dresses. Nothing jumped out for me though. I was never really good at this stuff. I never had such a desire to make myself look pretty for anyone. Last week's madness for my ensemble was not going to cut it for this guy. Nope. I wanted to look incredibly sexy, but not too overly sexy. Something subtle yet …oh hell who was I kidding? I just wanted something better than my damn jogging pants.

I was baffled at all the choices wishing Kasey was here to help. I swear, it was like her and I have a sixth sense thing going; because much to my surprise, she came waltzing in chewing on the rest of a bagel she had just got done making for herself.

"Whatcha doing?" She took a bite that left cream cheese on her mouth.

"Dressing up." I replied, leaning over to rub it off her lip.

"Dressing up? For what?"

"I don't know. I think I am just tired of blue jeans and jogging pants." I was really hoping she would just not ask any further.

"Because why?"

"I don't know I just want to."

She didn't buy my lame attempt at trying to sell a poorly written story. Neither did I. She grinned at me walking to her closet sifting through some outfits for me. She was always so generous with those things. Some girls are always so mean when people borrowed, but not Kasey. She would give you the shirt off her back if she had to. She found a great outfit for me to wear, she handed me a black top with a black skirt that came up right below the knee. The top was sheer V-neck that made me look like I was all of ten pounds. Yeah this was a great friend.

"What's his name?" She said nonchalantly

"It's no one you know."

"I might. What is his name?"

"Robert."

"Robert huh?"

"Yeah, see I told you, you wouldn't know him."

"How do you know..." She laughed in the middle

"That I don't know a Robert?" She finished by jumping on the bed.

"Oh sorry. Do you know a Robert?"

"Maybe."

"No, you don't know one. I know now."

"Why do you say that?"

"Because you would have definitely said yes if you did. Tell me I am lying for that statement." Now I was the one who laughed.

But I lay across the bed and told her anyway. I sat there and told her all about the encounter, she laughed and said;

"That was hot."

Go figure, I should have known. So she told me to help myself to anything in her closet and if I needed her, she was there for me. I personally think she just wanted to hear about the amazing sex I imagined we would have.

His next class, I was taking notes like everyone else; he had paused trying to let us all catch up with the massive overload he just dumped on us. When I looked to the board scrambling all his notes down there he was staring at me… well sort of.

He was fixated briefly on, what I thought was me, until I followed his amazing blue eyes to my legs. It occurred to me, that as I feverishly took notes, I had let my legs slip open. This should never have been, because I was wearing the skirt Kasey gave me. I was so used to wearing pants, I completely spaced the current outfit I had on, and the projection I was attempting to put off. He once again snapped out of his daze, now looked directly at me, then continued on as if nothing happened between us.

"Well." I thought. "That backfired epically."

His lectures were so demanding I just simply forgot I was wearing the skirt in my focus on class that day. He was a very intricate and detailed professor that loved going off on tangents. He always lost the class down rabbit holes of discussions. Keeping up with the task at hand was extremely difficult. I was struggling and rather hard.

After that one encounter, I never wore another skirt, and he never said a thing about it. There were looks and innuendos between us sometimes, or maybe it was a figment of my over creative imagination. But now, here it was close to midterms, and I was struggling rather desperately. I needed to ramp my studies up, because it was a paper we had to write for it. 'The influences of yesterday's Gods in today's society using personal life experiences.'

He announced on more than one occasion, about his office hours. Mainly for those like me who were going to fail. This was the only class that was dragging down my GPA and I wasn't happy about it. The professor knew I was trying like mad to keep up, and that made it worse.

One day he stated it yet again, this time at the beginning and end of class. I never looked up when he mentioned it, for fear he would catch my eyes in a tormented struggle of the offer. I had yet to sign up for the help. When the class ended he asked me to stay. I died when he said my name. I bravely gathered my things at the bell and then approached him. The kids had all piled out and he asked me if I had any plans on signing up for help. I stated nervously.

"I want to. It's just that..."

His demanding question and stare took me off guard as they usually did. I was trying hard not to look into his eyes. I was afraid he would see right through me, and know how much I was ravishing him in the back of my mind.

"What's stopping you? You're struggling badly, so when shall I put you down for?"

I nervously replied back.

"When do you have open?"

We made plans for tomorrow afternoon, at four. We met at his office. Fourth floor suite four eleven. I nervously made my way through the somewhat empty halls. Everyone was either at the library studying, or left because it was the end of the day.

I reached the elevator, and pressed the fourth floor button. It was rather a quick trip up, as there were no additional stops for students or teachers. My heart raced, and my stomach was in my throat. I had butterflies the size of softballs, and I kept getting dry mouth. I could feel my heart racing as the floors went up one by one. I had to shake myself into a reality check.

I convinced myself to role play this event out. I was hoping that if I character played, that might be enough to do the trick to get me through the meeting. Anything just so he couldn't see my real thoughts. Let's hope this worked because floor number four just lit up.

I made my way down into the hall, but not before stopping to take one last drink of water, hoping that would suffice. I approached his door that was slightly ajar. I grit my teeth and knocked softly, hoping he wouldn't hear. I could use that as an excuse to say I stopped by but no one answered. I thought I was too brilliant for my own good. Just as I started the turn to leave, I heard that raspy voice.

"Come in."

Crap. I took a deep breath in and let the grip of my teeth relax, and nervously opened the door.

"Miss Miller, come on in. Sit. Let's chat."

I quickly sat down, and reached in my bag for my notebook. I was prepared to take lots of notes to whatever was going to be recommended to help my paper get an A. He stood up, went behind me to close the door. I was sure he could hear my nervous panting as he slowly made his way past me.

"Have you decided what God or Goddess you're going to write about yet?"

"Yes." I replied having to clear my throat to do so.

"And? Who did you choose Miss Miller?"

"Oh you can call me Skye. And I chose Dionysus."

"OK Skye…why?"

"Why what?"

What the hell kind of response was that? Inside my head, I had a visual of me kicking myself while I lay curdled up like a fetus

"Why did you choose Dionysus?" He asked back.

"Dionysus is the God of theater. I wanted to tie it in with my major. You know kind of keeping the theme in line."

I nervously laughed appreciating my own sense of humor, even if he didn't.

"Oh I see, is that all you were going to discuss in the paper about him? Do you know his back story?"

"Well sort of."

OK I lied, I had no clue. I just knew he was the God of theater. I had yet to attempt any research on him. I had hoped I wouldn't make myself look like a fool, but I knew it was way too late on that one.

He sat back down at his desk, crossed his legs and placed his long lanky forefinger on his lips while staring at me. There was that confusing look again. I was trying so valiantly to maintain my composure. Seemed the only way to be able to do that now, was to *not look* at him in the eye. I tried to take a note, but there was none yet to take. So I had to look back up at him.

"Would you like me to give you some guidelines I think you should incorporate into the paper?" He saved me.

I melted completely in the seat. In the back of my mind I was screaming how much I wanted, whatever he wanted to throw my way. Including whatever else, like throwing me on the desk and just simply having his way with me.

"Yes please. Guidelines are good."

Great now I look like a rambling moron with no vocabulary. I composed myself quickly with a better reply to him.

"Yeah anything you think would help."   There, I made a remarkable save on that one.

"Well for starters did you know that he was the God of the grape harvest? He was the God of wine making, and of ritual madness?" He paused for me to start taking notes, before he continued."

"He was also the God of fertility and my favorite…" he had a mischievous smile about him

"God of religious ritual ecstasy."

Oh how this was going to be even more difficult than I could have ever imagined. I had no idea what I just walked into. I wanted to slap myself for not researching beforehand. The one God out of the millions that I chose and it lead to this. Crap! Now I was in trouble.

How do I write a paper about a God of religious ecstasy without making it sound like a porn movie, via words? If I were not careful in how I skillfully and scientifically narrated these words, surely my deepest fantasies and thoughts would be translated through this piece.

I couldn't even begin to express the lesson I learned at this very moment. Never procrastinate on anything, anymore. You know that saying "Open mouth insert foot? Yeah that was where I was at currently. Always research before we place our feet in to our mouths. Back in reality though, he was still staring at me awaiting my response while I pondered mouths and ecstasy rituals in my head.

"Um-no I should probably open a book on this guy huh? " That made him laugh.

I accidentally mumbled that out loud, and I was positive I was red from head to toe. I quickly jotted all the traits he just threw up at me. Sudden realization of that actual comment being said out loud forced me to look at him to see his reaction.

He hadn't lost his smile from the laugh. His piercing blue eyes were staring directly at me. Finally, he broke the awkward silence.

"I hope you're not already done picking my brain on the recommendations for the paper?"

Nervously trying to maintain my calm pretense, I straight lied to him.

"No uh-certainly not. "

"Alright then tell me what attracted you to him and or theatre?"

"He was my favorite God in high school when we did a play on the Greek mythology characters."

The realization of how completely dumb that statement was, as they stumbled their way out, made me want to crawl under a rock for the rest of my life. Could I have looked anymore naive at this moment? I was humiliated. I forced myself to look at him anyway, so as not to be defeated completely. I wasn't going to allow him that much credit for my own idiotic statement. Instead, he cocked his head and keeping his gentle smile for me replied back.

"He is one of my favorite Gods too. Want me to tell you why?"

"No," I screamed to myself. I don't want to have an orgasm here in your chair while you undress me with your words. Instead I barely uttered this instead.

"Yes, please."

Please? Please? Who says that? Then again, at this point who cared? Another guilty flush came over my face. I knew I was beat red, I felt the rush of heat take over me and stay there.

He tilted his head back when he saw that moment happen to me. While smiling as if in complete sympathy for my current situation, he continued with the story of why he loved Dionysus. How on earth could someone speak of a God the way he did, and make it sound like an orgasmic erotic love affair?

He described climatic ecstasies and rituals this God enjoyed. How could someone make something sound so hot? His words flowing like a romantic love novel. Holy shit, this professor knew what the hell he was talking about. I definitely wanted to collaborate on a screen play with him as the staring character.

I knew there was a good chance I was going home to the shower. I would now refer to my showers as religious ecstasy! I was dripping wet from hearing his stories. It didn't help that it was being narrated from the sexiest, raspiest voice I had ever heard. It was like music to my ears. If this mad man were to touch me at any moment I might just explode.

I had to gather myself from my happy place and get it back together to end the conversation with him. So far little notes had been taken. All I could do was just hang on his every word. His lips effortlessly caressing the conversation as he spoke about the God I happened to have chosen. I had to get home and do something about the soaked panties between my soaked thighs.

My whole cover of trying to pretend I was some journalist covering a breaking story was failing epically. He was breaking me; I had to get my composure back. When he was done, he looked at me with a devilish grin waiting for a response.
"Here I thought it would be a boring paper. Now I'm going to have a hard time not making it sound like a porn. Ha!"

Oh my freaking word. What the hell did I just respond with? Oh my God, I just failed the class. He smiled at me, simply stated, which again, blew me away.
"Just be creative then and tie it in with history." He grinned

I could hardly move at this point. I rushed the last of the notes then placed my notebook back in my bag. I wanted very much to leave at this point, but I was in a bit of a quandary though. I was afraid, if I stood to leave from where I sat, it may be a little drenched from this moment. I would have been embarrassed and thus never returning back to his class again. The humiliation would have been too great. So I couldn't stand without wanting to at least check to make sure, without being conspicuous. I sat there for a moment hoping he would open the door. I was filled with disappointment on his lack of delivery though

Instead he wheeled his chair around his desk to where I sat. He leaned in real close to me, almost having our lips meet. I was hoping he would just take me there, but instead he had one more pointer for me. This one took me over the edge.

At that moment things took a sharp left in the conversation. In explaining how their influences were held in today's society Dr. Davidson said we should use personal experiences in relation to the character we chose. However in my situation, we found there were no real experiences to use with my character, until that very moment.

Had I known Dionysus was a horny role model, I would have chosen to probably go with Athena. Instead my lack of worldly knowledge brought me to this one. Guess that's why I was the student and he was the teacher. I could come up with nothing.

He seemed surprised, rather delighted. He smiled as if to comfort me though. So we thought for just a minute, and then he suggested I incorporate the example of me wearing the skirt that day to class. The only skirt I had ever worn and the only skirt I will ever wear, thanks to him.

He spoke on how it was like one of Dionysus's muses in the woods playing and being mischievous in her nature, as they all normally were, but this muse running through the woods happened to have caught some attention. He told the rest of the story from the God's point of view. I found myself wondering if he cared about plagiarism at this point.

I failed to mention, that there were no underwear placed on me that day. That though, was beside the point. I may have subconsciously forgotten about them. OK I purposely forgot to wear them. But I wasn't going with the intention of flashing him; I just wanted to feel sexier for myself. Kasey suggested it, as sometimes she went without panties. She said it made her feel super sexy. I tried it out and didn't really care for it. Maybe I shouldn't have tried it out with the one person I fell head over heels for, but it's whatever at this point.

I continued to listen attentively, because quite frankly, I didn't think I was going to make it home that night without losing my mind in a climatic verbiage intercourse.

The only thing I can honestly say, is that what ever happened in that room was the most intense emotion I had ever felt. I walked out of there a whole new person and a brand new woman. There was no doubt about that. I was determined to not let him down on this paper. He was as intelligent as he was sexy, and ruthless as he was tall. He offered me a whole new realm to explore on this paper. I was baffled at that encounter to say the least, but in a very odd way. What an amazing moment for a meeting of the minds.

Was this all in my imagination, or did we actually just have intellectual intercourse? I was speechless, breathless, and completely exhilarated over that moment in time. I would never be able to look at him without imagining ravishing his body. That much I knew for a fact. All he did was use words, but both he and I, without touch, climbed there together, and that much I knew for a fact. I wanted this man more than anything currently, but I knew a shower was needed more so.

Was he like this with all his students? Or was it just me? Then it dawned on me, no... I would never have been the only one, but it didn't even matter. I just fell in love with intellectualism.

I was extremely light headed when the meeting was over. Observing my breathlessness from the conversation, he touched my cheek then made his way to offer me a glass of water from his machine in the corner. I needed more than water I thought, but I'll take what I could get for now. Time obviously ran away from us as it was close to seven in the evening when the "office consult" ended.

I had the same tingling and numbness I did when I was with Kasey. So when he offered me a ride home; I gladly took him up on it since Kasey had the car. We walked to the lot but there were no cars to be found.

"Where's the car?" I thought maybe it was stolen.

"I don't have a car."

I shot him a quizzical look then he pointed to a corner of the lot where bikes were chained. He rode a Harley, and I had to laugh and ask if he was related. He smiled and came back with; "I wish. Let's ride."

I was going to lose my mind. I knew I was already there, but now I was going for the guarantee. I didn't think I would be able to hold out. I felt a warm gush trickle down my panties while my blood surged with excitement. He straddled the bike and looked for me to follow. I repeated the motion, and then closed my legs around his middle. I could feel the warmth of my panties through my black leggings. I was sure he could feel it against the small of his back. I tightened around him. I clutched to his back from feeling all the reverb from the massive machine I was on. But the vibrations of the bikes engine...made my insides react with a buzz of their own in an aching desire. I was trying desperately to be sly about this amazing sensation.

As the bike hit the road, the wind blowing something fierce now, I couldn't help but press forward against him. The rhythmic nature of the tremors, made me have to grind my legs together. This powerful machine, with its pulsating leather seat below, was forcing odd emotions to surge through me. I couldn't help but hike my hips back and forth from the tingle it was currently sending.

I closed my eyes, and straightened the small of my back. In doing so, I instinctively gripped tighter around him. My hips were effortlessly and slowly grinding on the seat. I really wasn't trying to be obvious, rather quite the opposite. One more grind though. I had to bite my lip with the climbing sensation from the seat rubbing on my clit.

I opened my eyes to see, that out of my peripheral vision, he was staring at me, through the mirrors. He knew what was happening, he revved the engine and sped up. I couldn't help but let out a small cry from all the buildup.

"Fuck." I said softly.

I may have purposefully whispered that in his ear. I could feel his chest beating as hard as my pulsating walls below. I wouldn't be able to contain this any longer. Once more for his viewing pleasure I thought, because I was on the brink. Rocking my hips gently back and forth, with the vibrations of the seat, I tightened one last time around his back. I braced myself. I kept my thighs gripped tight around him, then steadied myself while the waves of ecstasy rode through my veins. I was pretty sure he reached too. His sigh said it all.

When we arrived at my house, I slid off the bike and could only look down to thank him. My body was still quivering from the ride and rather noticeable. He broke the silence yet again.

"First...bike ride?"

An overly nervous laugh blurted out.

"First ...yeah first ride." I was completely humiliated.

Still gazing down, he reached for my hand yanking me towards him. The way he pulled, with such force, caused me to bump into his straddled thigh. The sensation from my hips colliding with his sent an electric surge that told me I hadn't finished yet.

Clutching his leather jacket, I was forced to look up at him. They automatically tightened as though he were the seat. The unexpected eruption caused him to have to hold me until my body stopped its trembling. My hips uncontrollably locked on to him. He shook his head out of pure elation while crashing his mouth into mine for a kiss.

Secrets

So Robert and I now had something. What it was exactly, I didn't know. What I did know, was that I dressed for him every week with ulterior motives in mind. He was quite the professional though. He kept his distance from me in the class. In fact, he kept his distance from me the rest of the time. At one point it was almost awkward, and had me thinking the meeting hadn't even happened.

I found myself *always* daydreaming in his class. I had to force myself to do all the extra credit, because my grades on his exams weren't exactly stellar in their final marks. It was always so hard to not sit and fantasize about him. Every bit of his body was chiseled to perfection. His energy was just so demanding when he entered a room.

Sometimes he would glance in my direction, to which I could feel the intensity of the energy radiating between us. Even sitting in the very back of the room, it was obvious he and I had some thing, a connection of sorts? I don't know. The way he watched me when he thought no one was looking was nerve wrecking though. When people were too busy taking notes, I could feel his energy piercing through me when he would glance my way.

Nothing was ever brought up about it, on both our ends. If we managed to lock eyes, we never looked away, until necessary. It was a bit confusing.

I understood where it had to be with him. I wasn't angry that he was taking the professional route on this; I was more frustrated with it, but until the class was over, there was little I could do about it. So it was back to the professional professor and the studious student.

It was better off that way. I wouldn't know what to do if something were to happen anyway. For now, it was more of a turn on that I had a little secret with him, than it was to actually be with him. Maybe I was justifying the rejection of it all. That would be a bitter pill to swallow if that were true. The blaring of the bell brought me back to reality. I gathered my items sighing with a disappointment.

My friend Bart caught up with me in the parking lot that day after work. He ran to catch up with me while flagging me from across the way.

"Skye! Hey hang on a minute!" He yelled from across the way.

I stopped for him to catch up. He was completely out of breath upon his arrival.

"Dude you have got to quit smoking those damn cigarettes." I shook my head at him stating the obvious.

"Hey." Was all he could reply while desperately trying to catch his breath.

"You know the movie we did over winter break?"

"Yeah." I nodded in agreement

"Well the department gave me an A for that, but more importantly they want to show it at the competition for the spring film festival here."

"NO WAY! Get out of here."

"No shit, that's what I said. I thought I would tell you so you wouldn't be surprised when you see the advertisement poster they are creating for it, because it will be you blown up twenty feet tall for the creative arts advertisement."

"Are you messing with me? For real? Oh my God, what the hell...they really liked it that much?"

"Hell yeah and if it gets enough votes I get the prize."

"What is that?"

"It's a chance for the head department to send it to Moonlight festival, for backing to complete a real movie."

He was so stoked he could hardly contain his excitement. How could one really blame him though? What an opportunity for him or for anyone really. This was a great way for me to finally get noticed as well. The acting skills couldn't have been that bad for them to move it to the next level of competition.

I congratulated him on his accomplishment, he admitted he was nervous but there was nothing he could do about it until the end of the spring semester when the votes were in and tallied. I was crossing my fingers for him, and all the while knowing the following quarter I would be seen now by the students and faculty in my first professional acting job ever, well at least since high school. That had to help for exposure to the main stage.

Further into the quarter, people started taking notice in the halls, and were making comments on my skills as a budding theater student. Some of the kids in the film department had asked for me to star in projects, and so when there was free time in my shcedule, I was usually filming, or directing.

I finally finished my screen play and had Bart take a peek at it. He added another twist to the ending and said he appreciated the mystery of it. He asked if I would mind him tossing it around the department, and I had eagerly stated
"By all means, feel free."

But all this time I had still not forgotten my chance encounter with the amazing professor. Early one morning on my way to work, I was running late, and missed my stop to grab my coffee. So I was already flustered, but as I turned on the lights and got the phones ready, I heard a familiar voice from behind me.
"Hey, stranger."

I whipped around as soon as I heard the voice. It was Robert, what was he doing here? I was still his student. He hadn't said anything to me since that day and that was weeks ago in his office. I was all of a sudden quite nervous and ecstatic to see him at the same time, considering the last encounter.

"Robert!" I exclaimed

"How are you?" He said casually with that irresistible smile of his.

"Oh running a bit late, no coffee, tests to study for, you know...doing well and you?"

He knew I was completely startled by his presence. He knew how nervous he made me. My non responses always gave that away. We chatted for a bit, and then he asked what I was doing later. Of course in my mind, I was screaming, "You!" Instead all could manage to utter was one word.

"Studying."

"Want some company?" He asked.

"For studying?" I said a bit baffled.

"Nope." He smiled and I melted

"What time were you thinking?" I didn't hesitate to respond.

I didn't care what time he said, I would make time for him no matter what. No words were needed at this point as to what the evening would entail, because I was sure, both of us shared the same thoughts on it.

"I have a class later so maybe seven-ish?"

"Text me when you're done then and we can meet."

"Sounds good." With that he was gone.

The entire day dragged on, hour by hour, grueling and torturing me to the very end. Time finally caught up with my excitement so I clocked out and shut down the station. I could barely even contain the joy I was feeling at this point. Knowing in a couple of hours or so, I was going to be in heaven. Hopefully completely elated and exhausted from studying, or whatever was on his mind. Maybe another intellectual intercourse would happen, but who cares if it didn't? I was going to be with him, and he was going to be with me.

I raced home and jumped in the shower. It took me a total of two hours to calm the nerves and be acceptable enough to leave the house for him. He texted finally and we met at his place. The whole ride over to his place I was nothing but nerves and gelatin. When I arrived in his parking lot, I texted him like he said and he came down to meet me. We climbed the steep stairs to his apartment, and to my surprise, He lived a rather modest lifestyle. Outside his bike he was definitely not a flashy guy. He had a white cat that was extremely friendly. That in itself was a surprise. He didn't appear to be an animal lover.

"Love the kitty, Never would have taken you for being a cat guy. What is his name?"

"He was homeless and wouldn't leave. Every time I opened the damn door he was there, so I just finally let him in. He hasn't wanted to leave since. I just call him cat. It seemed OK at the time. Do you want a drink?" He asked as he poured himself one.

"No, thanks I'm good'"

Although rather large for an apartment, all the books that he had, made it appear clustered. Books were everywhere, in shelves that lined his walls, stacks on the floor. Some opened and some still in boxes.

"Wow." I was mesmerized at the amount of knowledge printed in the room

"Avid reader huh?"

"You could say that."

There appeared to be older publications well worn, and well referenced. There were hardcovers about Gods and Goddesses. Textbooks of every different mythological religion you could imagine. Literature publications as well as history seemed to have their own place in the apartment. The entire wall was nothing but books. Yeah I already figured I was going to fail this class.

I didn't dare attempt to touch any of them. They may be valuable. My luck, I would tear the page or binding of a million dollar book. He could be one of those guys that had his wealth in his items. But then it dawned on me what millionaire would be teaching at a local university? I came back to reality, still not touching anything.

The walls were painted a darker green, which made it appear to be a very studious theme in nature; the furniture was roughly placed in spots. His extremely large irregular sized dining room table was bold in its cherry wood color. The table had wrought iron legs, extremely heavy in appearance. It took up the whole room. How did he even fit this up those stairs? It was obvious this was where he spent the majority of his time. The rest of the furniture was completely opposite as far as beauty and elegance went; there was a couch that served just its purpose. None of the furniture matched, and he seemed more than ok with that. It had the feeling of being a place to put things in and not actually live in. I thought it was a bachelor thing, to never really finish unpacking.

The rest of the apartment, although rather mundane for my taste, seemed to reflect him pretty decent, though. I wondered what he did at night in this place, was he always alone? The answer seemed obvious to me with the amount of books in the apartment. But who knew really? I wanted to inspect every inch of his lifestyle to know what he was all about. On the dining room table, there lay a bunch of papers he was currently grading. I wondered if my paper was in there. I wondered what he would decide to give me considering.

I was lost in my assessment, when he came up behind me leaning in to place his drink on the rather large table in front of me. It caused him to have to brush past me. I felt his soft breath on the back of my ear and neck. It sent goose bumps down my spine. I stood there frozen; my nipples standing erect from the anticipation. I wanted him to touch me so bad at that moment. As if reading my mind, he took his hands and moved them under the short one piece dress I wore. From behind I could feel his masculine hands caressing my waist and exploring their way towards my breasts to unsnap my bra. They were ready, raised and swollen. His fingers reached the nipples. That sent a heightened tingle shooting straight through my veins. He cupped my breasts and turned me around to where his face was directly above mine. I was only as tall as his mid chest, so I was looking at every chiseled part of his frame. I couldn't even begin to look at him, I knew I was flushed all over; the heat caused me to let out small breaths.

He took his right hand and cupped my chin bringing it up to meet his eyes. I could tell by his look that he had already fucked me ten times over. I was light headed and closed my eyes to gain my bearings. I felt his hot lips touch mine. My moan from the sensation made his tongue rush inside mine, twirling around causing my knees to go weak. He had his hand around my waist, and caught me with such ease. He lifted me up as though it was pre-mediated. Straddling my legs over the dining room table, he pushed the papers out of the way. As they went flying, all I could do was lay back, and feel his hands now reaching for my inner thigh.

I was soaked all the way down my leg. He could hardly contain himself. When his hands felt my warm sensation running down to meet his rising excitement, a moan escaped from him.

He unzipped his pants, practically tearing his seam from the passion behind the intent, of what was to happen next. I reached for his sweater that was more along the lines of a causal turtleneck. Whatever it was called, it defined his amazing body and pecks splendidly.

I wanted him bad and I was going to have him. He took his lanky fingers and slid them up the thigh, then with his thumb, placed it at the beginning of my opening. He massaged his way around in a circle then slowly rotating the opposite way. I squirmed under the movement of his hand. He took two of the fingers then slid them barely inside where it was drenched with joy. He couldn't take it anymore. Robert took his fingers out, placed them inside my mouth, and then climbed on top with a thrust of vigor that took my entire breath away.

"Oh" I let a loud cry escape.

He stopped while holding me inspecting my eyes with a curious odd look.

"Are you OK?"

"Yeah…it's just…You're really big for me right now."

He had backed out for a moment to catch his breath. Then he looked at me again with an unfamiliar loving glare.

"I'm OK, don't stop please…oh please don't stop." I begged for him to place it back inside

He kissed my lips with a soft brush while his hand moved the strand of hair in my eyes to the side. He climbed back on top and placed his rock hard member inside. This time, however, he was slower and more rhythmic in his thrusts. I was taken aback at how large he was. I hadn't actually seen him naked, and my eyes were too busy closed enjoying the amazing sensations he was giving to me at the moment.

His mouth now entangled with mine, his sturdy hands massaged the small of my back. My own hungry hands were running down his masculine torso, stroking his pecks and abs on my way down to feeling his heat. He devoured my lips and continued his mission, but he didn't need to go much longer. I was already there about to erupt, when I saw that he could no longer hold himself either.

That set us over the edge. He stopped for a moment. His weight, which wasn't much at all, was on me. I could feel him tightening as he slammed deeper with each groan he let escape.

He buried his arms around my head kissing my forehead as he teetered on the brink of ecstasy.

"You're gonna make me explode. " He whispered into my ear.

He took a long deep breath and exhaled. I struggled as I drew my nails across the small of his back, leaving my graffiti for his memories later. I let out a soft moan and begged for him to finish with me. The sensation down there was tingling and unmanageable, I was paralyzed from doing anything else but grind against his absolute perfect waist.

He had pulled out to regain himself, but when I begged... and couldn't stop the rotation, he could do nothing else but oblige. He shook his head, and went back inside my womanhood to finish me. He was making a valiant effort to immerse himself in the wet sensation that cried for him to go deeper. He moved his hips in sync with mine, and then moaned briefly as he gazed down to where I was already staring back. I couldn't control what was building up from his movements. I was shaking my head, because whatever was happening wasn't like what Kasey and I experienced.

The rush of the sensations consumed every bone in my body. That was obvious by the goosebumps making their way up from my toes to the head. It was compelling every inch of me to stiffen up with the intensity of the thrust. When I relaxed, the pulsating would come rushing back ten times harder. I cried out once more. That last time I let go, swept my entire being into euphoria.

I lost my senses, and let a groan out from the feelings of the explosion that caused me to have to arch my back. The arch caused Robert to lose his gift for me at the exact same time. Both of us wrapped in the sweat from our exchange, and exhausted from the physical overload, we just stared at each other silently. He was caressing my now matted and soaked hair. I could do nothing but stroke his perfectly defined pecks.

"Robert."

"Why didn't you tell me?" He didn't sound angry, just more disappointed.

"I...I don't know. I just didn't think it would be a big deal. I really wanted to be with you. Was that wrong?'

"Wrong?" He said nothing more.

He just pushed himself back off the table, grabbing my hand to help me up from my position on it.

"No, not wrong, but it would have been nice to know in advance."

"If I had told you I was a virgin, would that have changed things?"

He just smiled as he grabbed his drink and went to the couch to sit.

"I'm sorry then." I went to join him on the couch. I bent over to clutch my short blueberry colored dress that had tiny little pink flowers sprinkled throughout. I quickly threw it over my neck to cover myself.

"Why do you cover yourself up?" He asked quizzically.

I had to stop and think about that.

"I don't know."

I really didn't know the answer. After a moment in silence, I glanced back over at him, who was still looking at me with his head cocked to the side, and a smile smirking from ear to ear. I knew he was waiting for an answer.

"I don't know.... maybe because my family is catholic and sex is a bad thing for us, unless we are married. I don't really feel too comfortable in my skin if you really must know. That is the reason I think....I never really thought about it until you said something. But I also am not used to being naked in front of a man either."

When I looked over at him I was ready to go again. But I was blushing from the humiliation. Every time I thought he would laugh at my inexperience, it seemed I got the opposite reaction. He had his mouth open and looked at me completely different now. I was completely turned on by this new look he had.

He shook his head

"You're joking right?" He said

"Which part? No, none of it is a joke, I wish it were. Does that upset you?"

"Oh God no…."

He said nothing more. He scooted closer to me staring at me with such intensity. I thought I was going to melt. He leaned in close to whisper in my ear with his raspy voice, and again, I was just a pile of liquid mess at that point.

"Want to hear a secret?"

"Ha…..ok! I like secrets"

He confessed how many times he had thought about me since the last encounter. Then proceeded to tell me what he fantasized about doing to my body. I was a bit taken back from hearing that. Something moved me when he confided in me, that not only did he fantasize about me, but this latest confession of mine to him, made him have to be inside me once more.

I smiled, and now suddenly I was the aggressor. I was so turned on by the thought of him inside me again, that I instantly leaped forward to touch his chest. He let me, and I, without hesitation instantly wanted to know what it was like to taste him.

I wouldn't forgive myself for not trying at least. I pushed him back on the couch, and then took my long sweat soaked hair and draped it on his chest. I massaged him all the way down to his full erection waiting in expectation for me to play. I opened my mouth and took every inch of him inside…I wanted to know what every bit tasted like. I slid my mouth down all the way to the base, choking on the swell of my new toy for the day. His hand pressed down on the back of my neck, he moaned quite loudly as he pushed my head encouraging gently, for me to take it all in. I succeeded at doing so, and then, I heard a soft request from his precious and swollen lips.

"Use your tongue babe."

That was a great idea. I needed pointers for sure. Incredibly aroused now, I had reached to suffice myself until I was done having my way with him. Using my tongue, I started to go back down to his base, trying to swallow the thick piece without gagging. It took concentration, but I was a success.

It was such a turn on to see him not have any control over his voiced pleasures escaping his mouth. After raising his head off the back of the couch he saw that I had to entertain myself. He instantly pulled me on top him. While he bit my nipples and massaged my clitoris, I placed him inside and rotated up and down. His hands fell to my waist as he guided me to another moment of earth shattering orgasmic ecstasy.

The night flew by without any rest or regard for time. Water was the only time we took a moment to regroup. We ended up finally making our way to the bedroom. From the evenings activities I had experienced with this man he had me asleep before we hit the sheets.

In the morning, he awoke before me. I finally opened my eyes when I smelled coffee. I tried to stand but was weak from the previous night's activities, so I slowly made my way to the bathroom to freshen up and splash some water on my face.

Reaching my goal, I closed the door behind me, so as to gather myself together in private, and appreciate what just transpired the previous evening. I went down to meet the sink, so I could use the water to pry open my sleep infested eyes.

When I could finally see the light, I happened to notice two tooth brushes sitting in a holder next to the faucet, one pink one blue. How cute. I opened the medicine cabinet and saw some female items there. I frowned with disappointment. He had a girlfriend.

I wasn't even upset about it. I thought it was cool that he wanted to be with me that bad he risked cheating on her. Then again, after some more thought, I kind of was disappointed at the false pretense we were meeting under. Never the less, I decided to shrug it off. At this point it didn't really matter. I got what I came for, and he got what he wanted. He was way out of my league anyways, so I was just thankful and completely turned on knowing I was his fantasy in the relationship! I believed that turned me on more.

I needed to get out of the bathroom or he would start to get suspicious. I wasn't sure if I was going to bring up the girlfriend or not yet, but knew the priorities were set to get coffee first. I walked out to him already standing there with a steaming cup of hot Joe for me.

"Good morning." He said in such a soft tone, handing me the cup.

"Good morning to you. Thank you for the coffee."

"Of course, how did you sleep?"

"I slept like a baby and you?"

"I slept for the first time in weeks, so very well Thank you."

"Robert..." I said reluctantly

"Yeah?" He responded while he walked back to the living room to sit on the sofa.

"Do you have a girlfriend?"

He looked at me while he tilted his beautiful head to one side, and said sternly;

"Yes, I do. She is out of town right now."

"Is that why you never called upon me until now?"

"Yes and no. I actually didn't start seeing her until way after you and I had our first encounter. She is a great person, but for some reason even dating her, I would always think about you. Let me show you something, you're either going to laugh, cry or slap me for, but I want to show you this."

I could hardly wait. I was happy he chose to be truthful about it, yet still reserved on the feelings for how I actually felt about being the "Other woman." But I think currently I was more than OK with being his "other lover.' When I thought about it, this amazing, intellectual, sexy man that was twenty years my senior was just simply a turn on in every imaginable way for me. His non-contact afterward with me, had me thinking the very opposite, but I can say after last night, I'm ok with any role in this man's life.

He went to a box and opened it revealing a disc; he placed it in his player and pressed play. It turned out to be some porn film, I looked at the starring lady on the cover, and I swear she was my doppelganger. She was a dead on match for me, and I was floored. I sat down next to him on the sofa and watched as intensely as he did, fixated on what she was allowing to have done to her. I looked at him, who at that point was already staring back at me. I was speechless, but he was not.

"I saw this movie and had to own it, it was a dead ringer for you and since then I watch this every time I think of you."

"Is this why you asked me here? To see if this could happen with me in reality?" I was so curious at this point.

He smiled at me, leaned in to kiss me.

"No..." He started to say

"I knew you were like this, the first time we were in my office. I knew exactly what kind of woman you wanted to be. It was so obvious, and I could barely contain myself that night. I had so many fantasies, which is why I couldn't help but kiss you that night. You had me so worked up. Then I saw this soon after and I just found it ironic that the one film I randomly chose to help alleviate what occurred that night looked just like you.

Last night was inevitable. I hope there will be other nights that are inevitable with you. I am completely in love with my fantasy."

Well what the hell does one say to that? I thought to myself. I was stunned and in shock. No words were forming, and no words were even needed. He reached and placed my cup on the table and then undressed me from the robe I had on. As the movie played out in front of us, we played out our fantasy once more.

Afterwards, no words were even spoken. They didn't need to be. We showered, got dressed and then left for school. Two people who obviously loved to meet under the covers of dark. I had my own boy toy and I was pretty sure I was in love.

Endings and Beginnings

Spring quarter was finally coming to an end. I was flying through all my tests with a small breeze by my side. Robert ended up giving me a 'B' in the class, and I was OK with that, considering I totally should have failed. It was a wash after we started to see each other. I tried my best to do the work, but I was horribly bad at meeting his expectations in class, but apparently I was doing fine in the bedroom. I understood he couldn't give the 'A', because it would look obvious, so I accepted it and moved on. It was worth the sacrifice of the GPA slip.

Over summer break, Robert and I decided we would try to get together before school restarted and in between his girlfriend playing Gulliver's travels. In the middle of all the amazing sex we were having, we did occasionally converse about matters of the heart. This was not easy, because I fell for him hard, emotionally as well as physically, but understood where my place was to be. He believed he was in love with her.

Jessica, whose name I learned later, was drop dead gorgeous. I saw one picture of her, and she was just as tall as he was, with the most amazing lustrous thick red hair one could ever imagine. Her flaming locks almost fluttering to the floor. The hair was perfect, even if she wasn't trying at it. She was model material. I couldn't hold a candle to this lady and her beauty. I could see why he was in love with her. She was Aphrodite, everything I was not.

I remember one time I asked him why on earth, when he had someone like her, would he even consider being with someone like me. He looked at me inquisitively and responded with the most touching words that solidified the love I felt for him.

"You are my fresh breath of air, in this mundane world. You do things, she could never even imagine. You arouse the taboo of it all, and allow me to be myself. You make me feel whole."

That was all he had to say. I was tormented and exhilarated at the same time. I was saddened and elated all in the same breath. I was in a whirlwind of emotion. How could I even be angry at that statement? He made me sound like I really was the only one who truly knew him, but clearly I could see I did not.

I grew to accept the connection he and I shared was a physical one rather than a mental one. I had to be ok with that if we were going to continue seeing each other under the cover of dark.

Leaving the last class of the day for the quarter I felt accomplished. I was getting ready to start working on some auditions for the third year productions, so I would be prepared in advance.

I got a text from Bart as I walked to my car after my test.

"Meet me in the arts center. Ten minutes."

I packed my items into the car, and then drove over to meet up with him. He must have found out the results of the film festival. My heart was thumping as to what it could be.

I actually found a parking spot with some ease. Upon entering, I didn't have to search him out, as he was there to greet me and he didn't have to say a word. There it was! The largest poster I had ever seen draping from the second floor balcony. It's was overwhelming, I started to tear up from the emotion. He stood under the poster with his hands open and said;

"We did it! We actually made the cut!"

He ran over hugged me and we just simply stared in awe at our accomplishment in front of us. We were going to the Moonlight festival in December. Well at least the film was, but I could hardly believe my eyes.

From behind the poster there emerged the cast and crew clapping for me and everyone. To my delight even some of the theater professors were there including three of my favorites. They were all here just for me and the crew with a reception of sorts. Everyone was stoked that a film from the department had been chosen to go to the festival. I learned later this was the first time in four years we were chosen as a school again.

This would do wonders now for me to get attention for main stage productions. I was beside myself with elation, because next year they were considering doing my all-time favorite production of Les Miserable. I wanted to play the part of Eponine, and I wanted that part badly.

It meant even more now. I could use the visual of Robert's and my relationship when I auditioned for her. It would be perfect. Hopefully now I had some attention, because I definitely was starting to have some experience.

One of the professors suggested I direct a play in the sub theater. It was for the other teachers to start noticing my wanting to be taken seriously in the department. Of course I put a thumbtack in that idea, because that would definitely put me on the map. But for now it was on to the summer festivities

The beginning of summer flew by with all the activities I participated in. Between work and theater projects, I had managed to have my screen play edited and produced for my own private library. It turned out really well and since Bart helped me write in a twist for the end. It had a darker ending leaving it open to a possible sequel if it ever took off.

One morning I was meeting the cast for another short production for a genetics lab. They commissioned a student to do their training video. My role was the single mother.

I arrived like I always did, and always earlier than most of the cast. I was sipping on the supplied cup of coffee studying my few lines that were written for me, when one of the cast members brought my "son" to me. I was introduced to the little boy that appeared extremely shy.

His name was Joey. I wondered if he was an actor or just someone's random child, being used just for the prop. Turned out the kid belonged to a theater student. Later I was to learn that when the cameras were turned on, this little boy seemed to come to life. He was going to be great in theater if he continued on at this pace.

The alleged father came in and sat down. I was quite stunned to see Cameron. He looked hung over. His hair was uncombed, his shirt was half way buttoned and over all a messy appearance. It was almost as if he hadn't slept in a week.

"You? You're the alleged father?" I asked shocked at his appearance.

"Yeah." He said disgusted "What's that mean?"

"Nothing." I straight lied.

With all the other actors in the department how did they choose him for this part? It made me laugh, because I couldn't really ever see myself with someone like Cameron, let alone have him be an alleged father. He was a great to hang with and even a better party friend but to actually be with him? Well I guess that's why they called acting.

He was almost cute in his disheveled appearance. He was definitely hurting this morning. I handed him the coffee and he smiled and gave a brief nod of thanks. This might be a long day for all of us with the state he was in. This man looked like he needed a bed.

Surprisingly though, the whole shoot went off without too much of a glitch. It turned out even with the child, and hungover alleged father, the crew and everyone was on point and executed the directors wishes right the first time we filmed. We finally finished around five that evening. Cameron had asked me if I wanted to go grab a beer afterwards, but I had to take a rain check.

I asked the director on the way out what ever made him choose Cameron. He laughed and stated that Cameron was always the fill in when the actors were not available. Well at least no child was harmed in the making of the film. Thankfully Cameron didn't believe in breeding as told by Kasey during one of their intimate moments together.

I couldn't wait to tell Kasey that Cameron was in a film with me. I was positive I knew what her reaction was going to be when she found out. I could hear her now;
"What drug did he have you do?"

I grinned at that because that was so him to do so.

But that afternoon Kasey had something else in mind to chat about with me. After I told her the story about my morning with Cameron and the film, I noticed her reaction was somewhat pre-occupied in its smiled response.
"What? What is it Kasey?" She had a serious tone when she spoke
"Come sit on the bed with me, I want to tell you something."

She took my hand and held it as she spoke. She had informed me that her, and her now fiancée had decided they were going to move in together. She said the house will look for another roommate, to replace her. I was saddened by that news, and thought this next year would be horrible without her here, but I understood, and was happy for her.

I did try to protest for whatever it would have been worth. I could tell that even in the newness of their relationship, there was something pretty serious about them. It was almost as if they had known they were soul mates that finally happened to have found each other in this lifetime. They were a strong couple together. I liked to hear her giggles when she spoke of him, and really appreciated that he cared for her as much as he did. She was my best friend and I wanted to see her treated right.

Their relationship was so wholesome.

They became so religious that I had to question her on the matter, as I felt he was more so convincing her that religion was the way to go, and I wanted to make sure that he wasn't trying to take her attention away from her friends. She assured me otherwise, and insisted the religion was her doing, and that Matt actually enjoyed when her and I hung out together. I bought it for now, and dropped the issue.

I found it ironic that her innocent relationship now was being put in place with a foundation of ethics and religion. It was such a new world for her, because this was nothing of what she was like. I found myself comparing Matt to Robert, and seeing how in my own relationship I was the second girl…the other one. I guess I had been OK with that title because we never stopped what we started. Although for the summer, it would be sparse to see him.

I was saddened when I remembered he and his lady were going to Europe at some point to travel for a vacation together. I wasn't even bothered by that title up until this moment. I was feeling a little sad and jealous over the second position in the relationship currently because I wanted him and me to be like Kasey and Matt. But I quickly escaped the thought by brushing it aside to finish the conversation with her. I would just have find comfort later when he and I eventually met up when we could.

The guys would be told that day, but she wanted me to know first. I sighed then hugged her afterward. I told her I loved her more than anything and she returned the sentiment with a soft gentle kiss on my lips.

Later, the guys at the house found a replacement without fail. It took all of a phone call literally to find her replacement.

Not sure how I felt about that one until I looked over and saw her glance when Aaron made the call. She was smiling at me as if that was a good sign. It was another one of the poker guys, and the house voted yes to his addition on the lease. I was OK with it because it was Shaun, another film major that was actually producing small films and getting paid to do them.

As people graduated or moved on, we just kept filling slots. There were never any shortages on someone wanting to move in and reside at the house. Things were pretty simple really, and since everyone now knew almost everyone in the departments, having someone come in at the last minute when someone moved on was more than usually acceptable for everyone. The landlord of course did not care; he just wanted the rent paid.

But one of the new roommates in the change of everything was introduced as Mike. He stood about six foot two, and had extremely thick brown hair, for a guy. He had a stalky build but rather tall so he carried it well. I had seen him in the groups around campus and socially in the circles. He had done a lot of main stage shows. He was one of those actors that always had the parts. He was a very versatile actor. He could play different parts with great ease. He played in Mice and Men too and played Lenny brilliantly.

He had a deeper voice for most, seemed almost perfect for a stage actor. He was of course extremely outgoing and friendly, with an amazing sense of humor. His specialty was improvisational theatre and was extremely known and loved by all. He had a lot of fans because almost everything that came from his mouth made people laugh. He was a senior, and seemed to be a perfect shoe in for all of us. All the housemates agreed that he would be a perfect fit. So it was settled he became the last of the new roommates.

We all pretty much did our own things, making sure though we all kept open lines of communications for the good of the house, and with her leaving and him coming in for the year, everything seemed to be moving along nicely and making the transition well. Thankfully no one had any issues hanging out with anyone else in the house when they were home as well. It was decided that Shaun would be the bill collector, since he was the control freak of the group.

The new roomies were great to hang out with, especially Mike as we were always laughing about something with him. We held the poker games at the house now on Saturdays, and we held multiple movie fests, where as a group, we watched and analyzed with our critiques. It was easy and cheap entertainment.

Shaun was always very adamant and vocal about his criticisms, and he had a lot of those to pass around. I had never seen any of his work before, but by the way he judged everyone else's work as harsh as he did, made me think that he was a compulsive perfectionist in his pieces. He must be brutal to work with.

Nevertheless, it was a fun time to hang with Mike and the guys. It was always enlightening to catch different views and opinions. I loved being surrounded by theater and film majors; they were all so well overly dramatic.

Chance encounter

One random afternoon Mike asked if I wanted to attend the play that was being presented in the stage downstairs. They had a summer festival that the students produced. I had heard a little about it, and was curious to see it. I gladly accepted the invitation to see the production written and directed by his good friend Greta. She was an amazing main stage performer. Very commanding in her presence and her voice was even more demanding. Her personality was very strong and her appearance reflected that.

I dressed for the theater, with my black dress that I had for what seemed like forever. It was always my go to dress, when I had to wear proper attire and didn't have anything to dress up with. A dress every female had in their closet that probably was used more often than not.

I slid each one of my black stockings one by one up my short stout legs. It's a good thing my thighs had some meat to hold the stocking up. I had diamond earrings already in my ears so there was no need to worry about the accents for the outfit, they were going to be it. I stared back at the short female looking at me in the mirror. Plain and simple, exactly how I liked to dress. I decided better on my pony tail though, so I took it out to let the hair down as that would have been the right thing to do for the atmosphere of the theater.

We arrived at the theater and it was bustling with plenty of film and theater students waiting for Greta's much anticipated show to start. A couple of professors were there as well. I was informed from Mike that, as a senior, such as she was, they were to write and produce a show for their final thesis. This was going to be great. I was ecstatic to hear that, I thought I had better get my other screen play back from the film department, I wouldn't want them to film something I could already be light years ahead on. I made a mental note to retrieve said script later.

My first year film teacher came over to have a conversation with us; his class was mind blowing to describe it mildly. We learned how to actually dissect movies, which was extremely enlightening to say the least. He was the reason we all stood around analyzing for hours on a simple minute cartoon about a cat and mouse. He was the reason people could never agree on Hitchcock's interpretations. I attended all his mainstage shows because as a director, he was simply brilliant, a true master in his craft.

"Skye" He said. He remembered who I was, that made me smile.

"Mr. Harrington, my pleasure."

"Oh stop. That's too much, call me Bill. I know I had you in a couple of my classes, and see that you are doing well in film. Are you going to be auditioning for the plays this coming year?"

I felt myself blush and said without fail.

"Yes! I was just really busy last year but this year it's all about mainstage."

"Great. I look forward to seeing your auditions."

He turned his attention back to Mike. They actually had rather a long conversation. They spoke of the current show and what was coming up in the department. The school was granted the rights to Les Miserables and he was chosen to direct it. That was going to be amazing. My favorite theatre teacher and my favorite all time show. As they conversed I excused myself to go interact with some of the students that were in my other classes.

Mike made his way back over to me after finishing his social rounds then accompanied me into the theater. The show was starting in a couple minutes, so we made our way inside. The theatre was all black except the house lights shining on the rows.

Seeing this was a Friday night, this was expected to be the busiest performance. Mike and I had our seats chosen for us by Mr. Harrington as he extended his hand out to the two seats next to him. I fluttered as Mike showed me the way towards the instructor. I wasn't sure how I was feeling seeing as I was sitting between the two. They were pretty chummy for a professor and student I thought. But then again who was I to question relationships like that?

I watched the crowd silently as they chatted around me. Last minute people pouring in the theater, to see Greta's show. I started to finally relax and get settled in, but lo and behold...there he was. It was Robert. What the hell was *he* doing here? I saw him saunter in with a man who seemed to be another colleague.

Oh my word, my pulse started racing and I melted to my seat, hoping, just hoping he would not notice me. Where was his girlfriend at? For someone who was in love, I never ever saw him with her. She was just as mysterious as he was. Well Damn.

I kind of allowed myself to sink a little further in the chair avoiding his eyes. I looked down in to the program they passed out at the door. I was trying to be slick and look up without any notice, but he was already staring at me.

Shit. I looked back down; I could feel the blush and warm tingle shoot through me. Dam it. If I don't look... he can't see me right? I couldn't help it. I raised my eyes once more and he hadn't moved. I cautiously smiled at him. He was already smiling back.

Robert had stayed in front while his friend climbed the stairs to see if there were any seats remaining that would give a decent view. I had no idea he even knew about the downstairs theater. He watched his friend climb the stairs all the while fixated on me. I could feel his eyes undressing me in the seat. I could barely look back at him, let alone Mike and Mr. Harrington to see if they could sense my tension. Thankfully they were into their programs at this point.

My stare still fixated on Robert, he looked at the two men who sat around me while grinning. My God he looked so spectacular with his mischievous glance and smile at me. He then called his friend to sit down front with him. His friend had no problem with that, and retreated back down the stairs.

Mike had asked me a question, but I was not even into hearing anything outside Roberts' voice calling his friend at the current moment. My heart was racing at the thought of Robert sitting here in the same theater as me.

Mike tugged at me, I responded with a generic answer hoping it sufficed his question. Instead he only looked at me more perplexed. I was saved by the bell, or well, lights technically. The lights dimmed half way, allowing everyone to find their seats. Relieved at the presence of the darkness I could finally breathe. Applause from the audience allowed Greta to grace us with her entrance and start of her senior thesis.

About forty minutes into the show I realized I had to use the bathroom. I whispered to Mike that I had to go and he said it would be acceptable to sneak out, they just ask that people be respectful about it and not slam the doors upon exiting. I was set to leave quietly when it dawned on me I had a problem with that. I would have to go past Robert. Now there was a dilemma. I had to pee but how bad, was the real question? I thought for a moment then decided I could hold until intermission.

Greta although a strong presence herself on the mainstage, seemed almost out of place down here in the tiny theater. Maybe it was the play itself that seemed to drag on for me, but it was taking a bit too long for me to want to wait it out at this point. I quietly excused myself from my seat, and headed towards the exit. I figured it was too dark for Robert to make out that it was me.

I made my way to the restroom; I had to splash water on my face to contemplate how I would handle intermission if Robert came over to me. Well I could just stay in the seat because I had already used the facilities. Perfect then, I thought to myself that was solved.

I unlocked the one person bathroom opening the door to see him standing outside waiting to use the bathroom.

I gasped. Not sure if it was one of delight or horror.

"Robert." My voice crackled.

"Hi."

"Where is your girlfriend? I thought you guys were leaving for Europe?"

"She is not due in until tomorrow and we don't leave until Saturday. I see you are surrounded by older men. You must have a thing for them huh?"

I laughed back nervously. For a moment I thought he might have been jealous over that. I looked into his eyes to see what hidden meaning it might have held. Then I just simply asked him.

"Does that make you jealous?"

I realized of course it didn't make him jealous. Robert didn't get jealous over his other women, although now I waited for the answer, so I gazed at his cherry colored lips awaiting his response.

"Quite so." He so matter of fact stated.

Wait What? What did he just say to me? He was actually jealous I was here with these two men who I wasn't really here with? Oh my word what does one say to that?

"Well…"

I didn't get a chance to finish before he backed me up into the bathroom and closed the door locking it with one hand behind him. He shoved me back to the sink, lifted me up like I was a rag doll here to do his bidding. I was alive with pleasure from it all.

He unzipped his pants; while passionately devouring my neck and adorning me with kisses. Now my body ached for him to be inside. I was on fire and I knew he was too. Just the thought of us here in the bathroom at the theater sent tingles travelling straight up my spine. He slammed himself so hard against my hips; I felt the effect up in my stomach. I gasped. He stopped, realizing his lust might have just been a bit much for me, he contained himself.

He started to take deeper breaths while slowly rotating his hips against mine. His hands fell to my ass, grabbing each one while lifting them up. He wanted me to experience all of him inside. He adjusted his speed, I bit his shoulder trying desperately not to scream or moan. He started again with the gyrating motion that told me he was close to release. I had to grab his hair. The pressure down below was building up with the anticipation. His lips seemed to swell with expectation and lust right back. He took my mouth into his, shoved his tongue all the way down my throat. His hands were too busy now yanking at my swollen nipples. I couldn't take it anymore, I couldn't hold on.

"I'm going to come."

"Come for me Skye."

That was all he had to say. I laid my head back and let out a cry with my legs stiffening, or convulsing, I couldn't tell which at this point. I let out a shiver, as he closed his eyes and moaned in delight. I felt the rush of him come inside as he continued to slam away at my now sore and swollen vagina. I could not help but lock up again, and meet his gift with a tightening of my muscles, which caused me to have a warm gush of liquid drip all over him.

We finally came to a slow stop then as he gazed at me, He kissed me on my lips and neck and then breast as he finally released himself from my liquid mess.

I climbed down from the sink. I pulled my panties back up wanting to savor every bit of this encounter. He did the same. I looked at him in the mirror standing so eloquently behind me and replied.

"You should probably get back before your friend misses you."

He kissed the back of my head and then unlocked the door to leave. So that was that I suppose.

Now I should find my way back before intermission. I bet Mike will want to know why it took so damn long for a pee break. I gathered myself and senses and crept back to the theater, sore stomach and all.

I made my way back to the play in progress, but was stopped outside the door by one of the helping hands. They informed me intermission was just starting in a minute and it would be better to wait outside. Perfect timing to come back, I thought.

Mike poured out with the rest of the crowd as I waited for him. He caught up with me and during the intermission we made our way through the crowd with Mike introducing me to everyone. Most already knew who I was because of the gigantic poster in the hall upstairs.

Oh shit, I never even thought about that. Robert surely saw that poster. Holy crap, is that why he had sex with me in the bathroom? Ugh, now I had to put a thumbtack in that thought to remember to ask about later. For now I concentrated on being in the current company conversation. I didn't really converse too much; because I could feel the burning of Robert's eyes on me throwing me off energetically. At one point, my back was towards him and I could feel the surge of energy tingling down my spine. I looked casually back to see if he was there. He was, and staring directly at me while conversing with his friend whose back faced me.

"Could we go back in and sit?" I asked as softly as I could to Mike standing next to me in discussion with the rest of the group about the play being performed.

"Oh sure." With that he escorted me right past Robert; where I caught his eyes following me until I turned the corner.

The play finally ended and Robert and his friend left soon afterward. I was relieved to see them gone; I could actually relax now with Mike. We hung around until the cast came out and his good friend Greta.

With introductions she was talking to me like she had always known me. I complimented her on the show. She thanked me but admitted she was nervous as she saw some of the professors grading it, and taking notes in the audience. Mr. Harrington was one of them taking notes.

"Did he give any clues?" She laughed asking Mike

"No none whatsoever." He laughed back

"Yeah he is always like that…damn. OK then guess I wait."

We laughed finishing the conversation. The cast and crew were going back to Greta's house to party so Mike asked if I wanted to tag along. Of course I said yes so we were off to her party.

Mike and I had a great time that night. There were lots of seniors there and they were all very talented. I had seen most of them in shows on mainstage and loved some of their work. Mike was always the life of the party though, even amongst his peers. I really had an opportunity to see him in his natural element with his classmates and they were really a strong improve group when they were together. Laughs were going all night long.

Mike was definitely well known, and well respected here. He's directed so many plays, filmed movies and knew lots of people. What a great guy to stumble on for a new house mate. I would have to definitely pick his brain later on tips he would give to a budding artist like me.

The party lasted to the wee hours of the morning, so we grabbed a bite to eat at the twenty four hour restaurant down the street before we headed home. I was famished, so we ordered some breakfast and I got to do exactly what I set out to accomplish, pick his brain and get some great tips.

Mike and I ended up going out as tag team friends for parties. I enjoyed hanging around the great actors in the department. I made amazing contacts for later. But over time I could sense Mike was starting to feel a little more for me than what I was feeling for him. At one point in the friendship he tried to make that "move" I anticipated. I had told him, hanging out with him was a blast as friends, but I wanted nothing more.

One evening, I had fallen asleep rather early and had a dream about a house. I was pretty sure it was my house because as dark as the basement was in the dream, it was still always cozy. I looked out the window of the basement to see people walking by. However, when I went upstairs to the second level, or main floor, it was just chaos, clutter, dark, and lonely. I was turning into different rooms, and never finding the same one even though there were only three rooms. There was an elevator that was in working condition to the third floor but not for me. I had to take the stairs, and the stairs were not letting me ever reach that final level. I was told to turn back around and try again.

So it was at this point that I needed to try and reach out to Nanny. I could not seem to shake the dreams always playing out for me when I closed my eyes, some were more pronounced than others, but for the most part my dreams were just always a lingering feeling of despair.

I had an energy that hung around me, very pronounced, that at one point I noticed myself becoming aware when it *wasn't* there, as opposed to when it was. One eventually becomes used to the constant breeze stirring around their feet.

Nanny would know exactly what energy this was that chose to hang by my side. The thought occurred to me to reach out to my sister to see if I could get her phone number or address. So I wrote in hopes that maybe I would hear back on how to contact Nanny.

One day Shaun told everyone via the message board that he had to make an announcement and that after work, there would be a house meeting. We were all there for him at five, relaxing in the living room, smoking out and watching some random b flick film. He made his announcement.

It was told to us that Monday there would be about a new roommate. He was letting us know that his girlfriend from California was due down here for the following quarter for school. She decided to be closer to her man, so we were going to have a new lady in the house.

Then he started to become upset and yell at everyone because of our non-responses on the topic. He was bothered, it appeared at the nonchalant attitudes we had. But it wasn't like any of us cared. It seemed like he was the only one who had a problem with his own announcement. We were all confused. Meanwhile he stood in front of us in the living room pacing back and forth rambling on. I think he just needed validation, or maybe someone to tell him it was not ok for her to come down for school.

"So she will be here, sharing the room with me, but split finance ways for the bills as an extra person, without the room charge."

"OK" Kevin stated then we some rose to leave as if the meeting had been adjourned.

"NO IT'S NOT OK!" Any of you care to say NO?" What is wrong with you guys? This is not OK, we had our living arrangements all worked out, so how does this NOT bother you people?"

At this point those very same people who had stood to leave sat back down, and quizzically we stared at each other in just as much state of confusion. So I asked for all of us.
"What is the problem? You told us she was coming, and we said no problem. So what has you all up in arms?"

But Kevin spoke before Shaun could answer.
"It sounds like it's you that doesn't want her down here. That is what that sounds like to me."

The rest of the roommates, continued to toke while nodding in agreement and mumbling the approvals back.
"Hell yeah I don't want her down here! We agreed that space was a good thing, and now....hell I don't know anymore."
"Well..." I interjected. "It's OK with me either way. But I have to go to work so whatever you decide just let us know."

Shaun had issues with committing from what I gathered later from Mike. Shaun was frustrated, he valued his "bachelor time'" I supposed. I for one was elated to hear that she was coming down, not that I minded, but guys were a full time job to clean up after.

Birthdays

My twenty-first birthday was in a day, which of course would mark a milestone for me. I had managed to stay above waters and swim on my own so far, events playing out for me seemed to be in my favor, and that was a wonderful feeling. Kasey had prior plans for that evening but we would do lunch that day together. I was going to have to be on my own for the evening's festivities. That was a bit disappointing to hear, because outside Robert or Kasey it just wouldn't be the same.

That morning, Mike appeared in my bedroom with a cup of coffee. He startled me trying to wake up, because I was staring out the window lost in thought.

"Hey you want some coffee?" He said handing me the coffee.

I was super appreciative at that point, because for some reason, my body was way ahead of my mind in becoming conscious that morning.

"So what is it that you had in mind for your big day?"

"Well I definitely want to try going to a bar and having a drink."

"Do you have any particular bar in mind?" He snickered

"Nope."

He offered to set up the evening and chauffer me around so I wouldn't have to worry about drinking and driving. I hesitated because my goal wasn't to go out to get drunk, but rather just out for a drink. I thought there was a big difference he wasn't seeing here. I thought better of it, and opted to agree with him.

"Great. We'll have fun…promise."

"Thanks." With that he left.

Reaching for my phone, I saw Robert had texted the previous evening. My heart raced.

"Need to meet tonight instead of tomorrow hon…."

His lady friend was coming in earlier than what he had anticipated. He was obligated to pick her up at the airport. I supposed that was the price I paid to be the" other" in his life. I had texted him back immediately.

Absolutely."

Then I asked for a time and a place.

Later that evening, we met up at a restaurant he chose, which from the outside was extremely formal and elegant. Once I pulled in to the parking lot, I had to bite my lip; I was terrified I was underdressed for the occasion. Stepping out of the car walking towards the outside entrance, I noticed him standing there leaning to the side. His hand so casually placed in the pocket of his black pleated slacks. A huge smile greeted me as if, in complete approval of my attire.

I found a short deep red, velvet halter dress at the thrift store yesterday I bought it with him in mind. Of course it was just above the knees, which were his favorite. I wore my diamond earrings and even had mascara on. But it seemed like anytime I chose to get dressed up I was still just a plain Jane. But that was ok for now; Robert seemed to like it, if only for a moment.

"My dear you are simply breath taking with your beauty."

I felt the heat rush through my body and up to my cheeks filling them with the same color as my dress. He reached for my hand and escorted me inside. Upon entering the gold doors that were as tall as the sky for me, I felt a bit overwhelmed. Stepping in the foyer I was suddenly frozen from all the gold lined décor everywhere. Robert asked if I was ok, and my response came unexpectedly.

"I don't think I should be here, this is way above my comfort level."

He smiled, took my arm in his and assured me, that I was the *only* one who deserved to be here. He had made a reservation for us. I was thankful to know it was in a very secluded part of the restaurant. The staff catered to us as if we were the only ones that were even there. Robert conversed a lot about maters of the heart that evening. He confessed he was having serious issues with his girlfriend, and was always thankful I was there when he needed to have a shoulder. Deep inside, I was honestly elated to hear it, but of course, I would never let on about it.

I chose to steer the conversation to happier moments like the chance encounter he and I shared at the arts center. My suspicions were correct. He saw the poster and was instantly turned on. When he saw me there that night, he knew it was a sign that he and I were to be together that evening. Well at least in his words, anyways.

"What were the chances you would be there that night, as opposed to any other for the duration of the production?"

That made me smile, because he was, of course correct. When I snuck out, he only assumed it was to meet with him. I hadn't really thought of what my subconscious was sending out, I was too busy trying to hide my conscious thoughts. He distracted me by placing something on the table that was wrapped in a shiny box. Another box followed that seemed to be wrapped like books. Still just as shiny, I just loved how he knew me so well. My love for shiny things will never stop.

"Ooh what is this Robert?" I gasped in reaction to the shiny box. He knew I was already appreciative because boxes seemed to be my other passion. Don't get me started on where that came from.

"What is it?" I asked again hardly containing my excitement.

"Open them and find out."

Before I started to tear the package open, he kissed my hand. I was like a kid on Christmas that was seeing Santa before her eyes. I opened the one that looked like a book first. It seemed like him to want to pass on one of his books we discussed once or twice in our escapades.

Imagine my surprise to find out, that it wasn't a book at all, rather that DVD. Robert said the DVD was a copy of the one that reminded him of "us." To my delight there were two copies even, but when I looked at the bottom copy I noticed it had no cover for it.

"What is this, another copy?" I had to laugh at that, because that would be just like him to do that.

"No the unmarked one is us."

"Us? Like in the real us?"

"Yeah, I couldn't help myself. I had to record us for when we couldn't be together. Is that bad?"

Now how could that be bad? I thought to myself.

"No. I'm truly flattered. I'm turned on about it, actually."

Robert's smile was just as big as mine when he heard my response. I giggled for a second then he pushed the box my way and said to open it, so I did. Inside was the most dazzling necklace I had ever seen. I was enamored by the stunning piece that sparkled so brilliantly with diamonds gazing up at me in all their glory.

"Robert…what on earth?" I was simply speechless.

"Happy twenty-first birthday, love." He kissed me as I melted in my seat.

Robert slid closer to place it around my neck. The piece was simply radiant as he situated it perfectly for me. I had no words, but I didn't need to. We sat there in each other's arms not having to say a word to understand that there was mad love we shared together. I was elated and heartbroken all at the same time, knowing he and I could never really be a true couple.

Dinner finally ended and we walked down on the river for the perfect ending to the night. His body was closing the space between, bringing his lips to mine for a rather simple kiss. He pulled back to gaze at me, but I saw his mind racing like mine. I could sense the energy was heading towards something physical, because that's what we were about. Grinning, he replied back in kind, we both leaned in to kiss.

There we were, watching the city from across the river. Not a soul anywhere around. Pitch black, except the lighting from the restaurant off in the distance. Both of us were on the same page wanting to make the best of this moment. Our lips colliding yet again, passionately as we did the first time we hooked up. His energy was always so animalistic when it came to touching me.

We found our way to the grass as he laid me down next to a tree. His body on top of mine, I allowed myself to get lost in moment. Closing my eyes I could feel the hot night air blow gently across my face, while his stubble scratched my chin from his warm intense kisses. My hands were running through his soft blonde hair. His strong body pressing hard up against mine, sending surges of nervous energy up my thighs. His fingers skimming slowly and softly now across my skin making their way toward my inner thigh, he crept up and bypassed the panties making his way inside me. He was so gentle right now, teasing me, making me plead more for him. Thoughts of this gorgeous man lying on top of me, having his way with me caused me to have to arch my back asking exactly what he had wanted me to ask.

"More please."

Slowly sliding further inside me he draped my neck in soft kisses. His fingers were working their magic. Struggling, it was rough not keeping my cries to myself. He brought his thumb up to stroke me while pushing even further inside. The pressure from his touch was too much now for me. I reached down and desperately tried to unzip encouraging more from him.

He opted to keep teasing me instead. I let out a small moan that was muffled by his shoulder. Our breaths were now completely in sync at this point. It wasn't going to be long for me; I could feel his growing desire below. It was always like this, intense. He was ravishing me with his fingers and I couldn't stop the sensation starting to sweep across my entire body. It was building up and letting me know as the goose bumps started to crawl up my legs to my stomach. I could feel the mounting pleasure from him when he caressed my skin following them up to my nipples. All at once, a feeling of ecstasy collided with a wave of sweet orgasmic pleasure forcing my body to shudder with delight. Another small cry of release escaped as he held onto me all the while just his fingers inside. It was over whelming for him I could tell, I could barely move from the numbing sensation I was trying to ride a bit longer.

"Oh Robert, I know we can never be, but damn I love you."

I realized what came out of my mouth at that moment and instantly regretted it. There was a slight awkward silence that I was desperately trying to figure out what to say to bring it back. But Robert smiled back at me and said softly in my ear before he rose to his feet helping me to mine.

"I love you too."

I left that dinner, completely confused and saddened that it was not in his cards to want to make me his permanently. It didn't make sense to me. I knew he was way out my league, so maybe that was why he just couldn't be with me. Was it because I could never attend functions that are required for people like him? Of course I was totally reaching for any logical conclusion as to why we just could not be an official couple.

I was no longer on the cloud nine as I usually was after our sessions, but rather quite the opposite. One would think I would be ecstatic that he told me he finally loved me. But it just solidified that he and I would never be. That was just so difficult to digest. Especially when I could think of nothing more I wanted in my life than to be with him.

It was a bitter pill to swallow that evening. The clock seemed to have made it a point to let me know I was not doing a very good job trying to convince myself otherwise. I remember the final time as it laughed at me, around three in the morning. My alarm went off at seven. So four hours I suppose, would be enough for me to make rational decisions the rest of the day. There was no used to going back to sleep after last night. All my thoughts were consumed about Robert. Wandering back again into my thoughts, a knock came loudly on the door to the tune of some short cheering rally chant.

"Come in." I tried to wipe the sleep and tears away from last night. I could tell my eyes were puffy.

"Hey."

Mike popped in to tell me to be ready around six. We were going to meet up with some friends at 'Eddies' later to start the evening.

"So just be ready around then OK? Hey you alright? You look like you've been crying." He came and sat on the bed to wipe my cheek.

"I'm fine, just a bad dream that's all."

"Are you sure?"

He looked at me the same way Robert did and for a moment, I had to close my eyes to get Robert out of my head. I was not about to admit, the previous evening was filled with tears. I knew my eyes were puffy.

Desperately trying to avoid eye contact with Mike, I kept them closed for just a moment to gain my bearings. I felt a brush against my lips. He was leaning in as if to kiss me. I jumped back from him and responded bluntly.

"I'm fine, thank you; just need a moment to wake up please." I stared at him and he stared back in awkward silence.

"Sorry I was just trying to give you a birthday kiss. I will let you wake up then."

With that he left abruptly.

"What the hell was that about?"

I mumbled to myself jumping off the bed to lock the door. His kiss threw me off. I was really hoping he wasn't thinking anything other than us being friends. I was going to have to set him straight later on when we met up. There had to be no misunderstanding of where he and I were at in this friendship.

I really didn't want to think nor be depressed anymore about the Robert situation either, so I pulled myself together, forced myself to complete some stretches to help me get out of the current funk I was feeling. I recalled the previous evening's events and appreciated them for what they were, then remembered my diamond necklace from him, still around my neck from last night. It brought a smile, enough to put him out of the brain for just a moment, anyways.

For now, I had places to go, so shower was first. After drying off and heading to the room, I slipped my favorite pair of jeans on with a casual sweatshirt. Grabbing my purse and phone I headed out the door.

First stop was the blood center. They had sent me my card that it was time to donate, so I thought I would knock that out first. It took a bit longer than expected. The phlebotomist had not a clue of what she was doing, so now I had a band aid, a sucker and a great big black bruise. I guessed eating some bananas was in my near future.

With that out of the way, it was off to spend the day going shopping with Kasey who officially purchased my first drink at lunch. She ordered two chocolate martinis and I guzzled it like it was chocolate milk. After showing me the proper etiquette in drinking the martini, I ordered the second drink. She reminded me to slow down and pace myself. I had a long evening ahead.

The second one was starting for my head anyway. The drink made me lightheaded, but Kasey told me it wasn't the drink, it was the donating of blood. I'll admit she was a bit upset I hadn't told her to begin with, that I donated. Apparently donating blood and drinking is not a great combination to mix, and I was learning that the hard way. I knew I definitely would not be getting hammered tonight as this was not a feeling I enjoyed. Kasey followed me home so I could rest and sober back up from lunch.

I fell asleep for a longer time than anticipated. When I finally came to, I noticed the clock said six p.m. That jolted me out of bed, considering I was supposed to be at the bar at six to meet Mike. I texted him to let him know I was running a bit late. His response was casual and stated not to worry he would be there.

Throwing on the outfit Kasey purchased for me that afternoon which was just a simple set of black leggings and a comfortable semi casual top. It was a deep magenta and perfectly highlighted the necklace from my secret love Robert.

Kasey loved hearing all the details and bought me an outfit that would make it stand out. I took a glance in the mirror; put my hair up in a ponytail so it was out of the way. I stopped to look at the official twenty one year old staring back at me and thought.
"Yeah, still nothing but a plain Jane. Only now I get to wear an expensive necklace."

It looked so out of place on my neck. But I wanted to wear it. I had two options. Dress up to the expectation of the necklace and its worth, or take it off and keep it safe.

So it was settled then. I placed his token of love back at my bedside and made my way towards my car, locking the house door behind me. I was on my way to a bar to legally drink as an adult. I laughed briefly and thought to myself as I raced to make the yellow light.
"Welcome to being an adult Skye!" I said to myself

I met Mike at 'Eddies,' checking myself once more in the rear view mirror. I had no makeup on and my hair was so just blah, but it would have to do for now.

The bar had blaring music there to greet me. I could feel every eye in that place make their way towards me as I entered the door. I was frozen in my tracks, desperately searching for Mike. My heart was racing.

Are they going to ask for my ID? I was ready for them in case. I actually hoped they wouldn't ask, because I didn't really want to be singled out. Or maybe they ID everybody? Was that normal? Oh man I was working my way in a panic and I hadn't even stepped two steps in to the joint. Skimming the room I finally saw him about mid-way down the bar talking to a buddy of his. I didn't recognize him though.

His friend was extremely tall, even taller than Robert. He had black skin tight jeans painted on with a chain hanging from his belt to his wallet, which was in the back pocket. He wore a T-shirt of some band with a worn black leather jacket to go with the ensemble. I was distracted by the amazing luster of his thick jet black hair that shined with the accent from the light above. It had somewhat of a wave to it but more looked scruffy, and untamed. His cheekbones reminded me of Roberts because they were just as high as his. Man everything was reminding me of him, I had to stop that. I shook my head to shake the thought, and headed their direction.

Making my way down the bar to greet them, Mike turned and welcomed me by placing his arm around my waist to introduce me. It was uncomfortable but I allowed Mike to carry on the introduction and then moved away from his grasp.

"Skye, this is Eric. Eric this is Skye. She's the one that got nominated in that film I told you that was going to moonlight."

"Hey Skye, it is nice to meet you. I hear it's your birthday, Want a Beer?"

No need to answer, he already had two in his hand, handing one off to me.

"Gee thanks."

"No problem, my friend. Enjoy." He headed back towards the stage leaving us to drink our beverages.

I took a sip and placed it back on top of the bar. Mike took a drink of his, and did the same.

"Is he in the theater department? I don't believe I have seen him around."

"No he's in my band."

"Wait you're in a band?"

Well this was something new. I had no idea Mike was that musically inclined. I knew his strength on stage, but to think about it, I never really heard him sing.

"Yeah, my band. That's why I asked you to come here, we are performing tonight. Why do you think I am always gone every Tuesday night? It's band practice."

"That's great!" I was truly happy for him.

"What do you play?"

"Vocals."

"Oh shit, well this will be fun to watch."

He laughed, and took another drink. I interrupted it though..

"Mike, I really appreciate you taking me out on my birthday."

"Think nothing of it. It's my pleasure."

"Well thanks anyways."

"Here's a toast to celebrate your amazing day." He raised his glass as I smiled to return the cheer.

"Mike, I wanted to talk about what happened earlier."

"No, please. Let's just forget it I was out of line. "

"I just wanted you to know that I do care for you..."

"I was in the moment. So again, you have my apologies." He was becoming rather upset.

"I understand. But I just want us to be friends. Is that too much to ask? I like you, I just don't want…"

He cut me off

"Yeah I got it. You like me but you just don't like me like Dr. Davidson. I got it. Now let's just celebrate."

He walked away leaving me like I was just punched hard right in the gut.

"Wait!" I yelled, livid at that last remark

First off how did anyone even know? Secondly, when did they know? Was it everyone or just him? Where did he get off saying that to me? I owed him nothing.

"What the hell was that about? Why on earth would you bring him up?"

"Skye it's not like the entire department doesn't know your banging a teacher."

Well that put my mouth back on the floor. Screw him for even going there. I reached forward and slapped his face without even thinking.

I was shocked at my behavior and a bit taken aback with horror at the thought of what I just did. I stood now with apologies falling from my lips for him. I could see the red starting to welt up from the impact.

"I'm sorry Mike, I am so very sorry. I just …I am…"

"Look…"

He took a step towards me and I took one, back away from him, I was still in shock and wanted not to be in the grips of his reach.

"It's not a big deal. No one really knows it's just me and the house mates. I'm sorry for saying it like that. But I get it. Now do you want to just go and have some fun? I have to get ready to go on stage, but hang out and relax tonight. The beers are on me."

He left for the stage. I saw some of the people looking over at me. Had they heard his comment? Or did they hear the slap? Oh well, at this point I was just going to have a seat at the bar and have my legally entitled drink. It was needed it after that conversation.

By myself, nursing the first beer, I took note that it tasted like piss. I could barely make it past three sips when I asked the bartender for a real drink. I needed something a little stiffer after that gut punch that he floored me with. Man this was just pathetic. The bartender asked what I wanted, I told him, it was my birthday and I wanted something not so girly. He smiled and returned with a Long island Ice tea.

It was stronger, and definitely a sipping drink for real. I calmed down a bit from the aftermath adrenaline rush he just gave to me.

Watching Mike and his band aptly named The Oxymoron's, play their pre-written, creative notes with skillfully crafted words allowed me to slowly enjoy the adult beverage. By the time the set was over, I was about half way done with it, but also completely done with Mike. Knowing how he really felt about things now, just verified this was not the evening to lose myself in an alcoholic stupor. After tonight, I would taper back hanging out with him. Their band on the other hand was extremely catchy with their choruses though. It wasn't hard to understand why they had a crowd at their performances.

Afterwards, we piled in one car to the next stop of the evening, The Bar called Loco's. It happened to be on a strip in the college town which of course was booming with the bar hoppers. Inside, a smoky haze filled the dimly lit dive bar. This was a neighborhood bar that had been here from the beginning of the prohibition it seemed. Even though it was rather small and cramped, it was a loved bar and had a relaxing vibe about it.

At one point I smelled weed in the air, but then realized it was probably me having wishful thoughts.

The rest of the band was already at the bartenders' heels ordering drinks by the time I made it inside. I had been distracted with all the vendors outside. Then distracted with the reggae band that was killing the jam they were performing. Who didn't like good Ole Bob Marley? Mike grabbed different beers for us to try while I grabbed a table towards the back of the bar for everyone.

The band mates were off the wall as far as views go, but they were fun to hang out with. All pretty much had the same sense of twisted humor that Mike did, but then again maybe I was the one off the wall.

Eric, the guitarist, was taller than all of them. He was the one at the bar when I first met up with Mike. He had pounded two beers to everyone else's one. It was truly astonishing how he could put it away for someone so tall and skinny.

Then you had Patrick, He was about five foot four or so with his hair all dishwater blond. He played the drums, as well as guitars. He had a stalky build, but looked like your average typical run of the mill brother just trying to get by. His hair is what seemed important to him, even if his outfit mattered not. Nothing he had on even remotely matched, but yet somehow it did. It kept with the theme of the highly eccentric dark image group. Maybe it was just for appearances but whatever the case, it worked for him.

Mark, did backup vocals and keyboards, He was the oddest of the group. He was also the one that interrupted my thoughts currently asking if I ever played in a band, or sang before.

"Uh-no, not really. It never came up to be honest."

"Do you sing?"

"Yeah.".

"You should come to practice sometime. We could use a couple of backup female singers for some of our songs."

The discussion of having females in the band created small talk for about thirty minutes. The beers Mike purchased for us were going warm now, I think as an adult I can say now that I really did not see the point to drinking any beer. Mike was smiling at me when he caught my reaction trying to swallow some of the beer. He continued to engage in conversation with one of the guys, while the performing band now was coming back from break.

Eric asked me if I danced.

"Yes I do very much so."

"Come on let's dance. Do you know the song?"

I listened for the band to play a little more, and then realized they were doing a cover from the Violent Femmes. Eric who had already made a dart for my hand pulled me to the dance floor in the center of all the tables. His build was the exact same as Roberts', so I felt an odd instant attraction to him. In reality though, I was sure it was just wishful thinking of me wanting him to be Robert.

Eric struck a conversation with me and asked if I thought Mike and I could be a possible couple. I was taken aback from the forward questioning, and replied back to him in kind.

"Why? Not likely. Does that answer you?"

"Yeah. I just thought I would mention it. He really likes you that's all."

"You have a girl?" I thought he would be just as taken aback from the forward line of personal nosiness from me.

"Yeah, my girl Julie. She is over there." It didn't even phase him.

I nodded while looking over to see what he was laying with every night. No kidding, she looked like Rizzo from 'Grease'. I shot him a puzzled look back. I was mystified, his girl matched perfectly like a greaser's girlfriend. But now looking back at Eric, he emulated one as well. Well now it all made sense. They were living up to their band name for real. I shook my head to the beat of the song so he wouldn't catch on that I was really shaking my head at them.

Afterwards we went back to the table as we sat there chatting it up. Midway through the drink, I became sick, almost nauseated and woozy. I kept thinking it must have been the blood donation and dancing, but it didn't matter at that point. I was not feeling well and I quickly became concerned. I had only drank about half of my drink so I know it wasn't the alcohol. I excused myself to go to the bathroom. I must have collapsed back into the seat because Mike was right there to catch me.

"Hey you alright?"

"Yeah, I think….I feel a bit off. I'm just going to go freshen up a bit. I will be right back."

"Oh…OK, do you need help?"

"No Mike, I'm good. Thanks though."

I made my way through the crowd that was now crowding the dance floor to some song I was not familiar with. I was becoming lighter headed. I fumbled over to the door and went inside to splash water on my face. When I reached for the sink, it all went black.

Hangover

My eyes opened slowly, wearily and with much effort from me. I was completely disoriented. Here now in my bed, there was a painful throbbing echoing inside my head. What on earth happened last night? I felt like I was punch drunk, and in a very bitter way. I tried to sit up, but there was an arm around me. I inspected the arm and followed to see who it belonged to, and there laid Mike. He was passed out face down with his arm around me. He had nothing on and neither did I.

I was sick. Lunging out of the bed making my way for the trash can, I hurled. I barely made it to the intended target. I was forced to stay there for a minute, as it took most of my strength too even make it there. Weak in my legs, my body cramped everywhere and was sore all over. There I was, naked with a man who I currently despised at the moment. What in the hell was he doing in my bed? I desperately tried to recall last night's events.

The sun was glaring down on my face, the brightness of its intensity made me squint my eyes. I couldn't even see him from its glare. Not that it mattered; I didn't want to look at him anyway.

I couldn't move, so I just sat in the corner grabbing a sheet that was on the floor to cover myself. My throbbing head just bobbing up and down from the trash, and having at this point nothing more than dry heaves, because there was nothing else to expel out of my body. My brain was raging with a horrible pounding, my heart beating hard through my chest. With what hoarse voice I could muster, I hollered at the beast that disguised himself as a friend. But that failed, instead came out a somewhat muffled yell.

"Why the fuck are you in my bed Mike?" I was fuming.

"Morning." He said barely rolling over

I said it again, this time even more demanding.

"Why the hell are you in my bed?"

"Damn, what's wrong?" He replied, barely lifting himself up to look where I might be.

"What's *wrong*? Why the hell are you *in* my bed?" I asked once more. I was overly perturbed at his more than casual remark.

"Well let's see." He was arrogant now and ugly with the tone.

"We went out last night, then you invited me into your room, then we had sex. Please tell me you remember it. I couldn't have been that bad."

Feeling nothing but a mocking tone at me for my question, I became infuriated at his cocky demeanor. How could he just say that like he was disregarding the entire event? His response and callousness set me over the edge. I had the courage to look him in his eyes when he moved out of the sun's glare and it sickened me. His smile and attitude about it was nothing less than appalling.

"Get out of my bed! I HATE you!" I was screaming.

"Calm down!" He leaned over the bed not honoring my only request.

"Get out of my bed and get out of my room now, or I am calling the cops."

He rolled off the bed slowly bending over to retrieve his clothes that were neatly placed, folded at the edge of my bed. How were his clothes all neat and mine were just thrown about? He scrutinized me as he dressed. On his way out the door, he pivoted back around glaring with a fierce scowl on his face, and pompously stated.

"I know what happened, I wasn't the drunken one. You wanted it."

I shot him a look of disgust. He slammed the door on his grand finale exit. How Dare he? How the fuck did this happen? I felt sick again. Reaching for the trash again tears started to roll down the face. I was curled in a fetal position now uncontrollably sobbing over what just happened. I was mortified.

How could he do this to me? *Why* would he do this to me? Was he mad because of Robert? This is so out of character for him. I was sick again. My head not stopping with the questions and all the pounding made me lightheaded from despair.

Inconsolable at this point I had nowhere to turn. Mike was nothing more than a sociopathic liar, disguised as everyone's friend. Being lost in all my questions about this, the more anger and rage built up with in me. How could I have let this happen? I scrambled trying desperately to remember anything from the previous evening.

My world was now shattered. How did I allow myself to be so dam naive? I remembered nothing of last night after the dance floor. Robert and Cameron were right on their assumptions of me. I was too naïve, too trusting in people. I had no reason though, to not trust this guy.

His stench was on me. I had to get it off. I grabbed my purple robe and made a bee line for the shower. I had no idea what time it was, but it seemed either it was very early and I was the only one up in the house, or I was the only one there, and it was later in the day. I didn't even care. I had to get this vile feeling off of me. I turned the hot water on as far as it would go.

I watched it pour just like my tears, nonstop. I cried and feverishly looked around for something to wash with. Grabbing the soap I sat in the bathtub under the water falling from the shower nozzle. It was comforting. The wash brush now being scrubbed all over me. I could feel him around me. I could smell his nasty breath. There were these terrible visions of him inside me. I lost myself and got sick again. It was comforting to scrub harder, especially between the thighs. It seemed if I stopped, the tears poured harder.

A sharp pain made me twinge. Down between the tears flowing, and the hot water splashing off my back, I had scrubbed myself into a bloody mess. The brush dropped from my hands so it could be replaced with my aching head. The physical exhaustion was consuming me. My mental state was completely crushed at this point. Slowly, painfully I pulled myself up to turn the water off. I barely had any strength left. I was dripping both with water and blood now and I could have cared less.

My robe went around me and instantly I felt somewhat better, or at least comforted. For the moment I only wanted to get back to my room without encountering Mike.

Opening its door I heard its creek. Was the monster around the corner? Peering around to see if he was lingering I was relieved, knowing he was nowhere to be found. I made my way to the room to lock and barricade myself in. Once I was secure enough for my mental state, I turned to the place he had his way with me. Tears started falling again. But now rage was having its way with me as I tore off the sheets. Somehow the thought of killing him seemed so perfect. How dare he do this to me? I was traumatized by his tenacity and arrogance.

I collapsed on the floor again. Now mentally exhausted, my pounding head was making me dizzy. I needed water badly. I grabbed bottled water from my bag lying next to sheets. It seemed like it only took one swig to empty the bottle. Every ounce of my being at this moment was seething with loathe and rage. I despised every bit of his existence at this moment. I wanted to kill him. I wanted to die.

Sitting on the floor almost trance like for what seemed like hours, I replayed the prior evening in my head for the umpteenth time, trying to figure the madness out.

It was a fact, that I only drank three, no-wait, make that two. I only had two drinks. The whole evening was one big blur. I remembered spots of the evening. I recalled reaching the second bar and then nothing. How did two drinks do that? Oh how the pain was deep right now with me. I was shattered with humiliation. How could I be so careless?

Well something had to be done. That was obvious, but what the hell was I going to do? I mean the man is my house mate. How would I handle telling everyone else? Do I even tell them? Would they believe me? Mike was known in the department. I mean, really known. Whose word would they take? How the hell was I going to handle this? Do I move out? One of us had to that was for sure.

There was no way we could live here together anymore. I couldn't bear to look at him after what he did. My head was now throbbing too loud for me to think.

"Well fuck me, now what?" I attempted to stand and throw the bottle in the can, but I felt a sharp tinge down in my groin area.

"Oh" I groaned being forced down on the bed. The pain of where I had scrubbed myself raw was extremely irritated at me currently.

"Ugh-I just don't know what to do."

I slumped down on the bed and cried again. Only this time no more tears came. The feeling of devastation wrecked me on an inner emotional energetic level.

I needed my friend here right now. That was it. Kasey. I hated bothering her on her vacation but I needed to talk to a real friend at the moment. It was agonizing to debate myself on sending a text that I knew would make her cancel her plans with Matt and come back for me.

I felt myself reaching for the phone then typing the message. "Oh Kasey, I'm so sorry I have to do this." I said as I typed out our word for each other when we were in trouble.

"Elephant."

I hesitated a moment before sending it, then finally just pressed the button. Not thirty seconds later the phone rang. It was her.

"Kasey?" I just started crying again. I couldn't even contain my anguish.

"Skye....what is wrong?"

"I need you right now, I'm so scared." I was uncontrollable

"Ok what happened...?"

"I ...I ..."

"Never mind I'm on the way. Stay right where you are, I am coming there. Are you at home?"

"Yes." That was the only thing I could say before she hung up.

What seemed like hours turned out to actually be about twenty minutes when I heard the sound of her car pulling up to the house. You could tell it was her car, because she had no muffler. It could be heard a mile away. I was never so relieved to hear that sound at that moment.

I refused to go out to meet her though. I couldn't bear to do it. I was already trembling at the thought of him coming back around to try and speak with me. I just needed Kasey right now. So seeing as the doors were never locked in the house, and she knew what room I would be in. I opted to stay right where I was.

I could hear the downstairs door open and close. Then I heard the sound of her faint footsteps coming up the stairs. She knocked on the door then tried to open it.

I ran to the door, my little pocket knife in hand from earlier when I found it on the ground.

"It's me Skye, let me in."

I undid the barricade to let her in. I poked my head in the hallway and looked to see if he was near then closed the door and re-did the blockade.

"What the hell is going on? What happened to you?" She genuinely sounded scared.

"I think…I …" the tears came back again

""What Skye…what happened to you last night?"

"I was raped."

Nothing less than pure raw emotion flooded from me while I poured it all out collapsing to the floor exhausted. The weight of knowing my entire being was taken in the most vulgar and cowardly way was too much. Kasey cradled me in her arms, crying as hard as I was.

Kasey finally asked me if I knew who it was. I nodded and replied back that it was Mike. Her mouth dropped.

"No…Mike? How sure are you that it was him?" She was just dumbfounded.

I said nothing. I just released myself from her gentle hold, so I could face her while I made myself perfectly clear on how I was one hundred percent sure it was that monster.

"It was him Kasey."

She was dumbstruck shaking her head in disbelief. She had a million questions and I had no answers to any of them. I told her everything that had occurred that evening. She was as baffled as I was. We both recapped again step by step. We knew that donating the blood may have played a part, but certainly not to make me black out. She even reminded me that I had napped again before going back out.

"It's just NOT like him."

"That's the thing, Kasey, I don't know. He wanted something more between us, he told me that at the bar last night. I had to set him straight though, and let him know I wanted nothing more than a friendship. He was upset at first…"

I recalled the scene perfectly back in my head. The gut punch he threw me when he brought up me casually banging my professor. Maybe he was angry at that and straight lied to me about his feelings on it.

"He was angry about it, but then reassured me things were alright between he and I. I made that abundantly clear to him, and he made it known as well, so why was he in my bed this morning?"

"I don't know." She responded

"Another thing Kasey, My clothes were thrown all over, and his? How creepy is this?" I jumped up pacing while I described how his clothes were.

"His clothes were neatly folded Kasey. Neatly folded!"

All she could do was shake her head and sit back down on the bed after getting up for the fourth time. She now paced back and forth in shock as well. For a couple minutes we both could do nothing more than to sit and pace trying to digest what had just happened. Then she stood up and started rummaging for something.

"Pack your things, you're not staying here."

"Seriously? Are you for real?"

I wanted to just crawl inside her at that point. I was over the moon to hear those words come out of her mouth. It had been so overwhelming for me with its guilt, anger, rage, disgust, and questions. When she said those words I simply weakened from the release of her providing hope for me. She grabbed some outfits and such things as she saw fit I would need, then she practically carried me down to the car to make the escape. I was thankful to have made it to the car without seeing any of the house mates.

I had not been to Kasey's new place yet, but now I guess I finally get to see where they called home. Not the best of circumstances, though. Their new place was a place out in the suburbs. The twenty minute drive allowed my eyes to rest with some ease.

The passenger side door opened startling me. Kasey went to the back to retrieve my bags. I heard the trunk close as I inspected the outside of the pretty yellow Victorian house with the white trim. She even had purple flowers in the front yard around a light pole still on from the previous evening . I was instantly in love with the huge wrap around porch.

Wow! She had she moved up in the world. What did Matt do again? Wonder what rent was on a place like this? More importantly what's it like to only have just two roommates? That must be a very quiet house.

"Hey…it's just a house. Come on in side so you can enjoy it some."

She had a bag in each hand and passed me the last of them. She led down the walkway to the house towards the front porch. I'm short so I look down a lot. I thought the nice solar lights that lined the walkway were a nice touch, so I put a thumbtack in that note to tell her later, but to suggest rainbow colors, instead of all white. That was so…well suburbia.

Upstairs, she opened the second door on the right. It adorned wallpapered with bright yellow and vanilla cream stripes with molding separating the look that finished its way down to the rustic bare wood floor below.

The bed looked like a cloud with its white fluffy comforter draping over its sides. The white laced curtains made it feel light and breezy.

She placed the bags on the floor. Then she headed for the tall framed wood door.

"You get yourself comfortable here OK. The second room is just a spare anyways so you will be no bother here OK?"

"Kasey, Does Matt know I'm here?" the tone a bit reserved in asking.

"Matt was with me when the text came through. He knows there is a very good possibility you would be here. Don't worry; he is more than fine with it. You just unpack and get comfortable. OK? Get some sleep."

She continued with her mission and I followed behind her to the top of the stairs.

"Kasey?"

She swiveled around with a smile on her face.

"Yes?"

"I love you."

She blew a kiss and headed down the stairs. I stood there for a moment. Relieved I didn't have to be at that horrible place. I wasn't sure if I could ever face him again. I finally allowed a sigh to escape from where it patiently waited down below. Twisting to turn back around, that same tinge went through my thighs. I stopped for a moment out of necessity. The pain was too intense from the brushing. Sadness came over me. I would rather feel this pain though, than him inside me ever again.

Lying on the bed I knew there had to be a decision; and I had to figure a way to move on from this. How was that even possible? I couldn't honestly look at him again without…it didn't matter. I couldn't do anything if I wanted. No one would believe me.

I would have to move. That would be not an option. If I had to deal with the wrath of everyone looking and gossiping about me, then I certainly wasn't going to torture myself and be around the rapist. Even saying that makes me think how stupid it would be to stay in the same home.

The light bulb came on and I realized I was completely screwed. I had to swallow a very bitter and nasty pill right now, and I wasn't sure how to do that.

Nausea crept back in. Lingering feelings of the despair taunted me. It made me sick from disgust. Utter devastation that I was going to have to just shut up and say nothing. I loathed him so much right now. I had to come to grips with this sooner than later though. How can you move a mountain when you don't even have a backpack? It proved to be too much thinking for me, because my head started throbbing again. Time to go back to sleep, this time I curled up clutching the pillow.

Coming back around to conscious level I barely noticed the time on the clock across the way. I knew I had to get up though. I eventually found my phone on the floor and the date showed I still had three days left on my vacation from work. That allowed me to make the decision, to roll back over in the fluffy white comforter and revisit sleep again.

That wish lasted about minute, when I heard a slight tap at the door, then another one. It was faint at first, and then gradually increased until finally the door just opened. I stayed hidden below the covers while the faint footsteps made their way across the wood floor to the bed.

"Hey" She whispered.

"What?" I muttered right back

"Ooh good you're up. Come on down and have something to eat. I want to talk with you."

She was gathering up my items I had stranded around the floor. I swear she was becoming my mother. I made the mental note to discipline her for becoming domesticated later on after food.

I rolled over and threw the pillow at her.

"STOP picking up after me. I got this. It is appreciated mom, but seriously I got this."

"Come on, I'm super excited to chat with you."

She left to go back down while I gathered my senses. Sitting upright in the bed I draped my legs over the side. I had to take a moment of pause, to rub my hands over my eyes and face. Then I just had to stretch, the cloud I slept on wasn't exactly made of Charmin. I was a little disappointed but thankful none the less.

I reached the kitchen and could smell the coffee.

"What time is it?" I asked wearily.

"Eleven-ish."

"Where's Matt?"

"Work, but he will be home soon, we'll do dinner and chat with him then. But I wanted to see how you were doing. Have you slept OK?"

She was now pouring the coffee and serving me some breakfast. It was nice to see she had made French toast and it looked absolutely delicious sitting there with a perfect scoop of butter and syrup on the side. She even detailed them down to the blueberries on top. Here it was noon and I was being served some great breakfast.

"OK yeah we need to talk about something alright. You just hear me out first before you jump in and go all ballistic in your answer too. OK?"

"I wanted…" I cut her off.

"No hear me out first then you can talk. I am rather let down a little at your becoming what I see as a domesticated individual. I mean look at you. You guys are living in the suburbs, you have spare bedrooms, and you even put blueberries on top of French toast you probably made from scratch huh?"

Kasey looked perplexed for a moment, cocking her head to the side. You could tell she had not even thought about that. I caught that glance too and called her out on it.

"A-ha!" I blurted out.

"See? You didn't even notice that did you? What is up with you guys? You're acting like real families do. Is it that serious with you guys now?"

She smiled at me and sat down next to me in the seat.

"Yes." She could hardly contain herself.

"Really?"

How does that just happen? How do two people meet and just know? How was this for a twist of fate? She was always the friendly outgoing one. She swore she would never get married, as that was not in her plan for world domination. Now here, she had what I always wanted. Well there it was. She was all in love and there was nothing going to stop her from falling for it. I was happy for her. She was the most beautiful soul on this earth and she deserved every bit of it. She was over the moon with joy.

"I love you so much and I am so happy for you and Matt. I also love my blueberries on top of my French toast! Which of course, are now getting cold, so pardon me while I inhale and appreciate the delicious home cooked meal you so lovingly put so much effort into."

I smiled at her from ear to ear than dug in. The taste was exquisite.

Kasey was excited to tell me the reason for wanting us to chat. As I inhaled the French toast she talked the whole time. I just let her go on, as the heavenly food on my belly was just as exciting.

"Matt and I were discussing what happened and we came up with a solution for you."

Now she had my attention. I stopped for a brief moment; shot her a look of confusion. Then continued back with the food.

"Hear me out. I know the last thing you want to do is to make waves at the department, especially against a very well loved theater student in the mix. Matt actually was the one to suggest it, but we thought maybe you should go ahead and instead of causing havoc for everyone…not trying to undermine the severity here…but we were thinking, that maybe, just maybe…well…"

"What Kasey?" I was feeling a bit of anger at the suggestion of ignoring what that piece of shit had done to me.

"Well, maybe you should just move out-"

"I thought of that, but I don't have anywhere to really go to…nor could I afford that."

"No see you can. Matt came up with it, and he thinks, as well as I do that maybe you should just move in with us. You know just to get you away from the situation. That way, you don't have to face it on a daily basis. No one knows the wiser as to why and no one will lose their credibility and standing with in the department."

Placing the fork down I sat there trying to digest the food and her solution. That was probably the best, and only answer available right now. If I chose to do that, it wouldn't be as difficult to find some closure to this. Maybe try and heal from the horrible memory. I nodded. Tears started to swell my eyes back up, all I could do was mumble.

"I just can't believe this happened."

"Me neither kid, me neither. I will never be able to look at him again without wanting to confront him about this for you, but right now, I feel this is the only solution to the problem. That will help you out."

She leaned forward to give me a hug, which I returned just as eagerly.

"Want to smoke a bowl to relax?"

"Do you have any with you?"

She smiled but almost offended at that statement she let me know it too.

"Of course I do. Just because I have been domesticated doesn't mean I gave up my vices."

With that we headed for the living room for a moment of clarity. About a half hour later or so the front door swung opened and in sauntered Matt. The sun was gazing behind him, lighting him up. His auburn hair so neatly combed back with gel keeping it frozen in its place. He was always all business all day.

"Hey ladies."

"Ooh babe, your home. To what do I owe this delight to?'

Oh man, I thought. It hasn't even been five minutes around him, and I already want to tell her to go upstairs and keep the love in the room far away from my bitter ears right now.

"Well it dawned on me that this was a pretty serious incident for Skye, and I wanted to be here for her, so…"

He walked towards the refrigerator after setting his rustic looking briefcase down on the opposite end of the table. It was more like a steam punk traveling case that reminded me of a Dr. Who character. You know the type of bag that just may be the epitome of the 'rugged gentleman look for all seasons?' I mean who knew? Maybe he was a man of fashion but just in the business sense.

He was the type that appeared to have a different look for different seasons. I placed a mental thumbtack in that thought to remind myself later to ask what Matt actually did for a living that would require such an expensive piece of attire.

"I thought I would be here to be supportive for her." He replied.

He looked directly at me, as he grabbed a beer and sat down where she previously had occupied.

"You." Now he was intent with his stare at me.

"Skye, I am so sorry this happened to you, we can't change it, but I want you to know that what love Kasey holds for you, I match in return. You are more than welcome to stay here, pay just what you have been paying so that you are not stressed about finances. We want you to be able to heal from this and we will do everything in our power to help."

Well shit. I had no idea Matt was this deep emotionally. His kind words embraced me with his sincerity.

"Matt…"

I started to tear up. He grabbed my hand and held it in place firmly.

"I want to help and I want to get to the bottom of this, but I have a favor to ask."

Shocked and taken aback from his last sentence my only response back was am agreement.

"OK, what?"

He swirled around behind the chair and with intent leaned towards his briefcase grabbing it from the other side. He reached and opened the flap taking out a box and handing it to me. I looked at it, and it was a drug kit. I was lost and shot him a questionable look. He anticipated that response I guessed because he answered my question without me even asking.

"It's a drug kit yes...."

"Um-OK, but we already know I have THC in my system."

"Yeah it's not what I'm looking for. It's for another drug. Kasey and I were trying to think of why you would have just suddenly blacked out, and it puzzled me the entire night. Then it came to me, the only logical reason for something like that to have happened...was if you were drugged."

It started to make sense to me then.

"What are the chances you would have left your drink sitting for any amount of time?" He asked inquisitively

"God, Matt...I did. I left my drink to go dance with Eric while Mike sat at the table..."

"Oh my God, see I told you Matt." Kasey interjected.

"Calm down hon. let's be sure." He reassured her.

My head now lost in questions, I saw Kasey's look of concern with the pity in her eyes. I knew she felt what was going on inside me. More tears yet again made their way down the cheeks. If Mike was that manipulative, how many others did he do this to? Oh how the anger started to rise back up in my chest.

"Hey-"Matt interrupted my thoughts though.

"Even though I know it won't help the situation, at least you can have an answer as to why. At least if it comes back positive then we know it truly had nothing to do with this being your fault…not that rape is any females' fault. I just thought you might want some answer."

Glancing up at Kasey once more, I then peered at Matt who held the look of genuine empathy for me. I leaned to hug him from the relief of his solution.

"OK how…what do I do?"

"Just go in and go to the bathroom, hold it under the urine and then bring it back. We will take it from there."

After deciding to be adult again and get dressed while waiting for the results, I wearily headed back to see if he had completed the test. The questions were racing through my head as I descended the stairs. What if it was? What if it wasn't? What ifs left and right shooting through my head. Pain from the thumping inside left me hurting now.

I took a deep breath at the bottom of the stair before joining them again. Kasey was behind him at the foot of the table where he was sitting with the test in his hands. Her arms on the back of him as if she was comforting him from something. His reaction when I walked in the room said enough. I was weak; I lost my knees and went to the floor. Mike raped me under a drug he slipped in my drink. I could see the pain in their eyes like they saw in mine. Kasey rushed to my side. I just cried. I was relieved, then I was angry, I was sobbing, and couldn't think. She wrapped her arms around me and I just sat there rocking myself along with her holding me. I was so numb. I was so dead inside.

It seemed like an eternity went by. Kasey finally rose to her feet, and grabbed my hands to help assist me up. I turned just a bit to peer back at Matt. My eyes were completely swollen and fire red with bloodshot lines.

I could barely see Matt but knew the sorrow in his heart was heavy. I felt that. I just let Kasey guide me back to the bedroom. I don't even remember going up the stairs, honestly. I think she had to call him for help at one point. I laid back in bed. Matt left the room once I was safely lying back down. Kasey undressed me again. Just paralyzed momentarily I guess. So much for playing adult today I thought. I closed my eyes to return to my safe space. My dreams, the only place I ever truly felt comfortable with.

The aftermath

Not sure what time or day I finally came back around on a conscious level, but my head was no longer throbbing. My face was a swollen painful mess from the aftermath of emotional exhaustion. A huge sigh of disappointment came out.

I had to take this blow and move on. The only relief was that at least I had an out to go with it. Finding out that I had been drugged, was going to have to be the closure for me on this. I had no other option.

I knew the consequences if I were to start an internal department conflict with another student. I knew the outcome would probably not bode well in my favor, especially against someone well loved and respected like him. My future would be casted in a dark shadow until graduation, and that couldn't be a good thing.

Then there was Robert. He would certainly have to back off seeing me as a result of all of it, at least until it blew over. Would he even still *want* to be with me knowing I would be in the limelight for a rape?

Yet another thing I would have to worry about. The lime light, was this how I wanted mine to be? Certainly this was going to remain with me for a very long while in my life. I was devastated at the thought of being just stuck.

What's that old saying? Stuck between a rock and a hard place? Yeah that's where I was at currently. Not a good place for anyone I suppose, alright then. I had made the decision, so now came the hard part.

Yet another exhausting sigh escaped. I had to get it together. I forced myself to sit up on the bed, throwing the comforter off of my naked body; I climbed out stretching to greet the sun. Glancing, I saw the phone over in the corner and that made me smile. Kasey plugged it in for me. Did I mention how much I loved that girl? I walked over to look at the date.

"Sweet."

I still had two more days of vacation. I grabbed a fresh pair of panties then headed for the shower. I figured I would raid Kasey's closet for old times' sake afterwards, but try as I may; I was not into wanting to reinvent myself, at least not without Kasey being here.

I opted instead for my normal blue jeans and dress top. I straightened the room that was soon to be my permanent one. I had to at least keep up the appearance that I was doing OK mentally, even if I knew I wasn't. Theater would be great therapy for me to learn how to mask emotions. I was going to excel in this field even if it killed me.

Downstairs I grabbed some juice and saw the note on the counter next to the fridge. I couldn't help but notice it, it was written in this metallic pink and purple writing with hearts drawn all over it. There was silver glitter around it too lighting the note up like a neon sign. The note was like that sign in that movie Beetlejuice, where the lights were flashing around at the hotel for vacancy. I had to giggle a bit, because that was so her to grab my attention that way. She knew how I loved sparkle!
"Went to the store...Be right back! Fifteen tops." Complete with the hearts and balloons.

I took a drink straight from container, which I simply did by habit because I was used to having my own. Shit, well they wouldn't know if I didn't tell, so I'll remember for next time. I closed it up and placed it back in the fridge.

The slam of the front screen door startled me, making a rather loud bang with no regard for any ears that were around. I looked behind and saw Kasey wearing a white cotton dress with a steep v neck collar. It was just above the knees. She wore this adorable daisy charm necklace. It was brilliantly cut with a yellow gem stone inside of diamonds for petals. It was so delicately placed around her neck.

She was a refreshing breath of fresh air. Here is where summer stood as a season. Her sandals were tied mid-way up her calf, and her hair just radiated with sheen. Obviously she had absorbed some Vitamin D for a hot minute. Wow, if I could carry that look off I wouldn't be here. I'd be on a runway somewhere. But thankfully modeling did not intrigue me, maybe because when I stopped at five foot, that aspiration was shot in the foot.

"Damn Kasey, You look gorgeous!" I exclaimed

"Yeah well I have a hot date with my man this afternoon, so I want to look perfect."

She walked to the table to put her bags down.

"Well….let me just say this. You nailed it." We both laughed

"Thanks. You look like you feel a bit better today."

I stood there watching her grace as she fluttered around the kitchen placing the groceries in their rightful place.

"Yeah I finally came to a decision, although it's not really the desired one, but it's the right one for now. I got it. I know what needs to happen. But I just want to let you know how much I absolutely cannot thank you and Matt…" She cut me off.

"Shhh, no more talk about that lets just make some arrangements to get your belongings from over there. I am going to go talk with the house mates. I am going to let them know something came up and that you just have to move in with me. Like I will just tell them something like, you need to help me with the bills or something. I don't know yet… but the point is, not to tell the real reason why you're moving out. So that no one is uncomfortable, and no one is suspicions. Does any of this make sense to you?"

She was searching for look on me.

"It makes perfect sense." I showed her the gratitude with a smile back.

"Okay then you just take care of you. I got the house thing. Matt and I already are on the move. Don't worry about having to look at him again, except of course on campus. We have your back."

She smiled and hugged me, and then up the stairs she went.

Only, I wanted to confront him. I was going to confront him too. I wanted answers. I wanted him to know he was a coward. He would know clearly that I saw right through his bullshit, but now this time, it was going to be done when I wanted it done. Luckily I had patience. I was not going to be a blubbering emotional mess when I confronted him on it either. No, he would not have that on me. I would be able to look him in the eye when I told him what a shit bag he was.

Convincing my brain to defeat the mental torture of something this horrific wasn't exactly as easy as my subconscious made it out to be. I found myself becoming a hermit, and my routine hardly veered. I hardly socialized outside Kasey and Matt. But they had their lives going in and out. It was surprising to see that Kasey was not as domesticated as I thought she may have been. Turned out she was always on the go. With those two living out their lives I had taken some time to just be alone away from people for a minute. I was trying to heal my mental ability with closure currently.

Robert was seeing his girl a lot more lately. It seemed as though she had slowed down on her travels for the time being, and they were actually playing couple for a minute. I was a bit jealous on that thought, but really didn't have the energy to think secondly or give any energy to it for long. At this moment I was feeling rather appreciative that she was home with him especially since I was still trying to heal down below. He may not understand. I didn't know nor did I care to speculate on the matter any further. I was just thankful he was not around right now.

Life eventually was making its way back into me slowly but surely. I ended my vacation completely devastated from my twenty first birthday. However now I had emerged a whole new person from that horrific encounter.

I transferred to the new coffee shop down her street for starters. That would make a great change. It was close and I didn't need to go anywhere near that side of town for any reason. I wasn't sure what Kasey told the guys, but I hadn't seen any of them for a couple of weeks now and I had wondered if they even cared, or if they knew? I wondered if they even really knew him? They had all gone to school for four years together and most had been roommates with him previously, so maybe they already knew why I abruptly moved out? Guess I will probably never find out either. On break one day at the coffee shop my phone buzzed.

"Saturday poker?"

It was Shaun; I was delighted that someone in the house reached out to me. It confirmed that they were not mad at me for just rudely not speaking to them again.

"I can't. I have to work."

I sent the reply back. I straight lied, but I didn't think I would be ready to face Mike yet, so I had to decline.

The phone buzzed again.

"Mike won't be there, he left for Colorado for vacation."

Why would he send that? My heart raced for a moment. Did he know? Did the whole house know? Now I was speechless. What do I respond with? I figured I could put him off for a minute, so that I could think about what he just sent.

"K let me get back with you...and hey, TY"

I stood there in disbelief. I may have to go to find out why he would have sent such an obscure text.

I finished my shift at the shop, riddled with preoccupied thoughts of the bizarre text from Shaun. I had to do it; I had to know what he knew. So I snuck off to the bathroom right before I punched out and let him know I would be there.

"Great." His response buzzed back.

Saturday approached and I was in my car, in the driveway before the start of poker. I told Shaun I would be a littler earlier than everyone else. I sat in my little white Toyota, rubbing the stick shift in worry. My car had been turned off, but I felt a moment of panic rush into my chest. A feeling of tightness filled my lungs and all I could do was place my hand over my mouth trying to prevent the surprised reflux of stomach contents from expelling. I took a swig of water from my half drank bottle that was at least a month old by now. It was what I had in the car at the time.

"Well let's get this over with Skye." I forced myself out of the car.

I had to do this if I was going to try and put this behind me. I knocked on the door and Shaun was ready to greet me. He opened the door and surprisingly hugged me

"Awe hey Skye Come on it, good to see you." His hug was genuine.

"Hey Shaun, how are you?"

We sat down on the well-worn leather couch. It was even more accented now in cigarette holes from all the smokers that have graced their presence sitting here. I could smell the faint smell of weed in the air, the conversations were buzzing upstairs, and I could hear Kevin in the kitchen getting the snacks ready. I thought I wouldn't be able to set foot back in this place after that night, and here it was, calling me back to the memories. Good memories at that though. I felt a little saddened, as I missed my former house mates in that instant.

The conversation was a revealing one for me. My suspicions and previous reading on the matter were correct. This monster was known for this. I was in disbelief sitting there numb from the stories I was hearing on him. How the hell could anyone not inform the rest of the house mates about such an individual, especially the female ones?

I was angered from hearing him explain all these sick things about their so called friend. He was a monster which was hiding behind an illusion of being a theatre student. What a hell of a con. I was heartbroken and shattered. I couldn't be that upset with the guys though, because they were just as much a victim in his scheme of things. He always had some explanation, or excuse. So they were not really thinking, they did what most friends would do…support and believe their buddy. Sadly it was a cost at my expense this time. Well that was that. I knew what I was dealing with.

I was growing stronger day by day. I was determined that he would never see me weak ever again. I appreciated Shaun's honesty. My old house mates were just as cool and apologetic about the whole thing. They eventually came through the room before the game to talk with me. My only consolation was that next quarter Mike would be moving to New York after his graduation. I was never so happy to hear that.

I still hadn't seen Robert at all that summer. He and his girlfriend must really be serious with each other. I hadn't heard a peep from him. Nor did I bother him, for fear it would blow our cover. I didn't want that for him, so I always let him text me. I took up extra shifts at the coffee house so that I didn't have to be alone in my thoughts all the time. The money was great from it too. I was too busy working to spend any of it, so it wasn't all bad I had supposed.

In to my third straight double shift; I had an overwhelming nauseated feeling sweep over me. I excused myself from the table I happened to be waiting on, fearing I wouldn't be able to hold my lunch down from earlier. I rushed to the bathroom and started dry heaving. I needed a drink but couldn't shake the queasiness. I took moment to gather myself together by splashing water on my face. I had to make it through the rest of the shift. I only had three more hours till close and I had a day off tomorrow. So if I stuck it out now, I could rest then. That was my logic anyways. But logic and emotion sometimes don't always get along, like right now at the current moment.

Logic is not listening to the emotional plea of my stomach to pipe down a minute. There it went. Emotion won. I was flustered as to why I was sick all the time now. Surely, it had to do with Mike. It was probably me trying to mentally stuff it down into a tight jar. I figured this was the physical side effect to the bitter pill I had to swallow weeks ago.

I made it till the end of shift. I was so proud of myself. After locking the store up, Larry took over counting the drawer for me. I was still a bit off from earlier. He told me to go home he had the counts and money. I took him up on his offer. I thought I better go pee beforehand though, I had been holding to for the last two hours. Seemed I was drinking too much water lately and having to pee every ten minutes. It was rather annoying.

I went back into the bathroom to take one last pee. It dawned on me that I hadn't had my monthly yet. That was highly unusual for me. Panic rose up again. A flush of overwhelming emotion came flooding right back in. I had to take a gasp of air in at that point, because my lungs didn't want to do it on their own.

"Oh my God...I haven't bled yet. Oh shit, Oh fuck, what do I do?"

I was racing in thoughts. What the hell would I do if I was pregnant? This was not even happening to me. I erased the anger from the thought of something like that out of my mind. OK maybe I was just stressed. I couldn't even logically justify the why of it. So I had to think quickly.

I had to tell myself to calm the hell down first off, and then I had to tell myself to leave the store before he asked me to do anything else. I snuck to the back and clocked out while yelling after him on my way out.

"See you later Larry."

I left and made a bee line for the nearest drug store. I pulled in the parking lot and ground it to a halt. Under the glaring neon fluorescent white lights inside the store the worker greeted me. I asked for the aisle where the pregnancy tests were. He pointed to behind the counter where he was.

"They're behind here. How many?"

How many? I thought to myself. How many does one need to know if they are carrying a fetus or not? On second thought, I purchased two.

I don't remember the drive home; I just remember climbing the stairs that were carpeted. It made a rather lame attempt at muffling the creek in the stairs. Those steps were sometimes quiet but not enough for when I came in late at night. I hated that too because they were morning people. I crept closing the door behind me. Stripping down to my panties I grabbed a shirt from my top drawer to throw over while I made my way to the bathroom. I assumed it was going to be just like the drug test, and sure enough I was correct. I took the stick back to my room to finish reading the instructions.

When I read how many lines counted for what, I looked at the test. It was a bright red line…and two at that. My heart sank I was pregnant with that monsters fetus.

Utterly devastated doesn't even begin to describe what was pouring through me at that moment. Completely wrecked and destroyed by this even in more than a million ways. Shattered beyond a billion pieces and there was no end to this madness in sight. What on earth was I going to do now?

There was no way I could have this child, there was no way. A deep sadness overwhelmed me at this point. I was so morally defeated now. An issue big enough I won't be able to rest the eyes at night. Not like I didn't have plenty of other issues prying for my attention.

The only thing left to do was to try and put it out of my head until morning, where I can talk to Kasey about it. Needless to say, that evening, I tossed rather continuously through the night. I was given some dreams though, in between the tosses and turns. I fell asleep and woke to the decision of a life time that was made for me while I slept.

My mind displayed some horrible revelation and in the moment of instantly coming to reality and consciousness, I sat straight up in my bed as the dream left on their way out.
"No!"

It was all I could muster being ripped from the dream in a moment of panic. The secrets left with the dream, with no remnants remaining for me to interpret. It left a very strong creeping feeling of despair. This dream was confidant on its message to me last night. Oh what am I doing? I had to let the emotion sink in that I was about to kill my first child. I shed a tear than went back under the covers to hide for a bit.

It was about ten when Kasey knocked on the door.

"Hey." She opened the door as she usually did before I could respond.

"Want some…" She interrupted herself on that one.

"Coffee?" I finished for her

She was still silent.

"What?" I asked

"What is wrong?" She darted the question right back.

"Kasey, can I get some coffee first?"

"Yeah here. Now what it going on?"

Here it went.

"Kasey I took a pregnancy test last night. That bastard got me pregnant."

Her gasp was loud.

"Oh shit Skye. Oh no! No… no… no … please no. Tell me this is not happening right now. Oh this has got to be a freaking bad ass nightmare."

"Yeah." Was all I could muster in response.

"Are you sure it's his and not Roberts?"

"Yes one hundred percent. That night I met with Robert, there was no sex that evening, well none that could have caused me to become pregnant. Yeah this is not Roberts."

I flashed back to a scene that made its way back to my memory from my previous evening's nightmare of a dream. That was it, that was why the answer was no. It was me wanting to know if there was that possibility.

"Skye."

"Wait..."

I had to cut her off; the dream was coming back to me. I remembered now. It was me standing up against a rock, upside down with my hands tied behind the permanent fixture. Ocean waves ripping at the sand and causing me to swallow, gasping trying to breathe. I thought I was being sentenced to death. That's what it felt like anyways. Robert stood pleading with me. I couldn't quite make out what he was saying. The wind was blowing so hard. I squinted my eyes trying to shield them from the splashes of water interrupting my lip reading. I could not hear him in the distance. He was standing on a rock secluded in the water and I realized it wasn't me that was dying. It was him. I told him about the baby. In the dream he kept talking though, it seemed he didn't hear me and my rhetoric. When he was sinking in to the water I told him about the baby again. He shook his head and I asked what was wrong? I see it clearly now as I remember him losing his bearings being swallowed by the ocean.

"No" he yelled at me although I could only see the lips moving.

I remember yelling at him "What is it Robert? Should I have the baby?"

There it was what jolted me awake. What made me yell the word no. It was his answer to my question about having the baby. That was why the decision felt so strong for me when I woke up.

"Well what are you going to do?"

"I can't have the baby, and yes I am one hundred percent positive it is Mike's child."

"Do you think you will tell Mike?"

It immediately came out as though it was just an automatic response.

"No, he couldn't tell me he was going to rape me so he doesn't need to know when I abort the aftermath of it."

That sounded so much colder than I wanted it to sound, but there it was, so maybe it sounded exactly how it should have.

I had to go see a doctor, so Kasey made the appointment for me for the following day. I had a week to back out of a decision that I knew would forever change, and mark my soul. I did my absolute best effort to try to push it far away from my mind and thoughts. But it consumed me, night and day, every second of every hour. I was so distracted at the slightest thing that crossed my path.

Ocean of tears didn't even cover the mental anguish my soul was being dragged through. I honestly just wanted to die. Pitch black filled my world. I could see people as if I was in some sort of dark tunnel. They were just passing by and through me. I would hear murmurs in the background when they spoke, but couldn't make out words.

I was robotic in my daily responses and responsibilities. I no longer socialized with anyone. I went from work to home to my room. I stayed there every night crying until I would pass out. The feeling of being stuck in a situation of overwhelming guilt and darkness devastated my entire psyche. My soul tormented at being a selfish, greedy, vile human being for even considering the only option I thought was for the best.

What did I even know about raising a baby? I'm not even close to supporting my own self let alone another human being who would rely on me for the next…well for a very long time. How could I even think to bring in another individual in to this world that was so messed up and chaotic?

That too, I felt was selfish. I had no family outside Kasey and Matt. That wouldn't be fair to place that burden on them. I know they would help, but I felt that too would be asking a lot. The constant agony of all the thoughts just swishing by like a huge tornado that is stuck the valley of my mind.

I knew morally and ethically I was going to burn in hell for this one. Catholics, they were very, very skilled at crafting guilt and torment. It was this very moment why I knew that religion was not for me.

I had three days left before the appointment. I contemplated doing another reading once I reached home, to see what they would say. I started to accept the inevitable fate of the thing inside me. I dare not say those words like child, baby or fetus. I desperately distanced myself from the tidal waves of emotions that would fill me from referring to it that way. It was some stupid justification to try and ease the pain, of the very wrong decision that was about to happen in two and half days.

I reached the porch with the door slamming behind me. Climbing the familiar stairs to my safe haven, Kasey was yelling at me to come eat. Eat, she says. That was a joke. What gave me the right to eat? Who was I to deserve a meal? I couldn't even remember when I did eat last. I yelled back that I was good and then went to the room. Besides, I could always snack on a pretzel or two if I got too light headed. But for now, I wouldn't be able to stomach it.

That day finally arrived. Kasey was at my door first thing at dawn. We made a very early appointment because she was concerned there would be protesters there. I certainly appreciated her every single day. She gently knocked on the door with a small tap or two.

"Hey you." She peeped her in and smiled.

"Morning." Was all I could respond back.

""I just wanted to remind you to wear something very comfortable…like your jogging pants OK?

She didn't have to remind me, I knew.

"Yeah, thanks. I'll be down in a minute."

"Okay. Love you."

"Love you too."

My heart sunk to the bottom of my stomach and I leaned over to the trash and threw up. I gathered myself for a moment. Empty inside with no emotions, and just tears to fill for the rest of whatever was left of me. Nothing was said the whole time. The ride down there she had asked if I was sure this was the right decision for me. I wish she hadn't asked that.

"I don't know."

"We don't have to go through with this you know." She was trying to be supportive, but I really just wanted no words at that moment, I no longer wanted to think.

"Shhh" I said softly then closed my eyes and laid my head back on the head rest. She got the point and put on some soft music and we rode the rest of the way just simply listening.

The parking lot was empty. That was good I thought. Maybe the early appointment would mean there no protesters. I unfastened the seat belt and stepped outside the car. Kasey waited for me to come around then she took my hand and walked around to the front of the building.

We turned the corner, and it shook me to my core to see there were plenty of them with their signs standing out front on the sidewalk.

""'Shit, Kasey." I started to shake. I already had the tears flowing. I was paralyzed with so much overwhelming anxiety at that moment, now just frozen in place, I couldn't move. My teeth were literally chattering from the over stimulus of emotion. Kasey held my hand strongly and yanked me forward to follow her lead.

"Keep your head down and hold on tight to me." That's all she said as we raced through the line to get inside.

I don't remember actually going through the line; I think I blacked out for a moment; all I can remember is being inside a dimly lit seventies brown paneled building.

All the dismal colors in here, made me feel even more disgusted with myself. There was nothing even remotely cherry about this building. Then again what was I expecting? Some pink and purple flowered poster saying something stupid like; 'Hey it will be alright?'

I was hoping something different I guess. I just tried not to think at this point. Kasey checked us in at the counter. She filled out my papers and handed the payment for them to rip something that should have never been. I watched in a haze as Kasey listened to everything the nurse was telling her about the procedure. All I could hear was the cheap elevator music playing in the background. I suppose it was playing to make one feel relaxed. I'm going to go with that theory, because the other guess is that they are just too lazy to turn it to a station with uplifting beats. Something positive in this would be nice.

When Kasey finished, she sat down next to me and grabbed my hand. Tears and tissues were today's theme for me;

thankfully I had lots of tissues. She was speaking but I heard not a word, just nodded in agreement. The exhaustion was making me sleepy, but thankfully the nurse called our name at that moment.

The hallway seemed ten miles long and was nothing but bare colorless white walls accented from years of dust and dirt. The floor layered with a cheap brown checkered veneer tile. This was a place straight from the seventies. I was hoping they at least invested their money in the modernizing of the tools that they were going to need for this.

Looking to my side I saw the nurse holding me up supporting me. Then I saw Kasey on the other. They were trying to assist me to the room. That only confirmed I was not here mentally anymore. I had officially checked out, and there was nothing I was going to do about it for the moment.

The nurse told Kasey she would have to wait outside at that point. I insisted she stay with me. But they informed me otherwise, she assured me Kasey would be right outside. The door slowly closed behind her, taking what little light there was in the hallway away from the nurse and I. The nurse had me disrobe and place the clothes on the chair. She would come back after I placed the blanket on top of me. I only had to undress from the waist down though. It didn't even matter really. I had big sweatshirt on, no bra, because it was pointless. I followed her orders than climbed up on the bed that seemed to have just one spotlight. It was directly above the bed. I felt as though I was going to be placed on display.

There was a soft knock on the door, and the nurse came back in. She told me again what was going to happen, I was going to be given a mild sedative and then wake up and be on my way. She made it sound like I was just going to take a ten minute nap for six hundred bucks. How casual her tone was, how matter of fact. There was nothing emotional coming from this extremely monotone, well-rehearsed nurse.

Lying on the table waiting for the doctor was painstakingly long. This was it. No turning back. I stared at the giant spotlight directly placed on top of me. I could see nothing else. It was pitch black. I heard the door and then the voices speaking back and forth. I was surprised to see it was a female doctor. That was a relief to know. I let a small sigh, finding a little comfort in that much.

"Skye… were going to give you the medicine now, you may start to feel some pressure, but you shouldn't feel much after that ok?"

I just nodded turning to see the nurse injecting me with their sedative. I turned my head the other way wishing it was already over with. The silver from her tools reflecting so vividly at that moment. I felt a slight tug, I closed my eyes. I felt a stronger pull. My body reacted, startled from the cold steel rubbing against my pelvic walls on the way up to her intended target. She took the first scrape slow. I felt every bit of it clawing at me like a sharp knife jabbing its way up to my bladder. I gasped arching the back screaming.

"OH! My God stop…. It hurts."

I was writhing from the pain of her deep relentless scrape. The clawing of the tool sent me over the edge, a cry escaped from the scraping. I was given another dose of medicine immediately to make me pass out. The last thing I remember was seeing the jar….I could see the contents. I threw up. The blackness finally came around

"Skye...you here with us darling?" It was the doctor, I think.

"Yeah." I managed to respond

"Come on, I'm going to walk you to the recovery room, your friend can come back in with you, if you would prefer."

Helping me to my feet the nurse held my hand as we walked down the same dismal hall. My insides now burning like the outside was a month or so ago. We reached a door to yet another dimly lit room. Climbing on the plastic recovery bed, the nurse gave me my instructions then promptly left the room. Kasey walked in a moment later.

"Hey you." She said in such a soft motherly voice.

"Hey." Was all I could say respond.

"You OK?"

"Not really."

I was having flashbacks of all the images, and feelings that had just transpired. Yet still more tears flowing freely.

"Yeah..." she stated "I didn't think you would be. But thought I would start the small talk. She said you would need about 20 min or so. Do you want me to be here right now?"

"Yeah...that would be great."

As Kasey tried to make small talk, I must have passed out again. The second time around I heard voices they were louder and clearer now. Both the nurse and Kasey were now talking. I sat up, slumped a bit over the edge. It took a moment to gain my strength. Both noticed my conscious state, and were pleased to see I had decided to join them. I tried to hop off the bed, which turned out to be a bad idea. The nurse lunged for me trying to save me from the fall I just took.

'"I'm OK."

I managed to blurt out a lie. That was going to bite me later. I was doubled over from the tinge of pain it left as a sharp reminder of my aftermath.

"Oh never mind." I managed to mumble.

I went to the floor. They were right in their assumption to run for me. They helped me to the chair and I sat back down with the cheap blue paper robe sticking to my body getting in my way.

"You can't do that Skye." Kasey reprimanded me.

"OK" I was not going to argue.

The nurse continued to tell me that I would need to take it easy for the next week or so. They were going to write a doctor's note for work, as they wanted me off for at least five days for recovery. Five days? I thought, Damn I wasn't told about that, or maybe I was told that. Who knew because the last week being such a blur to me.

After I was dressed and strong enough to leave that horrible place, I had to find more strength to face the people outside the joint again, all righteous in their judgments. I was upset that here they were judging so quickly, because they knew nothing of my situation. It may have appeared to have been an easy decision to cross that line, but it didn't make the mental decision any less easy. I shook my head watching them out the window, while Kasey finished up the paperwork that was left.

The mental anguish and torment that claimed my heart that day, would follow me through this life time and probably·next. A piece of my soul died that day. A deep scar had been driven into my heart.

Yet I had to still walk out this door and be judged by less than perfect individuals standing in front of me, calling me horrible names as we exited. That was a moment of clarity for me. It allowed me not to have to hold Kasey's hand when we left out those doors to go back through that line. I wasn't proud; I just was a different person after that.

I had shed all the tears that were going to be shed that night. I cried till I could no longer cry. I felt sorry until there was no more sorry to be had. I had been depressed, and spoke to no one. It was worse than the rape itself. Kasey was there during the duration of the five days I had to dedicate to this situation. Rock bottom had hit, but I had been trying to convince myself there had to have been a reason for this. I had to find it within myself to put this behind to move on yet again, but what was I supposed to do?

I slept. Afterwards I was forced to have to face life again. Force a fake smile after only five days of a quick mental and physical healing. Physically I knew I would be ok. Emotionally, well that would be a subject for a different day. For now, I had to rely once more on theatre skills to convince the world I was more than ok.

New beginnings

Kasey attempted every chance she had, to keep me positive and not dwelling on the past, I loved her for that. Thankfully, school was about to start back up, so I could immerse myself back into that and everything else getting ready to ramp up for me this year. It proved wonders to place that horrible summer far away out of memories reach.

I had the moonlight festival to look forward to, main stage productions to try out for, the coffee shop hours to work, and then of course there was my love, Robert. Not sure where he was going to fit in this quarter but I would desperately try to make it a point to find time for him.

Kasey and Matt started a new circle of the weekly poker game to be hosted at their house now. I supposed it was their way of trying to create a normal routine for me. On my way back from grabbing the refreshments for the evening, I pulled in the driveway. I was completely startled from a loud engine immediately pulling in behind me. I attempted peering in my rear view and mirror, but could see nothing but headlights glaring in my eyes.

"What the hell?" I was pissed at the lack of courtesy.

I jumped out of my car and looked at the asshole that was blatantly being so rude. After turning their engine off, they finally dimmed the damn lights. It was Cameron. I should have known. He was nothing less than short of arriving in his typical fashion: arrogant or rude. There is never an in between with him.

"Hey man, what's up? Where have you been lately?" He asked grabbing his bag and beer then heading my direction to walk me in the door.

I had been somewhat alarmed that he missed my presence. He had that same beat up brown leather jacket on, his hair just as un-kept as before, but this time it was in a ponytail. He wore these boots that made him look so out of place with the city guys. But he seemed proud of who he was. He handed me a fifth of rum to go with the rest of the beer that he carried inside.

"I had some personal issues to take care of."

I answered his question back.

"You stay here now?"

"Yeah, change of scenery." I lied

"Well let's go in and have a drink, you have my money in your pockets."

I smiled back. It was nice to see some familiar faces finally.

"Fair statement. The booze though is all you. I'm sticking to smoking"

He smiled at me handing me a bud from his pocket.

We climbed the stairs to join the game inside. The front screen door slamming behind, all eyes fell upon us. Cameron broke the awkward silence.

"What the hell's wrong?" He blatantly asked

"You all act like you saw God or something. Oh wait, you just did, carry on now."

Cameron strutted towards the kitchen with his beverages and I was left staring back at everybody that shifted from him to me and my bags. I shrugged with a remark on my way in the kitchen

"Like the damn plaque isn't he? Just can't seem to get rid of him." I smiled slightly.

He made himself a stiff drink, as I placed the snacks on the counter. Afterwards I sat down at the kitchen table to break apart the bud he handed to me releasing the flowering citrus aroma.

"It's Lemon G." He seemed proud of that name.

"It smells great, thanks a lot."

"My pleasure, smoke up. There's plenty where that came from."

Kasey yelled from the other room

"Come on! We need some players in here."

Grabbing the bowl now freshly filled, Cameron took his drink, handed me a lighter and we joined to play some cards. The game being called was named baseball. Shaun was explaining the rules while I adjusted myself and chips in front of me.

The slam of the front door came with a loud crashing sound. I didn't bother to see who it was. The rules were a little more important to me. The room suddenly became quiet. I could feel goosebumps at the base of my neck, my heart started racing. I heard the voice making me cringe.

"Having a poker game and forgot to invite me?"

I froze. I darted my stare across the table at Kasey, who was returning it just as equally confused. She was angered as was I. I knew she didn't invite him, so what the hell was he doing here?

I couldn't make a scene. No one knew what this monster did to me. What the hell was this asshole doing? He did this on purpose. My thoughts and emotions, boiling at this point, I wanted more than anything to claw his eyes out with the same scraping tools they used on me. I wanted him to feel every painful rip that knife tore through me that day. Instead all I could do was gaze at Kasey and steal Cameron's stiff drink to guzzle it.

Cameron was a great sport about it too. He broke the awkward silence that one could cut pierce with a sharp knife…like the ones that were used on me.

"Yeah sitting next to a great looking guy like me would make one want to drink for sure. Hold on though, this time I'll just grab the bottle for us." He was up and left for the kitchen.

Now my desire was to quickly lose my money to go hide back in my room. As fate would have it though, that wouldn't be the case. Mike attempted to join in the table, but at one point Matt informed him rather bluntly.

"I doubt there will be an open seat the rest of the night, so you probably won't need to stay and wait for one."

He chose to wait. Of course he did. His energy in the room was for a specific intent. I was finished with allowing this man to have control over me. I knew why he was there. I was sure he was checking to see if I had told anyone. School was getting ready to kick back up and he was graduating soon. Guess he had to make sure his 'reputation' was still intact.

I wanted to vomit; instead I seemed to have clung to Cameron's presence that evening. He was none the wiser as to why, he just thought I was actually being nice. He had a great time with it. He had me laughing during the evening more times than not. His crass abrasive views and remarks were refreshing to hear, and definitely called for laughs around the room. That eased the tension from the evil stares and glares coming from the snake that slithered in unwelcomed.

During the course of the first game I was shocked a bit to see I was holding my own, and pretty damn good too. I was trying to read everyone's expressions around the table, not so much for the cards they held, that part was easy. It was me wanting to catch their expressions as they watched and scrutinized the other players. I made sure to steer clear of Mike's eyes all evening. What were my expressions like to them? I was completely lost in that theory when my name was simultaneously called from everybody at the table.

"SKYE!" They all yelled loudly.

"Shit. So, so sorry folks. Got side tracked there."

I was zoning out from the weed they had going around. I asked what the matching bid was, and everyone laughed and said I was a fool. I was completely perplexed as to why, but then I saw that Cameron was the only one left in the bet. There was a huge amount of money in the pot.

"Screw it I'm all in." I decided to see his bet.

I had not a nickel to my name after deciding to match. How the hell did that happen? I just bought in for twenty dollars. Well I guess this hand was trying to tell me something.

The laughs continued and now some side bets were being placed. Who would take the first pot of the evening? Every nickel he and I had sitting in the pot. Everyone knew that Cameron never bluffed this bad, let alone the first hand, unless he had it in the hole. Shaun interrupted the thoughts flowing too freely from my mind.

"Alright, whatcha got Cam?"

I couldn't help but smile at him seated next to me. He was still in his leather coat from earlier. I had wondered if he ever had taken it off to sleep at night. It didn't matter, He was making me laugh and I needed that tonight.

Cam laid down his hand and the room exploded. This son of a bitch had four aces. Now what kind of hand was that on the first game of the evening? This is exactly why I didn't play this often. Good thing I had every intention on loosing tonight. However, it would have been nice to have it last more than five minutes. Was he this quick in the sack too? As the noise of the men rejoicing in the background over such an awesome hand played itself out, I took notice I was still holding mine up. I glanced down to make sense of what I had, and then it hit me. As I re-arranged my cards I let them bask in the moment of how amazing it was to see four aces. I silently sat there until they all calmed down.

Shaun's girlfriend Shelly who sat on my other side smiled back at me, all the while remaining quiet as if she knew. She rolled her eyes at me while they laughed and went on in his glory. I smiled back at her and waited for the room to die down.

I could feel all eyes on me at this point, yet for some reason, Mike's eyes were the only ones burning through me.

With all the excitement from his hand I could have sworn this was the highlight of their week. When it finally simmered down to a manageable tone Shaun finally addressed my hand.
"Sorry about that Skye, you just don't see that on the first round usually....let's see what you hung on to."

I said nothing but did exactly what he requested. I laid down my five red hearts straight to the king. There was complete silence, wide eyes, mouths dropped, disbelief, and devastation amongst the men. Then a great big camera flash from Shelly's phone, for my viewing pleasure later on...and socially.
The response was epic. Cameron sat there with his jaw on the floor, and I stood up and gathered my money. The room erupted again only this time, people taking back their money from the side bets they assumed on. Cameron raised a toast to me; I matched it equally, guzzled the shot then excused myself for the ladies room.

Mike's eyes piercing through me forced me to make an excuse to escape briefly. I had such an intense shudder of rage come over me, that it honestly was too much to handle at that point. I knew I was strong, but he was just flaunting his presence and taunting me with this torture. He just wouldn't leave. After locking myself in the bathroom to take some breaths for composure, a slight tap a couple minutes later knocked on the door. It was Kasey who I let in instantly.
"Let me in Skye." She said softly.

She entered closing the door behind her hugging me as if already understanding what I was feeling.
"What the hell is wrong with him? Who invited him?" I was so angry and fighting back the tears of rage.
"I don't know hon, but take some breaths. We have this. No one will let him hurt you tonight."

"I know that, but what the hell?"

"Matt is asking him to leave now… while the guys recoup from the devastating loss of that last hand."

We couldn't help but let out a laugh. The mind now had been made up. I wasn't going to let him have any type of control over me anymore. To do that though, I had to stick the evening out. That would require strength. I had it at this point I felt. My Last deep breath made its way to the surface.

"You know if he doesn't leave, that's fine. I'm done with him trying to think he is the one in control. I can do this. He isn't going to win like that."

"Yea, that's the spirit. He's just trying to get under your skin, so we show him it isn't working." She reassured me.

After I splashed water on my face I responded.

"Let's go. I'm ready."

It was a grueling couple of hours but I held my own. A huge accomplishment for me on an inner level, because it meant I was able to take some control back. The evening finally started winding down. We called last round and it finished with me being the big winner of the evening.

Cameron asked if I wanted to go back to his place to smoke out. I would have taken him up on the offer, but I was emotionally wiped out from the evening, so I politely took a raincheck.

"Well, text me, maybe we can shoot pool sometime."

"Sounds good."

Cameron took my phone from my hand and programmed his number. He handed it back for me to see that he programmed his name as 'big daddy.'

"Big Daddy?" I asked just as odd as it sounded.

"Yeah, that's me." He turned and sauntered out with the screen door slamming behind him.

If he thought I would ever text someone whose name was big daddy as a contact he was smoking more than just marijuana. I changed his name back to his birth one after he had left. That seemed the more logical thing to do.

I stuffed the phone in the pocket and started cleaning up when I noticed Mike standing in the corner. Why can't he just leave? Why was he being so creepy? Out of my peripheral I noticed he was headed my way. He purposely waited for this moment. He planned to leave last.

"If you are considering on dating Cameron, can I give you some advice?" He genuinely asked.

All I could think of was some sarcastic remark to pipe back at him like 'yeah asshole, give me advice from a rapist.' Instead I bluntly stated.

"What do you want?"

"Cam is a player, you now that right?"

"What does that make you?"

"Just be careful, he doesn't respect women, just uses them. Look I know you may think I am scum, but Skye, I never would have slept with you if you had not invited me in. I'm just saying be careful around him, I just want to tell you that friend to friend."

"We are *not* friends, you get that through your head."

There was just so much I wanted to do to this beast in front of me.

"OK its whatever, but you hang out with him you will get hurt."

"Yeah, I hear you. I'd be willing to place a bet that he'd hurt me less than you though…now get out!"

"That's Fine. Good luck to you then." He left slamming the door behind him.

The poker game ended and for once, I actually won at something, both with the game and with myself over Mike.

Harsh Reality

The first day of school finally arrived. I was never so happy to see the start of responsibilities back in my life. I loved my classes this year. They were geared more towards my field now that I got most of the useless classes out of the way. My job at the coffee shop seemed to taper into a nice routine as well. I wasn't working as many hours now. I didn't need to really work, because I had enough financial aid to cover my expenses for that year. But in my head, keeping busy was going to be the key if I was ever going to try to return to my old self.

Within a couple of weeks, Bart managed to get another one of my scripts picked up by a fourth year student to create for the second stage film crew night. I was beyond elated when I heard that. I chose not to be in the film, although the director tried desperately to persuade otherwise. But I had a film class this semester, and this would be a great chance to actually try and collaborate with someone who had experience in the field. The director was willing to have me assist him behind the scenes then, so that project was going to great to add to the portfolio.

One day sitting at the table by the window in the coffee shop playing on his lap top, Bart waited for the last ten minutes of my shift to end before taking off. I finished my side work and was taking care of the last customer when Bart came behind the counter to hug me goodbye. He finished his homework and was headed to the theater department to retrieve supplies he needed before the weekend. We agreed to meet up later and go over changes for a script.

I grabbed the towel to clean his table. It was the last thing to complete before I could clock out and be free. It was an awesome afternoon, and for the first time in a while, I actually wanted to be a part of society again. The sun's presence was providing its warmth for people to enjoy, and I needed to feel that today.

I planned on taking lunch and a slow stroll through the graveyard, right around the corner. It was a huge cemetery with magnificent statues, peaceful scenery and undisturbed history overlooking the city. The energy it offered was comforting. Turned out it was also a great place to do readings on people. They loved when we would meet up at the top of the cemetery hill, and have the reading looking down on life and city-folk.

I collected the last of my tips before heading over to the front window to wipe Bart's table off. I had to make sure it was clean for the next caffeine junkie that walked in. Glancing outside, I saw Robert. I hadn't spoken nor had I seen him since my birthday. His presence was exhilarating and exquisite to say the least. It had been a hot minute since I last laid my eyes on the most amazing body and perfectly chiseled face.

Lost in the breathtaking moment, admiring the view, he stepped out from the restaurant across the street. He buttoned up his coat, and then descended the step making way for someone else behind him.

Then I saw who, it was his tall red haired model which joined gracing his arm. They were standing outside the restaurant right across the street from the coffee shop. I was dumbfounded. I stood there with my mouth gaping like a three year old in a candy store. I was just beside myself staring at the most beautiful woman I had ever seen in my life. They were holding each other in a very affectionate embrace.

I was astonished actually. Here she was standing in front of me. I finally got to see her in the flesh. She was just simply a goddess with perfectly spiraled red hair flowing down with every strand shining in perfect radiance. Long luscious full curls that swayed with every turn the wind took. She was just as tall and matched him exactly in style. Her legs that went to infinity, dressed to the nines in a contemporary fall look that only celebrities could pull off in a small town like this. She was simply exquisite and dazzling with her energy, and the way she carried herself with nothing less than angelic. Every move this woman made was simply splendid. My mouth found its way back to the top of itself, but my shoulders seemed to have slumped with the crushing weight of knowing now why he and I could never be.

Overcome with jealousy and envy, my heart just sunk. I knew I barely held a candle standing next to the Goddess before me. I could only dream to be as graceful as her. This woman was so confidant; she had heels on and was killing it, for someone who might as well have been as tall as Andre the giant.

Then it happened, the kiss. He leaned in to kiss her, not the other way around. It wasn't both of them leaning at the same time. No, it was *he that wanted it.* That kiss was not like one that we ever shared. This kiss seemed so genuine, so heartfelt.

A very devastated empty sigh escaped. I would like to think, at that moment a light bulb switched on, but instead it was actually being turned off. I realized where my place was, and what he and I represented to each other. It was never clearer to me than right at that moment. I would never be anything more to him than just a call girl. That hit me in my gut. Well this was a harsh reality for me to have witnessed.

The kiss was soft on her lips. So gentle one could feel the love attached. I am not sure he ever kissed me that way. I had some crazy emotions stir up at that moment. I didn't understand what the big deal was, with being the other woman suddenly. I didn't even care, so why now was it an issue? The paralysis of the visual that just played out for me caught me off guard. By the time her turn to leave registered in my head, he had already noticed me standing in the window staring at her. Our eyes caught briefly.

"Shit." I said.

I snapped out of it long enough to finish the table. I lowered my head and felt the heated blood in my veins making their rounds.

"Oh please" I uttered under my breath.

"Please don't come in here."

I feverishly finished wiping down the table, while desperately calming the hearts anger down to a simmer. The butterflies were fluttering around hoping he wasn't going to walk in. I snuck a peep once more in the hopes that he had left, but instead his head did that tilt to the side, that it always did, and caught me off guard quite unexpectedly. I half wanted to run out of there, but instead, I was still, just frozen, staring right back at him. He smiled and started his strut my way. This was not what I wanted to deal with today.

I took off my apron while he made his way through the crowd to the front of the counter. He was right there when I came back after clocking out.

"Hey." I tried acting surprised. Not sure if I was excited to see him after that show I just witnessed.

"Hey you." He was grinning ear to ear.

"Want to go grab a bite to eat?"

"Didn't you just eat?" was my response back

"No, actually, I wasn't there for food."

That made sense. With looks like hers who could focus on anything else? Normally I would have jumped at the chance, but I was feeling a little down at the moment so I opted for a rain check. I made some excuse that I had to go pick up my costume for the Halloween party next week.

He opted to walk me to my car. I shrugged and agreed so on the way we conversed about how things were going. I insisted they were going well, although I had a feeling he could tell I was lying through my teeth.

He sensed that I was upset about seeing what just transpired and tried to make light of the situation. However, *how* it played out in front of me wasn't something I could just shake off. He turned sympathetic at that point, and honestly stated apologies for it. He didn't know I would be there, and I believed him.

It wasn't that. It was just everything for me. I was just drained from having any feelings on the topic at that point. I was exhausted from almost everything anymore.

I just wanted to drive away. Robert and I had been seeing each other off and on for a while, and now for some reason, seeing those two sent a feeling of final disappointment over me. I wasn't even sure why, I knew we could never work out, but when its displayed right in front of you as to why it would never work, well the feeling came through a little different than perhaps I anticipated. Maybe I had just realized that I was not actually OK being the other woman.

After quite a lengthy discussion on the topic, I smiled back as to reassure him things were alright. Subconsciously, I was already mentally in my car driving away. We agreed to text each other sometime to get caught up over how our summers went. I wasn't sure I would have the courage to tell him anything of mine.

I wasn't sure if he picked up the vibe on that, but I knew for a fact that while I had the most awful break, I was sure his was going to be the exact opposite. I didn't really want to hear how well his vacation went either with the most beautiful woman the world. There was no way I could tell him about mine. I steered the conversation to a rather quick ending, then hugged him before I drove away.

Would he think less of me if I told him what happened? Is it possible to think of someone less than a call girl? I doubted it. I finally reached home, my heart just drowning in the emotion of extreme despair.

I heard a hot bath and my robe calling for me. After grabbing the mail and fumbling for the keys to let myself in, I headed for the kitchen table to put the mail down. Flipping through the stack just purely out of boredom and nosiness, out of the corner of my eye I could see a hand written letter addressed to me. Who knew where I was staying to write me a hand written letter? Who even writes letters now days? I glanced at the returned address, it was from my sister.

My heart leapt out of my chest. I couldn't believe it was my sister writing me. How did she know where to find me? I had no clue but I was over the moon with delight. Finally! I ran up the stairs to start the bath so I could settle in to the relaxing bubbles. I was going to forget my issues for a moment. It'll be great to see how things were going back home. I could hardly contain my excitement.

I ran the bath then stepped in the steaming water with nothing more than my letter from my sister. The hot water stung against the skin. I could feel the first layer of my skin melting off as I slowly adjusted my body to the waters temperature by sitting down cautiously. It took me a minute to gain my bearings as the water was almost scalding, but once inside and used to it, I opened the letter to read. It was not as long as I had hoped it would be. In fact it wasn't long at all. There were hardly two paragraphs on the paper. I was shocked and even angrier now from this.

"I don't talk or see you guys in years and this is all I get? Damn way to make someone feel loved I guess." Then I read it. It was rather simple, direct and to the point.

Dear Skye,

Hope you are doing well, not that mom or dad care, but I thought I would pass this along to you as I know how close you and Nanny were….

I stopped. I allowed the letter to fall outside the tub when I dropped my arm to the ground. That was it. A letter to inform me Nanny died. Not even a hello, not anything. There was nothing. She gave me no update as to how, just simply wrote informing me about the death. What was I missing here? Were my sisters and brothers angry with me? Angry enough that not more than two paragraphs could be written? How do some erase a person from their minds? How can one pretend someone is dead while they clearly amongst the living? Why bother telling me about a death in the family if I am considered dead as well? I didn't even want to read the rest of the letter because there was no point. I think I finished it anyway though, because I wanted desperately to hear from my family, even if it was only a paragraph ironically about death.

I learned she had passed month ago. They debated telling me, but for some reason my sister decided she would 'sneak' off to write me about her death. This grown woman had to 'sneak' and tell me. I just let out a sigh but then the tears came soon afterward. I just sat in the tub and silently mourned for Nanny, me, Robert, my family, my unborn child, my everything at that moment. I had no idea why on earth I was even here amongst the living, when everything around me was meant for death. It made no sense to me anymore.

I was interrupted with the sound of the phone chiming in. It was Cameron, from poker. He had sent a text to see what I was doing.

"Not you." I sent back

He came back with a harsh response.

"Don't flatter yourself..." I laughed but the only thing I could think to say to that was something pathetic.

"Seriously?"

I was a bit taken off guard thinking, why the hell would you text me then if you weren't interested? Then the response came through.

"Lol...no silly, so what are you doing?"

"Truth?"

"No lie because it turns me on."

Another pathetic response from me was sent.

"Seriously?"

"Man...You are naive aren't you?"

"No!!! Whatever...what do you want?" I was becoming somewhat perturbed at him. There was just something about him, that either made you love him or hate him, I was not sure where I stood on in fence, but he loved pushing people off onto the hate side.

"Let's go shoot some pool."

I debated it for a moment but at that point shrugged my shoulders and decided why not?

"K. When and where?"

We met up that evening at the Top Hatters Tower. It was his favorite hangout. That wasn't hard to figure out, the way the bartender and he interacted. When the bartender has your drink ready for you when you walk in, I would bet to say that person would be considered a fixture. He bought an extra beer for me then strutted over and placed them down by the pool table I had just grabbed for us.

We shot some pool, played some darts, drank more beer and hung out with some people that streamed in later. Cameron was always fun to go out with. He had me laughing most of the evening as he told some jokes but just mainly just because of his personality, and the way he interacted with others. We stuck to small talk, as I really wasn't in the mood to discuss me and I could tell he was not about wanting to discuss anything deeper than a cue ball making it into the hole of his choosing.

Cameron's dirty blond hair wasn't in its normal pony tail, but he had his leather coat on. I was shocked to see he actually took the jacket off to play pool. He wore a yellow pullover shirt that highlighted his blond hair nicely against the pool table. He grabbed his beer from our table to swig one back.

"Your shot there pool queen."

He was obviously being sarcastic. I was horrible at the game and there wasn't even any pretending about it. The bartender shouted;

"Last call folks."

I hadn't realized we stayed that long playing pool that evening; as we were laughing and having such a great time. I was tipsy from the drinks he kept buying. He asked if I wanted to go back to his place, I asked how far away it was. I didn't think driving too far would be a great idea. He said two blocks away. Well that beat the shortest distance for a 'crash out' house.

Leaving the bartender her tip, we walked to the cars to finish the evening at his place. He drove rather fast for my taste, at one point I thought as I saw him hop a curb. Maybe he was just as tipsy as I was. That thought left my head though when I saw the cop up ahead. Cameron made a right down a back street. Great idea, I smiled in agreement with the shortcut. It turned out to actually be his street. He parked his van in front of a house that had the appearance of a rundown Gothic church. It even had the round spiral leading up to a rotunda. I stepped out of the vehicle and looked at the house in awe. He came from around his driver side and on his way past me simply stated.

"Come on."

With that he climbed the stairs two at a time. I closed my door and followed only one step at a time, taking in the view from the amazing piece of architecture standing in front of me. We reached the porch, and he flung the door open upon entering. He announced with a loud enough yell that had to be reprimanded for, when he finished.

"I AM HOME…You may carry on now."

"Knock it off Cutler…My baby boy is sleeping in the next room."

"My bad."

While the lady of the house, or so it would seem, reprimanded him for being childish, I glanced around to see the magnificent room in its entire elegance. It was definitely some sort of church. From what would appear to be the original markings and references to religion on the walls. The ceiling was a cathedral one, with stained glass covering at least half of it. Breathtaking reds and blues painted in their splendor. He must have introduced me at this point, because now the lady of the house was addressing me my name.

"Hi Skye, nice to meet you. I am Willow, and this is Laurel. "

I returned the greetings, and then peered into the other room, without leaving my current spot from where my feet decided to plant themselves. There seemed to be others lying on the floor and sofa sleeping. It appeared to be a commune of some sorts. Cameron didn't let me ponder for long; He grabbed my hand and pulled it into his needed direction, towards his room.

"We'll be upstairs if you need us."

They said good night, I smiled back silently then followed Cameron up the very steep dark stairs. Reaching the top, he opened the first door then went in while I stopped at the entrance, staring in to his room. I was in shock to see that his room had walls just as tall as Roberts walls were. They were a very dark, mundane earth green. But the tops of the walls were peeling and needed some love and attention. I was shocked to see an overwhelming amount of countless cages. Some had red lights, some had black lights, then regular lights, and some didn't have lights at all. There were cages from the floor to the ceiling on three out his five walls that he had.

He walked over to throw his coat on the mattress. The mattress, that I then saw lying on the ground. Normally, I myself would not have minded sleeping on the floor, but with the city Zoo locked inside that same room, I had a slight issue with that. In fact I had a huge issue with it. I wasn't even sure what it was I was walking into at this point, but it was too late to just drive home.

"You going to come on in or stand there all night?"

"Not sure. What's in the cages?"

He laughed. "Snakes. Come on they won't bite you."

I was slow to react and stepped in cautiously looking around trying to soak it all in. He told me to close the door, and without question, I followed directions.

"Is this where we are supposed to sleep?" I could barely even get the words out for fear of the answer back.

"Why? What's wrong?"

"Umm, well for starters the mattress being amongst the snakes."

"Well good thing all you're doing is closing your eyes. You'll be fine. Come on I'm tired."

I let out a deep sigh. I was well beyond exhaustion to argue with him. He kicked off his shoes, laid down then tapped the space next to him on the side of the mattress he was willing to share with me. He rolled over to pass out.

I figured I would sleep on the couch because there wasn't room on the single mattress size for both, unless we spooned each other. I looked over to see the couch was also filled with cages, but those were not snakes in there. I squinted hard in the direction of the cages. It was hard to see as the red lights were so dim, and the other lights were covered with a blanket over the door so as not to let light out of the cage. I walked over towards them, tripping over everything because it was that messy in the room.

He was defiantly a bachelor. There was no mistake on that one. Finally, I reached the cages, and leaned in for a closer look. I used my phone for a light to see that inside there were mice, and some were nursing babies. These little guys couldn't have been more than an inch in length. There were lots of them in this cage. Perring into the other cage, it looked like a bunch of little teenage mice. They all hopped around the cage. I had never seen something like this, so it was fascinating to me. Their tiny squeals were so cute.

"You coming over here or what?"

Cameron rolled back over facing me now mumbling. He could tell I was inspecting the cages under the blanket, because their squeaks caused him to wake back up. I giggled, and decided I was going to have to lay with him on the floor that evening.

For a moment in my light headed daze making my way over to the bed, I had wondered what it would be like to be with him physically, to experience Kasey's descriptive narrative on his sexual tendencies. He met my eyes, and asked what I was thinking, but shaking my head I said nothing. The thought of that both scared and turned me on.

I went to the mattress and took off the shoes, when I finally laid down, he inched closely next to and just simply reached his hand around my waist as if just to hold me. How odd and different this was. I actually started to relax, thinking he was being far more of a gentleman than his reputation projected.

I stared around the room as I lay there hoping to fall asleep. His place was un-kept. Food bags everywhere. The beer cans mixed in with clothes. Papers and cages were everywhere. I was assessing his cleanliness habits as he abruptly interrupted it with another disappointing statement.

"Oh I lost a snake so if you see one let me know, so I can grab it."

It took just a second for that statement to sink in. I jumped up out of the bed, freaked out from the whole nonchalant attitude of that statement. My stare burning through him, and my mouth on the floor speechless, while he responded.

"What? He isn't interested in you at all, so don't worry."

Well that presented a dilemma now for me. How drunk was I that I would risk a snake crawling around me as I sleep? I shook my head and after absorbing the shock of it, which took me a minute longer than I thought to process, I laid back down next to him. I was simply too tired, to even care at that point.

Finally, I dozed off and surprisingly slept well. The morning brought the rage of the hot sun beaming in through the overly exaggerated tall window that we happened to be laying under. We had fallen asleep with arms around each other, and for a moment, I laid there enjoying the comfort of a man's arms. I thought about Robert and then forced myself to stop because at that point I was becoming depressed and didn't want to start tearing up.

Exotic worlds

The sun added a nice touch to waking up alongside of someone though. As I was dozing back off, my vision, through the haze from my squint, saw a shadow crossing in front of me. I opened my eyes to see a very large, no less than four foot, shimmering black snake crossing towards the fireplace. It was slithering parallel from where I currently laid. The snake was heavy and fat, but the way the sun hit this majestic beast in the light made the black appear to be a deep violet. It was rather hypnotizing in its sheen.

Then I snapped back to reality and re-thought on the majestic beast part. I automatically did what a typical person would do if they weren't used to dealing with such exotic animals. I screamed like a baby. I jumped off the mattress and abruptly out of his arms, ruining whatever moment might have been… if woken another way.

He jumped up and rubbed his eyes yelling back at me. "What? What the hell Skye?"

"'"It's a fucking snake! Look."

I pointed in its direction which at this point was halfway across the floor. Cameron jumped to his feet and yelled "Grab it!"
"Fuck you! You Grab it!"
He laughed and stood up to grab the snake bringing it to me. I took steps back and fell back on the mattress.
"Calm down, they can sense fear. He won't eat you, nor will he bite you. Unless of course you smell like a rat or mouse."

He showed me the snake. I sat in fear at first just simply staring at it until he showed me how to pet it. I humored him by imitating his movement with the snake, just so he would put it away.

"See? I told you, they're not bad animals. They just get a bad rap. People can be ignorant in assessing things by their appearance."

How ironic I thought, and pretty deep for a man who does nothing but drugs and plays cards. Although as he handled the snake I did have a moment of clarity, because I had assumed the worst about him when I first met him; but last night he turned out to be nothing but the complete opposite. I felt a rush of guilt over my pre judgement of him. Now I understood why he enjoyed the animals.

"Where should we put him?"

"What do you mean where? Isn't that the snake that was lost? Where is his cage at?"

"No this is one I lost six months ago. So good catch."

"Oh my God, are you even serious right now?" I jumped back up because at this point I thought it be better if I went home.

"Well yeah, this bad boy was supposed to have been sold but I lost him right before the show. I've been looking for him, looks like he's been eating the mice and rats around the home. That's great too, cause now he'll cost more. So score for me."

Cameron eventually placed the snake in a cage that was occupied by another snake. While he watched for a moment to see how they would interact, he made sure to tell me a bit about the mixing and breeding that he did with animals to sell them at shows. How odd for a career path, I thought to myself. I had wondered how long he had been doing this, because he spoke as though he had been doing this all his life. When I asked, his response was exactly what I had expected to hear from the knowledge that poured from his lips with ease. All his life he had been into animals so he taught himself.

I was taught Lesson one on snakes that day. When he was comfortable enough for them to hang together, he turned his attention towards me. He smiled approaching me, where I hung behind peering over, around, and under to get a sneak of the massive snake he held with ease. I returned the smile, but noticed his was one of mischief. That made me smile a bit harder, and before I even had a chance to react afterwards, he closed the gap between us and rather suddenly.

His lips were less than an inch from mine. He cocked his head to the side and barely brushed my lips with his. He felt around my mouth with just the brush of the wind between our gaps. I thought he was going to kiss me, it was such a quick and reactive response for me to just lean forward with my eyes closed anticipating it, to no such luck, though.

He half carried and half pushed me back to the mattress. Laying me half way down before gently pushing me the rest of the way, he came crashing down on top of me, stripping his shirt off in the process.

I was already out of mine, with my nipples erect and tingling from the impromptu moment. He took my palms and interlaced them tightly with his. Raising them above my head, he had my heart racing, and heat rushing through the body. The sensation of his lust licking at my lips made me have to moan with pleasure.

He kissed me again, this time harder. He didn't have to pry hard though; his rising man hood had me ready and willing. My lips already wet and warm under his. He traced my lips with his tongue. My moan was silenced by his passionate kiss afterwards.

Pulling away, he stared at me in the eyes for a second before lowering his head. His mouth was kissing my chin and making its way down to my breasts. He nibbled on one, sending a pleasured tingle running through me. I could feel him making his way over to the other nipple, this one, sent me squirming. He bit that one; I was swelling with desire down below. I could feel the liquid drops burning down my thigh knowing there was no stopping now.

I must have moaned again, because he took his tongue and made his way down my stomach that was swamped with goose bumps from the sensation. He took his hand and placed it right over my panties, grabbing my woman hood with fierce intent. The thin fabric of my panties was now glued to him. It must have sent the same sensation back to him. He took his hand from the panties and finished pulling his pants down. I sat up to feel his chest, but he pushed me back down.

"No lay down. I got this" All I could do was shiver with anticipation at what was to soon come.

He pinned me down and said "I want to fuck you my way."

I let out yet another moan, I was breathless, and almost speechless.

"Your way?"

"Yeah…my way." He was relentless in his words.

He pinned me down, and brought his mouth down to my breast. He closed his mouth around one of the nipples while his stiff cock found its way towards my inner thigh. I sent a small yelp out of pleasure.

He shifted his hands so that he could caress my arms that he held above my head. I let him know by the shiver it sent through me, that I was thoroughly enjoying myself. I let my hand fall to his back where I couldn't help but gently rake my nails across it. He grabbed my hands again and pinned them behind me. He said not a word. Just shook his head as if I wasn't allowed to touch him.

His hands placed my hands where he wanted them to stay. Then he directed his attention to the waistband of my panties. They were soaking wet, I couldn't help the soft moan that escaped. He didn't even bother to take my panties off; he just moved them to the side. He went right in unceremoniously with two fingers sinking right into my soaking slit, then he plunged deep and very directly into that sacred space inside me that wanted all of his attention.

I cried out again, this time with his name on my lips. He was being so gentle with his touch and wasn't even remotely close to being finished with exploring this far inside me. I was a mess, arching my back and then clenching my drenched thighs. I couldn't take it any longer, and he knew this. He paused momentarily, long enough to switch things up. His thumb, had now gently found its way towards my swollen clit. He pressed massaging back and forth gently. He rolled so softly with just the right pressure. He was agonizing in his tortuous teasing, drawing out the anticipated release.

I could see his delight when he reached for the clit and felt how sensitive he made it. His look, made my thighs clamp tighter together. He was holding his hand in place, as I rode the wave of excitement. I was feeling lightheaded from it all. He couldn't take it any longer, and neither could I. He ripped my panties off, and climbing on top, shoved himself deep inside with a vengeance. I closed my eyes, I was already there. He stroked perfectly in tune and rhythm with my wave of ecstasy.

"Oh God..." I couldn't help but cry out.

"Just one more stroke, one more Cameron just stay right there."

Then I saw his teeth clench down while he pushed in even farther, rubbing and grazing my clit. He pushed once more deeper this time; I didn't think he could go any further.

Something about his look when he released did something for me and I lost it. The pressure, and swelling of it all, caused a glorious shatter of radiated pleasure pulsating through my blood.

He had lost himself inside me, and I had lost myself in him. I hugged his hips close to mine, cried out and let my shivering body pulsate in its utter delight. He threw his head back with both of us finishing together in this unrivaled bliss.

I must have passed out after that, I remember rolling over but that was it. A little while later, my eyes opened and he was sitting up next to me naked. I don't even remember when all his clothes came off during the fiasco. But I was impressed with his rather extremely defined masculine cut. I looked at him and moaned. My mouth apparently forgot that I had woken up. He looked down at me, gazing down at my lips first, then my still erect nipples. Cameron pivoted his torso to lean in to kiss me. Then he climbed on top of me and had his way once more before we called it for the day.

"Well that was unexpected." He said taking off his condom. I didn't even see him put one on. But it didn't matter, I was on the pill from the last mistake I made. He lit a cigarette, and passed me one.

"No I am good, thanks I don't smoke."

"Really? Ever try it?"

"Yeah, not for me….thanks though. But I will take a hit off one of these."

I rolled over to grab one of the many joints in his ashtray, then lit it to join the after sex smoke he was currently enjoying. I lay for a long time next to him that day. I listened to his stories, and just made mental notes about this new found friend of mine.

I left his house that day, not even knowing what to make of that. That was a whole new experience and nothing was bad about it either. I rather enjoyed him, and couldn't help but smile when on the way out he had asked.

"We cool?"

"Of course. Why wouldn't we be?"

"I don't know. Want to hang out again sometime?"

"Of course." With that I left him with his snakes.

I wondered on the way home if he was actually going to text me at any point and ask to hang out again? Or if what my mother always said was true. "Why pay for the milk when you can get the cow for free?" A revolting sigh came from within me and I turned up the radio to drown out the guilt.

It didn't matter to me anyways; I was good being alone for the time being. But hey at least I knew now to always trust Kasey when she said it would be worth a ride or two. I snickered at that thought.

I was a bit elated to know that after that encounter, he actually did send a text the following the day. He wanted to go to see a movie. It was nice to know the cow was worth coming back to. I smiled at the offer but had to raincheck it. The next couple weeks were filled with tight schedule productions and school. With the schedules conflicting, Cameron and I agreed to make time for the Halloween party downtown. I was curious to see if he would dress up for the event, but I probably could have taken a side bet that he wouldn't.

I sent him a message back stating I would love to go with him on Halloween but only if he dressed up. His response was typical.

"I'm going as a porn star…"

"Of course you are….wait, so does that mean you are or are not? Are you being sarcastic?"

"You'll see…

"So should I dress up?" I sent a quick question back.

"Yes." Was all he sent back.

Was his response sarcastic? I would figure that out later. I had to focus on everything else going on currently.

Halloween seemed to have whisked its way rather quickly to being around the corner, and as it approached I decided not to dress up. It seemed too much for me to really care about putting any effort into. Cameron chose to show up as himself, but made me smile when he said I was crazy for not seeing him as a porn star. I replied I did, but the problem was that no one outside his own head saw that. With that we left and had an amazing time down town. It was definitely entertaining to see the cast of characters and their costumes roaming around causing mischief for the evening.

After that date though, Cameron and I were hardly able to meet up for anything outside poker anymore. I was busy focusing on the film, play, and upcoming audition at school. He was busy doing his thing with the animals, so whatever it was we were pretending to have, would have to be placed on hold for a moment.

Accomplishing directing my first show in the theatre down stairs, proved more challenging than I had anticipated. What little time I could spare went directly towards Robert and our little escapades.

One day in the creative arts center I saw a glimpse of Mike with Mr. Harrington. I tried to dodge out of the main line of sight, but was caught by the professor. I couldn't wait for the end of fall quarter so that Mike could finally be gone from this place.

"Skye! Come on over and join us for a minute will you?"

How could I say no?

"Sure." I clamped my teeth and headed their way.

"I heard your working on a play down stairs. Mike was just telling me a bit about it, but he couldn't remember the name of it. I recognize it too, what's the name of your production?" He asked inquisitively.

I was angered by Mike knowing so much about me. It was as though he was stalking me. I was becoming a bit perturbed at him.

"Oh-"I completely ignored Mike and spoke directly with the professor.

"The play is Stage blood, by Charles Ludlow."

"Oh yes that's right. Great play I might add. Look forward to seeing it. Well alright then, I'm off to class, you two take care. Mike I'll see you this weekend."

He left the two of us standing there. Mike turned his attention to me trying to speak, but I was already hot behind the professors' tail. Not even considering giving him two cents of my time. I couldn't get out of there fast enough. I think I had an anxiety attack because I didn't remember anything but coming back around until I was in my car with the doors locked.

Breathing heavily, I tried calming myself down. I had no idea the effect he still had on me. I started the car, and headed towards work to start my shift, and shake this negative energy that was trying to attach itself to me.

At work, the fall and winter season were our busiest. I had been asked to work to fill some slots they had not anticipated, so I opted for the extra cash and pitched in to help out. I had been working so much and with the routine of school, I showed up one day after my class, prepared to try and squeeze my shift in before I ran home to rehearse my audition for tomorrow.

I reached the parking lot and could see the line out the door. I hustled inside, throwing my backpack on the floor, grabbed the apron and clocked in. I went out to help with the madness. Our manager Larry at the cash register, a bit flustered, but handling the pumpkin latte's and cash like a pro.

"Skye, did you feel bad for us or something on your drive by?"

"What do you mean?" I asked flustered trying desperately to tie my apron faster.

"Why are you here?" He asked perplexed.

"I work....don't I?"

I stopped mid tie and looked back at him now with wide eyes, with the possibility that I didn't have to be there.

"Your off tonight, you said you needed to have it for rehearsal on your audition in two days."

"OH shit, you're so right! Sweet!" I turned to go clock right back out.

"No, no! Please stay we could totally use the help."

"Larry…" I was already back with my back pack and mentally already in my car.
"Love ya man, but I have to do this audition, and I am scared out of my wits."
"I got ya." He smiled and I was out of there.

In the parking lot, heading toward good Ole Tessie the Toyota, a loud screech pulled in behind me, making skids to a stop, almost causing me to soil myself with the fear. I knew who it was before I turned around to address. It could be only one person. Cameron.

"HEY!" He yelled as he made his violent stop.

"Hey back."

"Whatcha doing?"

"Going home to practice my song for the audition at school.

"Want to hang this weekend?"

"Maybe, text me. I will let you know after the auditions!"

"Text me and let me know how you did!" he sped off and I followed.

On the way home, I contemplated how Robert must be doing, wondering whether or not I should send him a quick text to say hello. Then I thought better of it, in case he was with her. It had been a couple of months since we had spoken after that encounter at the shop, and I wasn't sure if it was on both of our parts or on mine. I could feel a distance between him and me growing. I was so desperately holding on to whatever we once had at the beginning of the affair. I wanted the old us back, before I saw her in his arms and the kiss. A kiss that was so pure and full of real love.

I tried to shake it, but the only way to really rid that feeling of disappointment for myself was to break it off with him. I really needed to end the relationship, if I was going to scathe out of this somewhat. I didn't want to become emotionally scarred from it. I wasn't sure who I was trying to kid, but Robert and I were just not meant to be together.

For now I would hold off though, at least through the auditions for Main stage. I had to focus on my character, and monologue so I could attempt to score the most ultimate acting role ever, Eponine. Even if it were only in College, it would still be my unparalleled role to have.

The next two nights, I spent every minute rehearsing over and over my lines and song. I rehearsed every which way I could think of, until I found the right delivery method for me. That second evening, I lost my voice, only then I knew it was time to call it for now. I knew it wasn't the fact that I had just recited the same paragraph for the past eight hours or so, but rather because my anticipation and nerves were becoming worse. I finally crashed out and slept extremely hard.

That evening I dreamt about some crazy play that ended in murder. I chalked it up to my over active imagination. The weather outside the next morning wasn't really being a team player on the way to auditions. It had snowed the night before so I was a bit late from having to dig out my car. After I exerted all my nerves out on shoveling snow, I finally reached the art center. I had entered the door with my cup of hot coffee in one hand and water in the other, bag in tow. As I entered the building I was once again filled with pits in the stomach, it was almost overwhelming.

One of my professors though, that I had in my first year had a way of calming me whenever I needed to be assured. I loved the old man's wisdom as he was rather worldly in his theatre knowledge. Walter, as he insisted everyone call him, was advanced in his age, and carried himself with a very distinguished walk. He was always very soft spoken. In taking his first year class for us novices, I had learned the "method" way of acting, through his knowledge and expertise. He was my 'go to' guy whenever I was feeling down in the department.

So it was even better to have happened to run into him in the center on my way to the auditions the next day. He was dressed in some gray plaid dress pants with a white long sleeve shirt underneath his always worn and favorite sweater. It reminded me of a Sherlock Holmes style sweater. He always seemed that he should have a pipe in his hand contemplating over a fire place of the next murder he would solve.
"Skye…love… come chat for a minute if you can."

I always had to make sure I had time for him, even if I was frustrated with myself because I was running a bit behind. "Hello Walter, How are you?"

Walter was also my interview expert in the field when I had to do a paper for one of my other professors. He helped me ace that class, so I was forever in his debt. The things I learned from that interview would stay with me for the rest of my days. He was such a brilliant actor and professor. He was even a published author, so I really appreciated his company.

"Getting ready for the audition today?"

"Yes and I am a wreck. I am so nervous. I am sick from it."

That was not a lie. It was the biggest audition of my life, at least at that moment, and I was terrified I would blow it.

He tossed his head back in laughter, as if he was thoroughly delighted to hear that. I was disappointed until he said this before he whisked off to his ultimate destination in the center.

"Aha- My dear, if you weren't nervous, you wouldn't be human. Nerves are the thrill of it. That is how you know you are truly alive. Don't just disregard those, you need to explore it, you surely will be delighted how they can help."

He sauntered off talking to himself, as he often did. Well that wasn't what I wanted to hear. But it was time. I would be up soon so I needed to go warm up the voice.

In the acoustics room, I warmed up the vocals by bouncing them off the back of the wall. I was trying to remember all the words to the monologue after that. Butterflies graced their presence in my stomach. The knot was so tight in my gut matching the knot I felt in my throat. I had guzzled the entire six pack of water throughout the morning, with some hot honey tea. Some theatre student popped his head in the door.

"Skye they are ready for you."

"OK. Be right there." This was it. For me, it was the audition of a life time. I made my way to the stage and entered in the spotlight trying not to squint under its blinding glare.

I took my stance dead center, and recited the protocol, first my song then the monologue. We were not given an option on the song for the audition. Mr. Harrington requested we all perform a song from the character we were wanting. He ask that we start the audition with the song first, which was usually opposite of auditions' normal protocol

I felt this rush of overwhelming calmness hit me at the moment I opened my mouth to sing. It must have been the endorphins finally settling, because there were no more butterflies in the belly. Instead, with the blackness surrounding and shielding me from the outside world for the time being, I closed my eyes welcoming the visual waiting to greet me behind my lids.

I sang the song as if in a world of my own. Never realizing how the ironic the duality that was being played out before my very eyes with Robert. I was the other woman; He was in love with his Cosette.

I was at the end of the song when tears filled my eyes. I cried at the last 'I love you.' It broke my heart, because at that moment, I wasn't pretending to be her anymore... I was her.
I closed my eyes and bowed the head to show the end of character.

I had to take a moment to re-gather the senses for the chosen monologue. About mid-way through though, He had cut me off and said that was all he needed, and then thanked me.

So that was it. I got cut off in the middle. That couldn't be a good sign. Damn I thought I definitely messed that up. I couldn't help the emotion of the song that hit me like a ton of bricks at that point. For some reason I was extremely emotional over this lingering break up with Robert. I knew it had to be done though, it was killing me and I think I had just killed my career because of it.

That evening I had sent a text to Cameron then met up with him for a beer. He was always a great company when one was down on their luck.

"I'm sure you did great...don't worry about it. There's nothing you can do about it now." He took another swig from his drink.

"Yeah I know, it's just that I had never been cut off before in the middle of a monologue."

"So what does that mean?" He asked

"In theater that can mean anything."
"When will you find out?"
"Tomorrow right before the winter break starts."
"Ugh." He laughed then took another gulp.
"Exactly."   We both lifted our glasses in a cheer to the anticipation.

That night back at the house, I could hardly sleep. I tossed and turned, then finally, dozed off for some dreams to come play out. The clock read four in the morning when slumber finally took its grip back.

The end of the new

The following day after an exhaustive night of no sleep, I couldn't contain my excitement and nerves any longer. I could hardly even take the stomach aches at this point. I had to know, so I made my way to the art center. I had to stop for a latte though, because my eyes did not want to be team players at the moment.

I felt a rush of emotion fill my body as I opened the doors. The center was so quiet, and it suddenly looked humongous under the skylight that greeted me with its ever endearing light. I looked up at the sun peering through the window and smiled. I took a deep breath, and then took the longest walk of my life, across the carpeted floor to the posting center. My nerves all a flutter, my stomach in my throat and then there was the sheet, hanging there for everyone to view.

CAST: Les Miserables

I scanned the characters and names

Jean Vale jean - Tomas Harlan

Cosette-Sara Parker

Fantine- Laura Whittier

Javert- Carl Jenkins

Eponine - Skye Miller

"Oh my ….."

I collapsed to the floor pivoting to sit down. Tears were streaming from my eyes. I couldn't believe it. I thought he hated me the way he cut me off mid monologue.

"Hey, young lady."

I looked up and saw Walter in his same sweater, only this time with brown checkered dress pants and a pink v neck sweater covering the white shirt underneath.

"Good morning professor." I was still trembling in the voice when I greeted him back.

"Congratulations my dear, I see you learned to overcome the fear."

"I can't thank you enough Walter. You working with me and guiding me with your wisdom could never be repaid." I was emotional on that response.

"It doesn't need to be. I eagerly await the performance." Off he went again, discussing something with himself about two poets.

"Oh man."

I just closed my eyes and appreciated every minute of that emotional relief. I was now officially wiped out. I had to gather what strength I had to muster through the day, for the last of my exams. I could not wait to get on with the winter break at this point.

My phone chimed, it was Robert. My heart racing once more, this whole day was going to be an emotional ride. I wasn't so sure I was ready for all the events that were about to play themselves out sooner than later. He had asked if I wanted to get together over the break. I had sent him a message back that we should meet up that night. I was done trying to put off the inevitable any longer.

We made plans to meet for dinner at seven. His lady friend was not due back in for Christmas break until tomorrow, so tonight seemed perfect and fitting to end the affair that should have never been. I was so desperately holding back on my emotions with him, I loved him and hated him all at the same time. I was not looking forward to dinner that evening.

What I actually did look forward to was Cameron coming around more often than not. I had no idea why on earth I was finding myself wanting to be around him constantly, the only reason I could logically come up with was that he was twenty years Roberts junior and energetically equally so. Physically it was like a volcano that was ready to erupt at any given time. He was completely new and exciting. He lived in a world where he made the rules up. He made me laugh though, that was a great plus in my book at the moment.

It was both fun and horrifying at times when hanging out with him. It seemed he had no problem living on the edge of the limits. Cameron was a different character, that seemed masked and angry at the world, but in reality he was a real kind guy to everyone it seemed but himself.

I shook the thoughts off and managed to get my things together both sense wise and energetically. This day was full of mixed emotions for me. I was almost robotic in trying to get to the two classes I had left. Last class flew by which was a blessing. I took a deep breath as I opened the door to the outside after the test. It was such a brisk hard frozen wind. The rush of air was bitter to the face and hands, which I completely forgot to cover before stepping outside.

I took three steps down towards the long walk to the parking lot across campus when I happened to see Bart walking slow with his head down, fighting the harsh wind that was beating up his face something fierce.

"Bart!" I yelled halfway across the yard.

I started the walk towards his direction. When we met up he kept his head down so as to avoid the frostbite he was currently struggling against.

"Did you hear anything yet?"

"Nope they said by seven this evening. Want me to of course call you ASAP when I hear from them?"

I smiled at him and stated the obvious.

"Well yes please." I thought I saw a smile emerge, but it just as quickly disappeared. I told him I would talk with him later and wished him a Merry Christmas.

I turned in the opposite direction and proceeded towards my car. I had a date with a bathtub and some bubbles and I was looking forward to it.

On the way home I stopped at the state store to buy something for the evening. I grabbed something light, and made my way back towards the cashier to finish checking out. I looked up long enough to see over the top of one of the shelves that there stood Robert. He was choosing something to quest his thirst as well I supposed. I wasn't sure how I felt about him seeing me there, so I cowardly ducked in the aisle looking down at an item I was pretending to read. I kept an eye on him, until he reached a decision of his choice, and made his way to complete his transaction. I was going to have a hard time breaking us off tonight, I honestly felt like I was in love with him. I allowed him to leave completely before I made my way up where the cashier stood, right in front of the window.

The bath ran, the drink poured and the bubbles were floating. I played with the water until it was perfect for me and my worries to relax within. As I placed my foot inside the steaming, oiled, and salted bath, I laid back and closed my eyes. I was imagining the scenarios playing out inside my mind with Robert.

How would he react to this? Does he even know what I am feeling? Should I tell him? I was lost in the agonizing contemplation over this that I didn't realize that the worry being that great had me doze off. It wasn't until the sound of the chime from a text coming through that I was brought back. It was from Bart. A simple one liner.
"We weren't chosen"

That was that. All that rush of emotion, from the start to finish ended with a one line text. 'We were not chosen.' I wasn't sure how I felt about that text, seeing as I was already saddened by the thought of Robert and I being over currently. A deep breath exhaled from my lungs. Not sure if it was relief, or disappointment, but it was what it was. So I responded back in kind.

"Well that sucks. It was great though, the whole ride. Thanks for the experience. Lol"

His response was perfect.

"Next film we kill it. Lol"

I smiled and poured myself another drink and continued with my mediation on closure. It seemed fitting that now would be perfect for the time to end everything in my life, starting with Robert. I watched as the water went down the drain reminding me again to just go with the flow. At this point I didn't need to do a reading; the bath was speaking volumes for me.

With the news of the play and the rejection of the movie, I was a bit in a trance as far as emotional feelings. I was pretty numb and I knew at this moment I was OK with it. There seemed to be a lot of endings for me in the cards currently and I had to be ok with it if I was going to move forward. I allowed my thoughts to wander as I was dressed myself for the last time my ultimate lover. This ending though was going to hurt.

I wore a deep violet v neck to accent his necklace. The chosen attire for the evening had a long skirt that flowed easily around my ankles. As always I reached in the drawer and chose his favorite lace panties. I slid them up my legs between the tights, which were now already wet with the anticipation of the evening, I wanted us to end on memorable note.

Sitting there I reminisced on some of the moments we had shared together. I remembered the feelings that shot through me when he would look my way in class. Reliving the experience after the office meeting the first time brought a tear to my eye. The rides on his bike, causing me to smile for the memories I would always have with him.

I finished dressing by adding a dash of his favorite perfume on my neck. Gathering the purse and phone I whisked out the door for an evening that would be forever marked on my soul. This evening had to be perfect, because I was saying good bye to my world and it tore me apart to think about it.

That evening played out absolutely perfect as it always did for us when we were together. He sensed that something was wrong, and after prying a bit more, didn't realize how much it really affected me seeing them together. He apologized, but I assured him, it was not his fault, it was completely mine.

He then stated they were having it rough for a while now. He also understood where I was at with it. He wished he could have changed my mind, and I had wished I would've had no problem letting him convince me if it otherwise.

He did inquire if I was seeing someone else. I lied and informed him that I was not. I just wanted to take some time for myself. Again he tried to pry, as if he could sense my deceit, but I held strong on that and switched the subject.

He then confessed that he felt bad not attempting to reach out to me more than what he had, but he was swamped with school and their conflict. I assured him it that I needed the space. Truth was, I really was not wanting to be the fall back girl anymore. So this was exactly why it needed to end.

We left the restaurant and stopped in the parking lot. He turned to kiss me. He cupped my chin in his palm and turned my head up to meet his. He kissed me so softly, which of course caused me to melt.

"One more for old times' sake?"

I nodded. He hopped on his bike to take the short ride back to his apartment I followed in the car behind, remembering the first time he and I shared our first moment together. When we reached the door of his apartment, he opened it, backing me to the couch. I started to speak but he dismissed me. I found myself completely disarmed by the look he had in his eyes at that moment.

He was filled with so much lust, and fire. I could feel him burning my bare skin with his hands. The door closed behind him. I took a deep breath and swallowed, allowing my body to adjust to the sensation he just sent surging through me. My legs already parted for him by the time I was hoisted over the couch.

The wine from dinner was swirling around in my head but right now, the only thing that mattered was his touch on my skin. My body relaxed the closer he came in to me. He wrapped his hands around my waist; I could hear the drizzle of the rain outside.

The living room filled with darkness except the street light showing the silhouettes of our embrace. The darkness welcoming the taboo of what we were doing. That turned me on and then we did what we always did, and it was like it always was….incredible. We took full advantage of the evening and at the very end, when we were exhausted emotionally, and physically, he rolled to where I was and this time whispered in my ear.

"I want you one last time…from behind this time."

"Robert…I'm not …" He didn't let me finish.

I wasn't going to argue. I wanted to leave there sore, for a week. I wanted to remember him and this moment for the rest of my life.

He took his hands and stood me up before turning me around. He bent me at my hips and needed no direction to know where to enter. He slid inside gently, and took such care when he grabbed my hair yanking it back to his so he could kiss me. I had to fight back a tear knowing this would be the last time.

I tried to force that thought to the side as he was growing thicker within me. I let out an animalistic moan from the intensity of his movement. My walls flooded with my own juice, as he rocked back and forth, his penis growing with every stroke.

He let his length slide in and out of my now engorged woman hood. The grinding sent my head back as I reached my hand down to squeeze my breasts, squelching with every one of his thrusts. He was ready to fill me up and I was ready for every last drop of him. I could feel nothing but his rigidness between my thighs.

I squeezed one last time before the orgasm had cascaded over me causing me to lose my bearing and drip uncontrollably over his couch. I trembled in delight. He followed while hugging me close to him as he finished off deep inside me. I tightened my muscles again; it was the natural thing to do.

My body was insistent on not letting go of that feeling. I had no idea what overtook me, but I wouldn't let him release from me. I started the movement back up, and then I rode him until my body reached its peak again, I had to close my eyes and shake once more from the feeling of pure delight. Robert of course, ready to receive me again. It was the most perfect ending to the most perfect man, in an almost perfect relationship.

The following morning, we woke and went for breakfast. The snow had covered the ground through the evening, so it had the appearance of shiny diamonds undisturbed on the white blanket used to cradle them. He and I talked for a long time that morning, and when it was all exhausted out of us, we gave one final kiss goodbye then went our separate ways.

I was a mess of tears pulling away from him that morning. I was beside myself as I saw him standing in the rear view mirror as I pulled away. I had a whole break to go, and no one now to spend it with. I just wanted to go home to curl up from the world for a month.

I made my way back to my bed and passed out. I slept hard through the day; I hardly heard the phone buzzing the next morning for my usual morning wakeup call. I shut the alarm off, and then went back to bed. I found myself moping around an empty house for the holidays. Kasey and Matt were off taking a winter vacation, so it looked like it would be me with the tree this year.

After a day or so I sent a text to Cameron to see what he was up to. Cameron was basically the only one hanging around for break, as his family lived ten minutes away from him. He didn't have to worry about traveling for the holidays. It was just a simple text that I sent, honestly expecting no response back.

"Hey want some company?" I pressed the send button.

"Well, that depends…" was the response back. Almost immediately, which took me by surprised.

"On…?"

"How bad is it if your company is high?"

"I don't care."

"Then by all means come on by."

Ride to hell

I grabbed another cup of coffee for my ride over to Cameron's house. He informed me the side door would be unlocked so I could just come up the stairs Once there, I crept trying not to wake his friends in the process. Knocking gently on the door he whispered.

"Who is it?"

"Skye, silly."

He unlocked the door. I entered and handed him a sandwich with a large orange juice from the restaurant I was just at. He showed his appreciation by kissing my cheek with an excitedly childish response.

"Ooh, Thank you." He immediately un-wrapped the sandwich making his way back to the couch to inhale it. I sat down beside him and watched him quietly eat. Nothing outside that sandwich mattered at the current moment for him, so who was I to distract him from it?

About three quarters into the egg and cheese bagel, he asked me if I had any sleep.

"No, why? Do I look that bad?"

"Yeah." He laughed in between bites

"You look like you had a rough night."

"Yeah it has been just an overall rough week."

"Well did you get the part?"

"Yes, I got the part!" I had realized that I had not texted him like he had asked me to.

"I am pretty exhausted, really."

"Want a pick me up?"

"Like what do you mean? This is like my fifth cup of coffee so I don't need any more. I'm pretty sure I am good."

""Not like that. Like this."

With that he leaned down to pull something out from under the couch. It was a piece of small tinfoil about five inches long and three inches wide. Along with it, was a tube, actually looked like a pen case without the pen inside.

"What the hell is this?"

"It's coffee but ten times better."

I tilted my head to the side, not really sure if I had wanted to try this from him or not.

"Have you already done it?" I asked. He laughed at that remark.

"Look at my eyes; I've been up all night too."

I thought about that statement for a minute. So both he and I were up all last night, and for very different reasons. This probably was not going to be the best decision I was going to make in my life, but one time I could justify it for. I had simply been too tired to actually debate the offer, so I reached over grabbed the pen and waited to inhale.

Once I inhaled, a massive tidal wave rush washed all over my body, from head to toe. It was like wings coming down from the heavens, swooping me up in their grasp and carrying me for a minute above the world and chaos. I leaned back closed my eyes, as it was almost too euphoric to even think about placing words for a description. I could hear some acoustics in the back ground. I was pretty sure he was trying to converse with me, yet all I heard was just a muffled question that echoed in the back ground as though I was far inside a cave.

"Hey…" He snapped be back from it

"You OK?" He tugged at my arm.

"Yeah…Shhh let me enjoy that for a minute. Please."

I kept my eyes closed while he laughed and took a hit following behind mine. It lasted about a minute or so, and then when I was sure there was no more wings to be flown, I opened my eyes and saw him sitting there gazing at me in awe.

"What?" I said looking back at him

"Nothing, I miss the innocent days, where feeling that kind of euphoria was done with just a hit. That was awesome to watch. Sure wish I was that way."

"This is making me feel weird…like wow. I feel awake. I mean really awake."

He smiled at me.

"Yup, have any plans today?"

"No, not at all. Actually school is out and everyone has left for the holiday."

"Great, then you can hang out with me and we can watch TV or something."

"OK sounds like a plan to me."

Twelve hours went by but for us like it was three minutes. We occasionally would return back to the couch to feel underneath for the 'cup of coffee.' At some point he once again became hungry. It was completely opposite for me though. I could barely even consider anything going in my stomach on this new found coffee substitute. He ordered a pizza with some beer. The delivery service was running about thirty minutes behind normal run time. Which meant it was about thirty seconds in the world I currently existed within.

He devoured the pizza but it was a close tie on which ended first, the beer or the pizza. He insisted I eat a piece, stating I would actually feel better once I had eaten something. I forced myself to slowly take the bites; I was full after that one slice, so I stopped there. He popped open a beer and handed one to me, I took a swig of it and placed it on the floor. He then reached underneath again for the foil, and we once again, lit up.

This was the craziest feeling I felt in a long time. It made me feel like I had the ability to save the world of all its problems and still be back in time for dinner to happen at the grand gothic palace, I currently sat in.

Cameron and I spent the rest of that day, and every day thereafter for the duration of break, together. We stayed in his room mostly. Sometimes we ventured out to the store down the street or to go grab a bite to eat. I learned that even if I had no desire to digest any substance, on this, it was a requirement, especially if one happened to find themselves in the boat we currently were in…not having slept for four days. I could hardly believe it had been that long since we actually had any sleep. My mind after day three seemed to be playing a bit of a trick or two on me. I thought I was starting to see some shadows, but he reassured me it was just a result of no sleep.

I got to know Cameron, on a really deep level. When one doesn't sleep and all they do is converse with one person for ninety six hours straight, they get to know the person sitting beside them doing nothing but the same thing. He spoke of his dreams, and his business. He spoke of the things that actually scared him as an individual. Why he does the things he does and why he does his drugs.

He spoke of his obsessions, his mental torments and his ultimate enemy that had a hold over him which was drinking. Something he was convinced he would never be able to overcome. To see someone struggle with such inner demons on a level that he was struggling with, was hard to understand.

Watching someone sit in front of you admitting defeat from it all, took its toll on him. He drank a lot to numb his thoughts. His anger was being repressed from the drugs he chose to do. His past revealed times where the emotional scar was a deep one on his soul. Still he was a strong individual on the outside.

Cameron spent every day with me and I returned the favor, spending it right back with him. Mostly, we discussed conversations about life, dreams, fears, and normal every day mundane things.

He confided in me that he dreamed as well. Like I did, but his are of evil and horrible thoughts. He scowled at the images flashing across his eyes as he spoke of them. The parasitic ones that made him completely paralyzed at night, unable to move at all. His drinking allowed him not to have to see them at night.

Here I had dreams completely opposite. His always shadowed the evil things and he would rather not see it. It was enlightening to say the least. It was mortifying to hear of all the evil that could exist in one's head, or maybe in reality. Whichever it was, it was very real for Cameron.

The break finally came to exhaustive end. I finally said goodbye to Cameron a day before the quarter was to start back. He had asked if I wanted to get together again and I eagerly said yes. We would try in between schedules to see each other. We agreed to text and figure it out though later as I had to get back for school.

Decisions

The experience with Cameron was intense to say the least. Hanging out on that level took me by surprise. It was a thrilling crazy time and good break from reality, civilization and every other responsibility I didn't want to have to mess with.

The coffee shop was a great break too. With all the kids that left home on break, they decided to close until school came back. So I can honestly say I had a vacation even if it was spent holed up with some grunge hippy doing illicit drugs.

After the break though, I hardly had time to see Cameron. Robert, now nothing more than a distant memory; I was swamped in film classes, work and rehearsals for Les Mis. Rehearsals at First were certain characters at certain times, then eventually a couple months into it we started coming together to share the downstairs theatre with others for the production rehearsals.

The production had to be executed without any issues and performed on a Broadway level for Mr. Harrington's approval. We would be rehearsing for months before we even were able to make it up to the Main stage for final rehearsals. I was swept up in the production of a lifetime. The show was on a tight schedule for rehearsing on main stage because there was already another play being performed in the beginning of the spring quarter. So sharing the stage was going to be somewhat tedious at times with the other production. We managed to work it all out and rather well.

We all breezed through the spring quarter. I was never so elated to see I managed to carry my GPA at a three point eight on a steady. The play was moving right along and I was starting to feel a bit overwhelmed from everything. I had lost weight, I assumed from the stress of the production and with work hours being long and grueling.

Rehearsals were really ramping up and I was starting to cave with exhaustion from it. Well into the routine, towards the end of one of the rehearsals, a very nauseating affect took hold of me. It forced me to stop in mid song and take a moment to regroup. I was so light headed; I ended up backstage with an ice pack on the back of my neck. One of the stage hands was trying to get me to sip some water, but my stomach just couldn't handle it.

"Stop I'm OK on that. I just had a spell of something temporarily, that's all."

They nodded and whisked off. Mr. Harrington came back to see if I was alright and asked if I could continue. I assured him I could, I guaranteed him I would. There wouldn't be any reason I would not be able to perform this role.

That evening at home, I continued getting sick.

"Maybe you're pregnant." Kasey blurted out.

There was complete silence for a minute that seemed like an eternity. I shot her an angry glare when we met eyes on that remark. That rush of horror consumed me.

"I'm on the pill though." Reassuring myself but unconvincing of it.

"That doesn't mean anything. Did Robert use protection last time?"

I smiled because I was wondering which time of that last time she was referring to? He had not used protection.

"He only ever used it once." Panic came rushing in then.

"Kasey stop, your making me worried."

""Well when's the last time you had your monthly?"

I had to stop on that one. I had been so busy I hadn't even paid attention to it. I naturally assumed it was stress, seeing as I was on the pill so that would have been perfectly rational.

"Kasey…" I believed it finally hit me; I dropped to the nearest chair available. Now I was spinning.

"Hey, don't worry, let's just find out first. I'll stop by the store and you just focus on your work for now. Smoke a bowl if you have to."

"Fuck, not again."

What would I do? I certainly couldn't go through what I went through the last time this happened. I was almost done with school, and so were Kasey and Matt. They were finishing up and getting married after that. They didn't know if they would stay in the area though, so I had that lingering over my head for the start of winter worries. But for now it was not what my energies were concentrating on.

We were stuck at the theater every day until sometimes midnight with all the tech rehearsals. Things were so busy at the time; I completely dismissed Kasey getting the test for me the following day. I walked in my room and saw the test on the bed with a note. I snatched the note as I rolled my eyes.

"Don't you want to know?" was all the scribbled note said.

I exhaled throwing my back pack on the floor, and the test on my night stand. I would worry about it in the morning. Exhaustion took its toll that night; I passed out dreaming of babies. I had to remember to thank Kasey for that one.

The morning sun radiated its morning heat on my naked body. Making me toss and turn then forced to sit up drenched with sweat from its morning hello. Rubbing my eyes I gathered my thoughts for the day. My hair was matted from the previous evenings make up call, and I was sure my face had the remnants of it as well. Shower was a must currently so I could get ready for the day. I crawled out of bed and was reminded of the pregnancy test that now made its way to the floor through the evening. I stepped on the box and cursed.

"Dammit. OK Fine!" I took the box and my freshly washed clothes and headed for the shower.

About an hour later, after the shower was taken there was a knock on the door. I hadn't realized I was still there sitting on the floor forgetting that Kasey or Matt may have to use the facility.

"Hello?" I called out.

It was Kasey, peeping her head through as usual. She said not a word, she didn't have to. I held the test in my hand and looked up at her.

"Seriously?" She gawked at it while she slithered in like she was a teenager sneaking out for the evening.

"Yeah, seriously. Kasey I was on the damn pill."

"Your family is just freaking fertile myrtle." She nervously laughed trying to break the tension.

"You think? What the fuck Kasey?"

'What are you going to do?"

"It's not an option. I have to keep the baby. I can't go through that again. I just can't."

"Understood." She replied. There was a long moment of silence as she sat on the toilet above me. Then the dreaded question that followed hit me in the gut.

"Are you going to tell him?" She was biting her lip with anticipation.

I was silent. I didn't know. I had not a clue

"Do you think its Roberts?"

"Yeah, I know the baby's Roberts."

"Hey…" She tightened her grip on my hands.

"Are you going to be OK with this?" She was honestly concerned.

"I will have to be, because there is no other option…I simply cannot go through what I did before. I will figure it all out later. Thank you" I kissed her cheek and stood up to leave.

"Hey, we will help in any way we can, you know this."

I smiled at her, because I knew that was true.

I made the doctor's appointment for the following week. I made a decision and it was going to have to be made a priority now. It was rather difficult to fit the appointments in between rehearsals and everything else. In my head I tried not to think about it, so keeping busy was key. It helped to have the prenatal pill though. My body was feeling much better after that started. Who knew a baby could suck that much life and energy out of someone?

By the time summer break came I was beginning to feel the toll of it all. I decided I would take time off from the coffee shop during the summer because I was more tired than not, and more often than not. I simply had no time to dedicate to Larry and his needs to supply endless caffeine for the kids. He was saddened to see me take the leave of absence but yet happy for me. Thankfully he understood.

I had to slow it down even more so during the summer I limited things to just the play. My once tiny bump was becoming more and more prevalent. I desperately tried to hide it underneath some oversized clothes. Thankfully I was small framed so nothing really showed

When fall quarter came along, I was well over the morning sickness and the baby was doing fine according to the doctor. Still no one outside Kasey and Matt knew what was going on with me. I finally had to approach Mr. Harrington though to advise him of the current situation as we had final dress fittings and he needed to know they were going to have to make some adjustments with me. I had a bump that was making itself known to the world. It needed to be addressed as soon as possible. It was no longer able to be hidden without some effort. I was surprised to see how supportive he was, and then he let me in on a secret.

"It's all good Skye, I already knew." He smiled softly at me.

"How did you know?" I was humiliated.

"My wife has had three my dear. A man can tell from the look a pregnant lady has to her. They simply for some reason radiate and glow with a beauty all their own."

"Oh…well is my bump that noticeable?" I was scared of the answer.

"No not at all…it's simply just the look, that's all. No worries, we have you all taken care of." I was forever thankful to him for that.

That evening, the last tech night before premiere, it seemed to just fly by. It was about eleven thirty at night when we were wrapping up. I made my way out to the car with some other cast members. Bart hollered at me from across the way. "Skye…did you want to join us at the bar for drinks? The cast is going to head down for some pre-premiere drinks."

"Pre-premiere?" I laughed distracted in my thoughts.

"Yeah come on, it'll be fun. I promise. You seem down for someone who is killing their character in the show. Let's just go for one."

He gave me his puppy eyed look, the one that stated he needed a backup as a tag along. He had plans to pick this girl Lisa in the makeup department up, so he needed his tag team partner to help him go to bat.

"You really need me?" I said lowering my tone so she wouldn't hear. Lisa was in her car driving past us, when she rolled down the window and in her flighty voice that matched her flighty blond hair she said;

"Bart, I will see you there then."

She giggled while she flashed him a shot of her must have been double D's. I glanced over to him who looked like a salivating dog in heat.

"I'm there lady."

He gave her thumbs up. I couldn't help but roll my eyes. She drove off and I crossed over to look him in the eyes.

"Dude, you're so going to have to place your hand over her mouth if you fuck her. That voice alone would make anyone shriek in pain. It's grueling on the ears. Are you sure you need me? She looks like she is totally into you anyways, you don't need my help."

I had just really wanted to go home and think about the little one growing inside me.

"Yeah I totally need you." He ran to his car and yelled as he pulled out like he was in the Indy 500.

"See you there!"

I sighed and thought well I could always drink water. There would be no more beers or drinks for me for a while. But I went for Bart. I arrived at the already packed out bar. There was hardly any room for one to make their way across the floor. I finally weaseled my way where the bartender was pouring two other drinks. He didn't even bother to look up at me before he asked

"Whatcha having lovely lady?"

"Uh-water please."

"That's it? Just water?"

"Yeah, thanks."

I grabbed the stool next to me as the overly ripe bottomed lady who wore cheap red lipstick slid off. She melted her way into the crowd as if to leave. She looked out of place anyways. She may have been in her mid-thirties, but the rest of the bar was packed in freshly painted twenty year olds. I slowly looked around the room to see if I could notice where the cast was and saw no one from school. What the hell I thought. He did say 'Shenanigans' I thought. So I sent a text and waited.

"Hey."

I jolted turning around to the familiar voice that was suddenly behind me. It was Cameron, holding a beer.

"Is this seat taken?" I shrugged my shoulders. He sat down and offered me his beer.

"No I'm good."

"Is that water?" He asked pointing to my drink.

"Yes." I didn't really want to talk for some reason, but he pressed on.

"Why?

"Why what Cameron?"

"Why are you drinking a glass of water in a bar?"

OK that was a fair question.

"I was waiting on my cast from the play to show up but…" I was cut off from the buzzing of my phone. It was Bart.

"Wrong bar dork."

That's all he wrote. Not even what the name of the correct bar was. I rolled my eyes in disgust. Obviously I spaced that part of the conversation. It buzzed again.

"And I don't need you there after all, turns out; she invited me to her place already, so were cool. And THANKS."

I roiled my eyes again. Cameron caught the look of disgust and asked about it. I let him know I was at the wrong bar.

"What's wrong with you?"

"What are you talking about?" I quickly retorted back at him.

"Why are you so distant?"

"Ugh, you don't want to know."

"Try me."

"No."

"I won't take no for an answer."

"Cameron, I don't want to talk about it."

"Yeah but it looks like you need to… so what's going on girly girl?"

I saw his eyes glaring at me with purpose and intent. It wasn't one of lust like before. Could this be a look of true concern from him?

"Why do you want to know so bad Cam?" I just wanted to vent but I didn't think he should be the one to throw it all at.

"Contrary to what you may or may not think, I'm actually a really good guy. I do well with listening to people and their problems. Try me, I bet you'll be surprised."

He smiled at me. I couldn't help but look at his most perfect teeth, remembering when they collided with mine in our search for pleasure. I snapped back out of it and pondered for a moment.

"Okay, you want to know?"

"I'm still sitting here aren't I?"

"OK fine…..here it is."

For the next two hours I poured out my entire soul to him. I held nothing back. But as much as I hated to tell him, the relief of just sharing my twist of fate with someone was exhilarating. Cameron was an extremely great listener. He said not a word the whole time I spoke. I had tears flowing nonstop. Reaching over the bar, he grabbed some napkins for me. I had no idea how utterly releasing that conversation would be. When I was completely out of anymore words, he took my hand and led me out of the bar.

"Come on. You don't need to be here, let's go back to my place and hang out and fall asleep. You look exhausted."

I wasn't sure what to make of that statement. Was he trying to take advantage of me being as weak as I was? Or did he honestly mean what he just said. I shot a confused look up at him. He shook his head and pulled me before I could respond. We climbed in his van and left.

I fell asleep in his arms that night. I woke up with his morning sun shining back on me, like the first night we slept together. Only this time there were no free roaming snakes wandering on the floor. I rubbed my eyes and moved his arm that was around my waist. He rolled over and then called to me softly as I sat up from the mattress.

"Hey."

"Hey, I didn't mean to wake you."

"No it's all good. You sleep OK?" He asked with concern.

"I slept amazing, thank you." That wasn't a lie either. I hadn't slept that well for the longest time. Lying next to someone really helped me relaxed to wake up feeling almost new.

"Want to grab a bite to eat before you go to the show?"

"Oh Cameron, that would be great."

"Perfect, let me jump in the shower and then we'll go."

While Cameron showered, I prepared myself for the show mentally by rehearsing my lines in the room. I had to look away when he appeared back in the room, I was becoming flushed. His body just glistened with wet drops in the sun's rays that he ignored from the shower. Cameron had no problem dropping his towel to get dressed in front of me. I guess it makes sense seeing as we had been together before. Guess he felt there was nothing to hide.

I had to look away though. I caught a glimpse of him and could not help the few drops that escaped from my inner walls. I bit my tongue, because having sex with him was the last thing I wanted on my mind for the show. He threw on some jeans he had laying on the couch that were freshly laundered. I smiled because I remembered that he never wore underwear. The first night I found that out.

He brushed his fingers through his soaking dirty blond hair. Then he sat to put those forever boots on. He grabbed his jacket and my back pack and then kissed my forehead.

"Let's eat." We headed for food.

Cameron drove me back to my car and we decided to just walk down to the restaurant down the street to grab some food before we parted for the day, but on the way to the restaurant Cameron had a chilling conversation with me.

"I was thinking…" He said with one hand in the back pocket and the other combing through his thick luscious hair.

"Yeah…" I mumbled back focusing on the broken sidewalk cracks I wanted to avoid for some silly reason.

"Skye, you said you were going to keep the baby. Well I can help you with the baby, you know. I would like to try and be around to help raise him…or her, if that's cool with you."

I had to let that comment sink in for a moment. So there was a moment of silence, then I had to stop and take a good look at him. He continued a step or two until he realized I had trailed behind in my tracks from his offer. He stopped and waited for me to catch up before continuing.

"I really mean this. I thought about it long and hard. Look I really like you a lot. I know I have a bad rap around town, but it just seemed like you and I connected on a deeper level, and I would hate for that to end for whatever reason."

We started the stroll again.

"Cam, do you know what you're saying here? I mean I'm sorry, of course you do. But that is like some serious commitment."

"Yeah I know, but I could really help you. I thought about it, and I would be willing to step up for the baby and be its like…you know role model for a father. You know so the baby doesn't feel like it doesn't have one or like a male figure or something."

I could see he really put some serious thought behind this idea. I could also tell that he was extremely nervous in offering it, maybe for the fear of rejection. I had no response for him. I was shocked, quite frankly.

"Why? Why would you want to do that? You want to suddenly dedicate yourself to a child you have nothing to do with just because we connect mentally? That makes no sense, because for you to help me raise the baby means you would have to be around for a longer than a night or two. Do you know what I mean?"

"Listen Skye, I know you don't want to tell Robert, I don't blame you, I get it. I disagree with you though; I wish you would tell him. I mean if some chic did that to me I would be upset but the choice is yours. But if you make that choice your going to need help because babies are not easy. You see the house I'm in with all the kids…"

He laughed at that thought then finished his speech.

"…the baby would fit right in with the others at the home. I'm just saying this as a possible solution for you and me, I like you. I actually like you a lot more than I'm comfortable with, but that's beside the point. I am here as a friend, first and foremost. But also because you're pretty cool."

I was speechless. I had no idea what to say, but thankfully we reached the restaurant, and food at this point was the only thing now we wanted to talk about. I thanked him profusely for his offer and told him I would definitely consider it.

I took his offer to mean, I would move in with the hippies so I could their help with the babies. I had a decision to ponder on. Kasey and Matt were going to be graduating anyways and I was unsure of where things would be with them, so it was rather nice to have this olive tree being handed to me.

At the end of breakfast we kissed on the lips and then walked back to the cars. I told him I would text him later and we would catch up after the show. He was excited to see it, although I had no idea he had purchased a ticket for the play. He had told me he had to act fast because all the shows had been sold out.

My mouth went to the floor. I had not heard that at all. "Sold out for real?" I was ecstatic.

I wondered if there may even be some talent scouts in the audience. That was my dream anyways.

"Well yeah Skye, It's Les Mis. What other college has the money to pay for the rights to produce it at a local college?"

He was right. I hadn't thought of that. Now the pressure was starting to build for me and the butterflies fluttered in suddenly causing me to want to lose what I had just digested.

"Shit Cameron. Holy shit. I am so freaking nervous."

"Hey stop that you are going to kill it tonight."

He tried to shoot a boost of confidence through me but it was too late....all nerves were on deck.

On my own

I arrived at the Creative arts center two hours prior to show time. Nerves, butterflies, and worry all in tow behind me. I kept trying to focus on Walters' words that played like a repetitive tape recorder in the back of my head.

'Nerves! Embrace them! They are the thrill of the profession.'

Bullshit popped up every time though right after, so I stopped thinking about it.

The center was buzzing with energy like I had not felt before. There were stage techs scrambling to address the last of the issues with the set. The caterers were buzzing around, getting the tables ready to receive the sold out crowd. The cast members all jammed in the back, singing and warming up their throats for the notes to be sung later that evening. Costumes were being tucked and pinned with last minutes measurements.

I made my way down the stairs to start with the costume crew. My first costume was one of a peasant. If we weren't singing on stage, we were usually filling in extras needed for somewhere else on stage. So I had multiple characters to play. Eponine was the only speaking role though. With how the makeup crew made everyone up, the audience would barely be able to tell we were all multiple characters for the evening. I was being dressed, pinned, wrapped, powdered, and prodded in every which way they learned to master in class.

Up until this moment, the downstairs always seemed so big. But tonight, it was almost packed to its capacity. I could hear as time crept closer the people starting to arrive upstairs. Time was sneaking upon us. The director called down stairs and ordered a huddle for the cast and crew. We all came pouring out of rooms and stood around in a circle.

He gave us the pep speech, and said his Thankyou's to everyone respectively. In turn after he was finished with his speech, we presented him with a token of our appreciation. Not only was this to be his biggest production here, but it was also to be his last. He was offered a job directing with a troupe for off Broadway productions and he was delighted to take the offer. So this performance would be bitter sweet for him. We were all going to make sure he went out on the front page.

I snuck away from the group long enough to go upstairs to take a look out at the sold out audience. I climbed through the dark wings of the theater. They were pitch black, and hardly visible to anyone. There would be small night lights placed strategically on the floor for the set crew. No one was to be up in the wings at any time unless you were on stage. I peeked out; I could see people filling in their seats. I saw the ushers helping those that were confused, and the extra hands going around making sure everyone had a program.

I didn't really recognize anyone, because there were so many. I started backing up, and then caught a view where the orchestra was gathering their music sheets. There in the third row, almost directly in front of my mark for Eponine's solo. It was Robert.

I glanced to see who might be next to him, bracing myself for the impact. I was relieved it wasn't her. I had to force my breath. OK well at least he wasn't with her. But shit this was not going to be an easy performance. I had to make sure I wouldn't lose it. Damn me for being so nosey.

How was I supposed to be non-emotional when that was all I've been for the past month? I am carrying this man's baby and he has no idea. How am I ever going to make through tonight? Well like everything else currently, I have no other choice but to figure it out.

I tensed up with fear. How ironic was this whole dam thing? The crazy thoughts with the nerves caught the better of me. I fell back from being light headed; thankfully Bart was right behind me.

"Hey…" He whispered catching me

"What are you doing here? You can't be up here yet."

I was startled, but nodded back. He helped me to a lighted area just off the wings. By now everyone was now starting to make their way up.

" Are you going to be OK?"

"Think so." I lied straight through my teeth.

We could hear the music start. My heart fluttered. This was it. I wanted to run and cry, but Bart grabbed my hand and whisked me with the rest of the crew now piling in the wings.

The audience applauded as the lights dimmed. The start of music from the orchestra started slowly at a rhythmic pace. The building anticipation of the skillfully crafted crescendo from the instruments started to lift the theatres energy. The actors entered the stage to their rightful places, starting to sing their well-rehearsed lines.

'Look down, look down don't look 'em in the eye
Look down, look down you're here until you die'
The first convict sang his notes right on cue.
'The sun is strong…. It's hot as hell below.'

"Look down…Look down…" The words encapsulated me. I peeked at Robert who watched intently, as the actors on stage performed a brilliantly directed prologue.

The costumes were dazzling, and the voices even more radiant. Mr. Harington chose French revolution costumes that were brilliant in all their colors.

His character assessment of Jean Val jeans' appearance was rough in every manner. The makeup crew triumphantly etched two loveless decades onto his face, his pale worn skin exposed his sense of vulnerability. His wardrobe was created to retain his nature of being humble. It had earthy tones, trying to reflect his modesty. His distressed vest, with the number 24601 printed on the breast.

They effortlessly displayed his supporting and unfailing honesty. His look was soft but worn. It was going to be interesting to see this character develop tonight on stage. The actor had come a long way in trying to portray the goodness that will eventually turn him, from hating a world that, in his eyes, had always hated him.

"Look down your standing in your grave…"

The lyrics flowed and My heart now focusing on my story unfolding as my own character started to emerge from within me.

I was dressed as a vagrant for the first half. So I was wearing dark brown pants with patches and holes. I had the peasant shawl to go with it. The costume department was very detailed all the way down to the peasants not having any pockets, because in that time apparently only the wealthy had them.

I listened to Jean Val jean belt out his words, and then I entered in the shadow on my mark for the finale of the first song. Robert hadn't seen me yet. The music blaring and the characters in full march, the light came up on me to where I was standing singing in unison with the cast on stage. I tried like mad to not look anywhere in the direction of his seat. We had finished the intro, and then we all scrambled off stage.

I went back to my place downstairs quickly and out of the way of others. I could hear the music just as loud and clear down stairs. I was in Paris…at least I felt I was. There was so much energy from the buzz of all the actors roaming all around down there. Everyone dressed in their character, speaking in their accents while the show above us played out. I knew this was probably going to be the best it will ever get for me.

With the baby now I was going to be limited, I understood this, and so for tonight, I would give the best performance I could in my short lived career in theater. I was being called again to the stage. I hopped up in my sandals and rushed to help with 'Master of the house.' I was playing a prostitute extra....well that character felt fitting.

My solo didn't happen until the second act, and seeing as we were all being used as extras in the play, we hardly sat. It was physically exhausting to say the least. But I was more than fine with it.

I wondered If Kasey and Matt ended up making it tonight. I flashed to Cameron and remembered he was in the audience as well. I had yet to notice him. But I wasn't able to really see with the lights down. I could feel Robert's energy and that was enough for me for an evening.

The first half went off without a hitch. Some last minute scrambles here and there but overall, almost perfect. During Intermission, The cast was to stay downstairs the entire time. They had to change some of the set upstairs, and with the packed house above, there were to be no actors mingling with the audience until after the show.

I sat down below drinking my water, in the make-up chair. They were getting me ready for my big moment on stage. I was on cloud nine with the jitters. I sat in the seat, thinking of Robert who was upstairs probably hoping I would sneak off into the bathroom. Ha! I had to laugh at that. But then realized that's what got me where I was now. Never mind on that thought.

The stage hand came down to tell me some last minute adjustment they were going to have to do. He seemed panicked in his voice when he told me the mark had to be changed, and hopefully I *wouldn't* miss it. The light somehow decided to break and now, it was stuck in a position that wouldn't have been on me for my solo. Well shit. Not like any added pressure was needed.

"Okay, Okay…I got it, no worries. " I had to reassure him. His final grade was riding on this play.

They called fifteen from above. My heart leapt into my throat. It was time. I rushed quietly to sneak upstairs to get in position.

My heart racing as the lights started to dim. The crew was silently sneaking around me. Make up girl still trying to do last minute touches. The lights went black. The music started, and the cast piled on stage. The audience now back in for the second and final act. The music started, then the applause. The brilliantly executed sound of the woodwind and brass section, surrounded my soul, and I could feel Eponine and her spirit rush inside me. I closed my eyes, I had to catch my breath, because at that moment I could feel myself transforming into the harrowing lost woman, whose fate was sealed before it started. I was recognizing the own horrifying agony of my own fate being sealed, with the little one I now carried within.

There it was. I could hear the low-pitched bassoon leading me out into the light. The soft stroke of the oboe slowly built the anticipation for my moment. There I stood on stage in the shadow, directly on the first mark wearing a well-worn brown skirt, a distressed off colored white peasant top. I wore a tattered brown jacket that fell to the knees, complete with a page boy cap that covered my long chestnut colored hair. My hair that looked just as tattered as the jacket. The make-up artists painted soot on my cheeks adding to the careful detail of my character and her turmoil. No one would be able to see the bump that was now making its presence known.

I walk down the streets of Paris to deliver my letter. I stopped on my mark. I open my mouth and let the words fall perfectly in tune with the music.

"And now I'm all alone again, nowhere to turn no one to go to."
The words were flawless as they escaped my lips.
'Without a home, without a friend, without a face to say hello
to...'
The words stung with the reality behind them. I continued on.
'But now the night is near, and I can make believe....he is
here."
I locked eyes with him as I started the song. He was so radiant
sitting in his seat just fixated on me.
'On my own...pretending he's beside me...all alone..."

I don't remember the rest of the performance because at that
moment, nothing else existed in this world. It wasn't until I saw
a tear in his eye that I seemed to snap back into the
performance. I remember barely whispering the first 'I love
you' from the end of the song. Then once more only directly at
him

"I love you...but only on my own."

I held the last note for what seemed like an eternity. I took a
breath finally, and the whole theater rose with vigorous
applause. I had no time to relish in it; I had to get ready for the
next scene. On the way out of the wings, getting ready for the
next number, I was patted on the back and heard wonderful
praises. But none of that actually mattered to me. I guess my
own performance was just as bitter sweet that evening.

The play continued, and finally after what seemed like a
decade, we reached the finale. The cast rushed around backstage
trying to get in place for the final song of the evening. We were
all exhausted, but we were ready for the final song. Mr.
Herrington's final curtain calls here at the university.

The chorus which was comprised of the character spirits of
Enjolras, Gavroche and all of the revolutionaries' were heard
singing in perfect pitch and tune with the others. We all made

our way to file out on the stage. In unison together we all chanted together.

"Do you Hear the people sing lost in the valley of the night?
It is the music of a people who are climbing to the light."

We finished then once more rushed off stage to make our way in line for curtain call. The orchestra had come up with the curtain music for all the characters as we took our places on the stage for our personal bows, and applauses.

I followed after Marius and Cosette. I was by myself when I came from the wings down the front of the stage. I took my place to the left of Cosette. The audience were already on their feet praising the performers with their thunderous claps and loud vigorous whistles. I shot a look to where Robert sat, and saw him professionally following suite of his colleague in the praise. He had a smile that was just for me. My moment had just come and gone.

We ended up receiving three curtain calls. The director appeared on stage the second time after we called him up to help take the credit. When we were released from curtain call, the actors either scrambled to change and leave, or stay in their characters, so they could socialize with the people in the audience.

Mr. Harrington asked that if we were going to socialize with the audience afterward, he would have preferred for us to stay in costume. Most had no problem doing so, as they rather enjoyed it. One didn't need to ask theater people to stay in character for anything. They love those opportunities.

I, however, chose not to socialize. I couldn't bear to take the chance running into Robert after that. I was devastated on a personal level, wrecked on an emotional level, and hormonally challenged from something I chose to accept and keep.

There was no way I could face him right now, so I quietly went back down stairs. Snatching some toiletries I headed for the shower, so I could wash up here instead of the house. My thought process was that by the time I was done, most people would have left the theater by then,

I finished but not without scrubbing my face raw from all the makeup they piled on for authenticity. I grabbed my change of clothes, which was nothing more than a pair of jogging pants and a great big sweat shirt. I was months along and the growth in the belly was too much for me to want to deal with, so I opted for the overly baggy look so as to look inconspicuous.

I said good night to some of the crew that was still cleaning, prepping for the next day's show. On the way up the stairs I was stopped by Mr. Harrington who graciously praised me for what he said was the performance of the lifetime for me. I smiled, wishing I could have remembered it. I hugged him and politely told him my thank you and that I would see him tomorrow first thing.

"You're not going to the cast party?"

"No."

I had actually changed my mind from earlier in the evening. I was all set to go until I saw Robert, and then things kind of went south in my eagerness to hang out with the crew that I just spent over twelve weeks with, day and night.

"I'm exhausted really. I think I have been fighting a cold to be honest with you."

"Oh well then, by all means please go home and get some rest."

"Thanks and I will see you tomorrow."

I snuck out the side door to avoid any more conversations. Two steps and I heard that gorgeous raspy voice say my name.

"Skye."

I took a deep breath and closed my eyes. I was so wishing he had left, but yet here he stood right in front of me in his entire splendor.

"You were breathtaking tonight."

I wanted to let him know he was just as much so, in his perfectly defining outfit he chose tonight.

"Did you know I was in the play?" I asked out of curiosity.

"No. I actually didn't know until I read the program. I must say, you blew me away."

"Thanks. How are you?"

"Fine, I suppose. Jess and I have decided to break up finally but that's whatever. How are you?"

"I'm doing well." Again I straight lied through my teeth. I was hoping he couldn't tell.

In the background I could hear the song 'Master of the house' being played over the speakers. He stepped closer to look at me; I looked down to avoid his piercing gaze. He took his hand and cupped my chin raising it to meet his eyes.

"You look so exquisite right now, Radiating. Not sure if it's you blushing or just straight exhaustion, but you look splendid this evening."

I nervously smiled hoping he wouldn't brush up against me fearing he would feel the protruding bump underneath the shirt.

"I'm tired that's all. I'm going to try and catch some sleep." Was all I could muster to say.

"I'll send you a text OK? Maybe we can get together for some coffee."

"Sounds good." I lied.

He kissed me so tenderly on my lips. I couldn't help but return the love, because I knew I wasn't going to be able to return his text.

Changes

For the duration of the production, every note I sang from the song was a constant reminder of where my life seemed destined to be. It wasn't long after that the quarter finally ended. I was never so relieved to see school finally over with after that. I must have slept for a week straight.

I made the decision not to enroll in the winter quarter for the last year, because of the baby. Cameron was a huge help surprisingly. It seemed we were spending more time together as a couple, than just as friends getting ready to raise a child.

Kasey and Matt decided to move closer to his family out west. So the day after graduation, they packed up and started their trip and their life. Kasey wanted to make sure I was going to be fine before she would commit to leaving with him at first. I assured her, I would be. Matt dragged her to the car to escape before she changed her mind as they were leaving. I must say she made the transition for me rather an easy one. I was going to miss her something awful, but she assured me she was only going to be a text away. I sought some comfort in that.

Cameron and I decided to take over her lease. He would still have his own room and I would have mine. But we would share the home responsibilities and kind of share the baby. When I asked again if this chaos was what he really wanted to jump into, His response back was almost too candid and alarming.

"I'm not doing anything else better at the current moment, so why not have a kid?"

He laughed like it was a commodity. I had to explain to him that this was not like breeding exotic animals for resale. He needed to understand that babies weren't reptiles; they don't go in cages, or under heat lamps. I had to reiterate how they needed fed more than once a week, and I made him promise he wouldn't flip the baby for resale like he did every other living object so easily.

Cameron agreed that he would keep all the drugs from his other business outside the home. He was rather content with this arrangement, and had no problems adjusting to the new lifestyle. Subconsciously, I believed the baby was like a new beginning for him as well. Whatever the case, pieces seemed to finally be falling in place for once.

The baby inside was growing bigger every day. I was contemplating the agonizing stories I would read about labor. Cameron tried reassuring me, telling me I was being a typical theater person and being over dramatic about it. I replied; maybe he ought to let us know how over dramatic we are after he experienced it. He laughed and stated he wouldn't be caught dead.

We painted the nursery, opting for the greens and yellows as I wasn't sure what I was having. The baby squirmed all the time now, and my stomach moved in sync when the little bugger would roll over or turn. The pregnancy itself was rather a simple one so far. This baby always seemed to have hiccups with me. I was told of this old wives tale about having heartburn when you got pregnant. It meant the baby was supposed to have a head full of hair But time would tell though.

It was getting close to the due date, and I was packing my bag contemplating the final names I had chosen if the baby was a boy or girl. My phone buzzed and instinctively I picked it up to read, expecting it to be Cameron. It was Robert instead.

I caught my breath back. I felt the surge of emotion through my veins. My heart raced. It had been almost two months since I had seen him. I was way bigger now. I read the text.
'Hey stranger.'

I hesitated on texting him back. But I couldn't just ignore him. I wanted to know how he was doing. My heart skipped its beat hoping he wasn't wanting to see me, especially now.

"Hey you, how are you?" I sent back

"What are you doing?"

I had to think and fast. What could I say that would be believable? I searched my head for ideas, and then the perfect one hit me, so I typed in my response.

"I'm out of town for a month. Visiting some friends in Colorado"

"When do you get back?"

The question was quite direct. I had to look at a calendar on the phone to calculate when I was not going to be carrying around a baby.

"Mid December." I had managed to push it off as far as I could. The baby was due any day now, so I would not be able to see him anytime soon after the delivery.

"Will you let me know when you get back please?"

"Of course…but why?" I had to know.

"I have something I want to give you."

I loved surprises and he knew that.

"OOH what is it?"

"LOL." Nope. You have to wait."

"Darn." I sent back "Guess I will have to wait then. Miss you." I couldn't believe I accidentally sent that last part; it was just always so routine. The buzz came back quickly.

"Miss you more than you know."

Really? I couldn't believe he just sent that. I let a depressing sigh escape. It wouldn't have mattered anyways. But the thought and fantasies were nice.

Cameron finally made it home from work, and he brought with him some vanilla ice cream and chicken livers from down the street. It was my absolute favorite meal to consume at the moment. We sat down and had dinner while I told him of my surprised text.

Cameron always felt strong about wanting me to tell Robert that I was having his child, but I couldn't bring myself to tell him. I knew where Robert stood on the whole kid thing, so this was the better option, I was not about to burden him because of my selfish decision.

Cameron sighed at the same response he always received when we discussed this topic.

"Are you going to hook up with him after the baby and see what it is he wants to give you?" He watched for my reaction.

I made sure not to give him one; I think Cameron was feeling a bit more for me than he led on currently.

"I don't know, maybe. But Then again I just don't know."

Cameron nodded and stuck a fry in his mouth from his fast food dinner. I just stared down at mine, now losing my appetite at the thought of facing Robert again. It was then that I felt a sharp pain in my stomach. It doubled me over in an agonizing way.

"Hey." Cameron leaned in to me and put his hand over mine, which happened to be precisely where the sharp stab was a minute ago.

"Yeah…I think." It took my breath away for a moment, I had to sit and allow the twinge of it dissipate away.

"Holy shit that was rough Cam."

He laughed.

"Yeah it looked it." I just stared back at him bewildered at that moment. Then it hit again, this time causing some tears to swell in my eyes.

"Oh God."

I went down to the floor. It felt like a knife being stabbed right through my abdomen. Almost like agonizing menstrual cramps times a million. It was much more intense though with the pain shooting all through my lower back. My insides were being twisted, pulled, and squeezed in all different directions.

"Cam I think it may be time. This is not normal."

"Cool…let's do this then."

I could only look up and him and let a small nervous laugh out.

"Yeah, if I can get up off the floor."

He ran upstairs to grab the overnight bag that I had just finished earlier that day. The cold cheap linoleum actually felt good on my bare legs that were covered only by the long fall skirt I wore. It came complete with the elastic waistband for fat people.

Another one came, and this time lasted longer than the last. My water had not broken yet so I started to time them as they came on stronger with each one. Great I thought, here we go. I had to laugh after that last stab thinking of Cams' response on how over dramatic women could be.

I sure would love to see him sitting here feeling this to see if his reaction would be just as colorful. It seemed like ten minutes went by while Cam was fumbling upstairs for something. Another one came on and I felt myself just instinctively starting to breathe short breaths.

If I fought the pain, it only became worse. Once I surrendered and accepted the pain, it was more bearable, but not too much. The contractions made my lower back slowly seize up. The muscles inside were slowly twisting harder and harder until it became almost unbearable. My breathing was short and shallow matching the intensity of the pain right back. Then at the point I could no longer handle them, they would slowly subside. This was much more painful than I had imagined it would be.

Cameron finally came back in the room, with keys in hand.

"OK the bag is in the car, let's go."

"What the hell took you so long?"

"Had to take care of something."

"Cam… seriously?"

"Shhh…come on dear, let's go have a kid." He smiled grabbing my arm to help me to my feet. He had a bead of sweat trickle down his forehead. It made me smile in appreciation.

"Hey Cam, Thank you."

I didn't hear the reaction. The next pain made sure of that. We made our way slowly to the car, he was trying to figure how much time we had, in relation to the distance to the hospital, I had to tell him not to worry, and just focus on getting me there. He agreed and then sped out the driveway.

They received me well at the hospital by immediately placing me into a room by myself. Cam was pacing back and forth like this was his child that was getting ready to come in to the world.

After my water broke completely is when I really felt the real pain. At first, it was a tightening that got more and more intense and then it peaked, and tapered off. If I could have had this particular pain once an hour or even once every 15 minutes, I'd have been able to tolerate it. But as luck and nature would have it, just as soon as I got through with one contraction another one would set in. That's what wore me down.

At one point it became so fierce that I had imagined that I drifted away from my body. I imagined myself walking on the beach next to the crashing of the waves, which felt just like the contractions I was feeling. Of course, that didn't work for long and my next memory was begging the nurse for the epidural. I was over the insides being wrung out like a dirty dishrag. She smiled at me, and informed both of us she would be right back with one. I let a sigh of relief.

In the corner Cam was texting his friends, I could only assume. Without lifting his focus from the current message at hand, he asked me if I needed anything from him.

"You need some ice chips or something?" He asked so calmly

"No…" I started the panting with the next contraction again

"I'm good. You OK?"

"No, not really, I just got word there was a drop and I need to be there to get it."

I knew exactly what he was referring to. I felt a wave of disappointment come over me, but told him to go do what he had to do. After all, this wasn't really his kid anyways, so he was not obligated to be here with me. He felt compelled to stay until I insisted he go. He struggled internally for a brief moment and then came to kiss me.

"I promise you, I will be right back. I will be here in time for the baby to come. OK?"

I think he was trying to reassure himself more than me. I smiled slightly and nodded.

"It's okay even if you don't, just be careful OK? I don't want to have to worry about you and having to give birth…" I laughed unconvincingly.

He kissed my forehead and out the door he went almost slamming in to the nurses as they were walking in. He yelled at them on his way out.

"I'll be right back…I have an emergency to attend to!"

"Not sure what other emergency one would have to top a woman in labor." The nurse mumbled to her coworker now approaching me.

If they only knew, I had thought.

I saw the size of the needle in the second nurses' hand. 'Oh this can't be good.'

After they sat me up, a nurse stood in front of me and one behind. The one in front had me look into her eyes, as she matched my breathing in sync with the contractions. Oh how painful it was, but she remained extremely calm and professional, and her voice seemed so soothing to my entire body for some reason. She had me focus on her lips and breathing, I felt a cold pinch at the small of my back. I was informed to take a deep breath, but that part wasn't needed, my breaths were happening how they wanted to happen. I felt the gush of the cold fluid crawling up my back to my neck. It was an almost immediate in its heavenly relief. There was almost little to no pain left. My eyes must have widened with delight, because the wonderful lady in front of me, smiled then laid me back in the bed.

They gathered their things and asked if there was anything they could do for me while I sat there by my lonesome, awaiting the birth of my child.

"No I'm good really; I just want to close my eyes."

"Great idea. You should try and rest, you will need it."

The nurses started on their way out dimming the lights for me so I could regain some strength.

A while later, I was having to push, something awful. And it felt good to push. I was having trouble with the correct kind of push though, so it made it a bit more difficult. The nurse tried to instruct me on how to push; I remember looking at this lady like she was crazy.

"Push like you have to take a poop."

The deranged look I shot her made her laugh.

"Seriously, trust me on this part. Have I steered you wrong so far?"

I had to smile, and then lay my head back because the baby was coming either way.

I don't remember much after the crowning of the head. That sent such a burn through me that made me have to leave my body for a moment.

I must have passed out at some point because I remember opening my eyes, and hearing the two doctors who were in front of the blinding white sheet they placed in front of me so I couldn't see. I saw the mirror above me, reflecting the top half of my body back at me. The light was so intense back in the eyes. I wearily looked to my left to see the nurse administering something in my tube. Everyone seemed now to be cleaning and dismantling surgery items. I turned to my right and there he was. It was Cameron. A tear ran down my face in disbelief that he actually made it in time.

He was dressed head to toe in blue scrubs; I remember smiling at the funny way the hat sat on his head. His head was not meant for that horrible cap. He sat there holding the little bundle that was wrapped in a blue cocoon. He was holding the tiny little hand and talking to him.

"Boy?" I smiled at the color of his receiving blanket they wrapped him in. Cameron looked up at me with a smile that was none I had ever seen from him before. I was taken aback by the love I could feel radiating with that look from his eyes at that moment.

"Yeah. Sure is. He's a cute lil' fellow too. Wanna hold him?"

"Of course I do, but not sure it's a good idea, seeing as I am all laid out on this bed with a sheet over half of it. I will in a minute."

"What are you going to name him?"

"Karl." I replied back

"Why Karl?" He looked puzzled.

"I just kind of like that name." I lied again. I wanted to name the baby after Roberts's ultimate paragon, Karl Jung.

"What is his middle name going to be?" He asked even more intrigued.

"Oh…you know I hadn't quite made it that far."   I had contemplated on even giving him a second name at this point now.

"Well then could I give one to him?"

I pondered just for a moment and said without any more hesitation.

"Absolutely."

"Maxwell." He said rather proudly. As if it were already premeditated.

I repeated it back for the sound alone.

"Karl. Karl Maxwell Miller. "It had a nice ring to it.

"I like it. So Maxwell it is."

He smiled and continued right back talking to the baby. I closed my eyes and fell asleep.

Choices

After Christmas things were settling in quite nicely. Little Karl was a perfect baby too. He mostly slept through the nights, hardly even crying for feeding time. His soft cry more of a whine just letting me know he needed something.

I tried to breast feed him, and the few times I had been able to were just simply amazing. His tiny little lips which were all of Robert's genes, clasped on to me ever so perfectly.

Unfortunately though, my body wasn't having any of it. The milk dried up after only a week. It bewildered the doctors as well as I. Cameron said it was a subconscious thing. He thought it had to do something with on an inner level with the whole birth and mental torment I was putting myself through. Maybe he was right on that one.

Karl's eyes were just as blue as Roberts, and to think of it Cameron's as well. But Karl's were more piercing to the soul like Roberts. His delicate skin against mine, always reassuring me that I would forever have a piece of Roberts heart. I struggled looking down into his innocent eyes, about the possibility of letting Robert know. I felt the torment of the decision with every stare at this perfect little human.

The constant nagging dilemma hung over my head like a thunderous cloud ready to unleash its fierce storm any moment.

I hadn't done a reading in a while. Honestly I couldn't even remember how long. So as little Karl napped, and Cameron was off doing what Cameron does, I thought I would sit for a moment and contemplate a decision on the matter.

I searched out my cards, and then headed down to the living room, where my coffee still sat, from earlier in the morning before feeding time. Sitting on the couch I spoke with the cards for about an hour. The conclusion the cards came to was that I needed to let him know. The tower card reared its ugly head. "Always the inevitable with you Robert." I sighed.

I sat back trying to plan it out. I grabbed my phone hanging out on the table making sure I turned the baby monitor up in the process, so I could hear Karl's angelic cry when he woke up.

I nervously sent the text to Robert.

"Hey stranger."

I could feel my heart start to palpitate in anticipation of a response. What if he didn't respond? Ugh all the torment in my head for nothing then. I would know if it was really the right thing to do, by his response… or lack of. I almost hoped he wouldn't. Maybe I was even praying for him not to respond.

The phone buzzed. My eyes were closed. I waited thinking maybe it was Cameron, It was of course Robert.

"Hey lovely lady. How r u?"

"Good." I typed back

"What are you doing?" He asked.

I had to think of something quick, I wasn't ready to deal with this right *now*. I had to mentally get myself ready, so I had to make up something on the fly. I needed a get out of dodge card just for the minute.

"Working on something. Did you still want to meet up sometime?"

I thought by saying 'sometime' that meant like a month or so.

"Absolutely. When do you get off work?"

Or I guess 'sometime' could have implied this evening. Yet another sigh escaped from my lungs. This sigh escaping was now completely out of fear. I had to make up a time. My heart was beating a million miles a minute.

"Uh- eight."

What kind of response was that? Great, now he'll think that I don't want to see him, which actually was the truth. Crap, now I was confusing myself. The waiting was killing me.

"☺ "Was all that came back.

So I sent the same vague message back.

" ??? "

"So meet me at eight thirty then, my place."

My heart sunk. I was going to be a wreck for a hot minute. This would be rough, my nerves trembling in the what-if of it all.

"OK, see you then…"

"I can't wait to give you this gift I have been holding on to. I think you will really like it."

"☺" was all I could send back.

Little Karl slept the whole afternoon. Meanwhile, I was an absolute wreck, lost in worries in seeing Robert. There were emotions flooding my body, causing me to shiver from the overload of it all. I cried. I sobbed out of panic, fear, and worry. I tried to erase the tears away so Robert would not see the face being swollen later from the streams.

I wondered how I was going to look to him, after just giving birth? Did I still show the pregnancy weight? What would he look like? Would he look older? Did he put on weight? Will there still be the attraction and connection we had, which seemed to be so long ago?

Our energies would certainly be different. The thought and dread of it all was too overwhelming for me to be alone any more on. I looked over at Cameron's bowl that was loaded with some green from the night before. I took a deep breath and thought to myself.

"Well thank God Karl is on formula." I headed for the bowl.

Later that afternoon, Cameron came rolling through the front door, with bags of goodies, and what appeared to be dinner for himself.

I had sent him a message earlier asking if he would mind watching the baby later. He of course jumped at the chance. Cam carried bags to the table, threw his jacket off, and pulled a chair out so he could inhale his fast food burger he bought on the way home.

"You want a burger? I got extras."

I had stood in the doorway just watching his madness of the all the bags and food unfold. I thought it would be better to stay out of the tornadoes way than to try and assist him in his turmoil of getting situated.

He saw me and gasped as the fry was hitting his mouth. He stopped just short of his teeth and stared, mouthed gaped open.

"Close the mouth Cam, unless you want a fly in." I pointed to the overly grown fly that looked beefed up on steroids buzzing around his head.

"What the hell, Skye? You look….wow. What is the occasion?" He was able to finally eat the fry.

"I'm going to tell him Cameron."

He put the burger on the table, leaned back in the chair as though a ton of bricks just came crashing down on his head.

"I'm watching the baby for you to go tell Him?"

"Cameron! You were the one that told me to tell him. Why is it now an issue? How can you tell me to tell him and then act this surprised when I tell you that I am? Cameron don't do this to me, you're the reason I am doing this. YOU told me to! I'm already beating myself up over this …"

I started to tear up again. I didn't think I was going to be able to handle it. He stood to place his arms around.

"Shhh…I'm sorry, it's just that….well I wasn't prepared to hear that, I guess. I'm sorry. Your right, you need to do this."

He was hugging me now. I just focused on trying to get myself together, for what the evening was about to unfold. We spoke briefly on it, then I left him with Karl to go face my fear.

Pulling in his lot, I found a spot under the only dimly lit street lamp. It was darker than normal as I noted while looking up to his window. His light was on, and in came the butterflies. I turned the car off, stepped out into the brisk cool air, and tied my belt around my sweater that was acting as a coat for the time being.

Climbing the stairs to his door, I remembered some shared moments we had in the private stairwell which made it nice for some of the rendezvous we had. I made it to his front door, and paused for a moment. I could hardly move, from all the nerves that were flooding my body right now. I found myself shivering uncontrollably. I could barely raise my hand to knock on the door. I heard the classical music playing from within his apartment. I held my hand in place, contemplating on this moment.

I didn't think I could do this. I was right. I couldn't go through with it. I caught my breath, snapped out of the panic attack and ran back down the stairs. I reached the bottom so fast, that on my way out the front door, I heard his door unlock and him opening the door. I ran to the car, jammed the keys in and took off.

My breath was panting like a lap dog, and my chest heaving up and down from the emotions. My heart was just racing. I was screaming, crying, cursing, yelling, all while pounding the steering wheel, in such rage and anger. Never have I felt so angry and disgusted with myself. The coward's way. That's what I kept hearing in my head. Oh man what had I done? I had to pull over in some restaurant lot to try and gain some sort composure back, but instead passed out.

It must have been a good hour or so. I heard the buzzing on my phone a couple times. But that was thrown on the floor in my rage. I dare not look at it. I couldn't. I had no idea why I just did what I had done. I heard the buzz again, so I fumbled for it. I found it under the back seat of the passenger side. It lit up once more

"?????" It was from Robert.

I didn't respond. Instead I just stayed in the parking lot, with closed eyes. An hour or so later, I woke from my endorphins crash, looked down at my phone to catch the time. Surely Cameron would be worried. The brightness of the screen took me off guard so I had to squint to see that there was another message on the front screen.

"Going to sleep then. Take care" it was from Robert.

I let a deep breath go. A horrible painful reminder of the bad decision I had just made earlier in the evening. I threw it to the passenger seat and headed home.

I closed the screen door as carefully as I could so as not to disturb any of the men in the house. That damn screen door still made a piercing loud creek even after being repaired. I started towards the stairs, but there Cameron was, waiting eagerly in the living room for the outcome of some movie saga. All he was missing, I thought was the popcorn."

I just blurted the ending out as if the ending didn't matter.

"I didn't go through with it."

"What? Are you serious?" He was up off the couch and in front of me.

My head hung down like I was a school girl being scolded for a bad grade or something.

"What the hell Skye? Why did you even bother going over there? Did you even see him?"

"STOP IT!"

I yelled at him, maybe secretly hoping little Karl would wake so I had an excuse to leave without explanation.

"Did you even see him?"

"I couldn't. I tried Cameron, I did try. I got all the way there, I climbed his stairs but when I got to the top of the door, I just froze. I just couldn't bring myself to do it."

"Skye, you have *got* to tell him. "

I was done with the conversation at this point. I grabbed the baby monitor and headed for my room. I didn't sleep that night. That was a shame too, because it turned out to be the little bugger's first night sleeping *all* the way through. I could think of nothing else. I was plagued with guilt, and disappointment in myself.

The depression was consuming me and it was becoming rather noticeable. Daily courage was scarce to try to fake my way through it anymore. Cameron was more than right on this. Even immersing my energies in the baby wasn't helping the thoughts and anxiety I held.

Approximately two weeks later, I was in the kitchen warming little Karl's bottle. My knees buckled for a moment causing me to instantly become light headed. I had an overwhelming emotion rush over me. It was a very sharp, deep sadness that consumed me from head to toe. I couldn't breathe for a moment. I think the revelation came to me that I had no other choice. I instantly and instinctively, reached for my phone. I could not shake this feeling.

I sent a text to Robert. I had to tell him. At this point I didn't care or worry about the outcome, because at least now he would know. I waited for the text back.

There was nothing. I sent another one. No response. My heart sunk. This was not like him. I could understand though, he was probably pissed at me so I backed off sending the multiple messages, trying to reach him.

Later that evening I asked Cameron if he would mind watching the baby while I ran to the store. I didn't want to tell him where I was really going. I didn't have the heart to face the fear and anger that met me before when I failed.

He had no problem of course with it. I took off not even thinking about the 'what ifs.' I just wanted it to be done. I pondered how I was going to tell him, but that didn't matter, I thought, just go with it and see what happens. It will come out eventually.

Clouds from storm started rolling in to greet me on the drive over there. Some rather large drops started on the windshield sooner than expected. I saw the lightening flash behind his building as I pulled up to the block. I focused too much on the drops to notice the sirens and lights in his little parking lot. The same lot I raced away so frantically from that night. I looked up at his window and stared for a movement.

What was going on? There were lights from cruisers, an ambulance, and now a Coroner pulling up? Tears filled my eyes as I saw the people wandering outside the bottom of his place. I raced past the policeman whose back was turned speaking with a man and made the same climb I did that night.

At the top of his steps his cat was calling out to me. I remember thinking how odd, he was never outside. I reach down to pick him up. Great way to break the ice, Cat. I reached with him in one arm and with the other was getting ready to knock. I had to step back because I thought I was seeing things. What the hell was this on his door? It was yellow crime tape taped all across.

I placed Cat back on the floor. I took another step back and just stared at the fluorescent yellow tape in front of me screaming in its color.

"Crime Scene- Do Not Cross."

My knees buckled and I collapsed outside on his stoop. The cat rubbing up against my folded legs now as I just stared blankly at the door. It felt as though someone took a shot gun to my head, and pulled the trigger point blank. I was in total shock. My heart shattered. My whole world now pasted with crime scene tape. What the hell happened?

"Oh God Robert. No, no, Robert."

I was sobbing uncontrollably. The door below opened. It was the man and a police officer.

"Miss Can we help you?"

"I looked down at them barely making them out through the swollen eyes.

"Where is Robert?" Was all I could muster up.

"Ma'am? Are you any relation to him?"

I said another lie, and didn't even question it.

"I'm his fiancée."

By this time the cop had made his way up to help me down the stairs. The air was cold and the rain was pouring down on us as he desperately tried to shield me from all the angry drops. I could feel the cool wind blowing from the blackened sky.

Suddenly the wind increased intensity. The trees were bending, precariously to one side like feathers being blown around.

I jumped back at hearing the loud roar above; it startled me to my core. The turbulent rumbling of the thunder dancing and howling with the wind drowned out his words. His head trying to duck between drops, I saw the lips moving but nothing being heard.

Yet again an extremely boisterous sound of thunder came rolling by. This time the thunder sounded like a gigantic train approaching, although it certainly was not that. I probably would have welcomed the train more than the storm. The sound of its rage was deeply unsettling. The tears mixed with the rain, I couldn't tell the difference.

Flashes of lightning lit up the darkened sky now continuously, followed by more cracks of thunder in reply. Just like this cop standing here replying to my question asked what seemed like an hour ago.

The responses from all the thunder were immediate and deafening. Its fury was almost spectacular if not given the current situation I was in.

I don't remember the flight down the stairs, but at the bottom right outside, with me cowering in the storm trying to make sense of his lip movements is when he uttered those words. Words I finally heard through the storm's delight. A conversation I would never forget for the rest of my life.

"Ma'am, Robert is no longer with us. It appears he shot himself."

I just shook my head back and forth. I had no idea he even owned a gun, which of course solidified how much I didn't really know of him. I let out a cry of despair and collapsed again. I was just as dead as he was now. There was nothing left. The hopelessness and the despair that filled my heart emptied what little emotion I had left. The guilt from it all was too much. What was it he wanted to give to me? I will never know, nor will he now of little Karl. What had I done?

The cop reached down pulling my soaked and shivering body back inside the lower stoop to get out of the angry rain.

"Ma'am do you have someone that you can call to come get you?"

What was he talking about? I shook him off of me and in a haze, systematically walked to the car, and started the engine. I left them standing at the bottom of the stairs. I tried to make my way from the chaos that just unfolded. I must have blacked out again, because I don't remember anything but calling Cameron then meeting him at Laurel's so they can watch Karl.

After reaching their house I saw Cameron's car already there. He met me outside and walking to the driver's side, opened the door for me. I could only make it to the front porch before I had to sit down and let the tears fall again. Cameron said not a word but just calmly rubbed my back.

I asked him for something to take the pain away for a moment. I couldn't bear this feeling anymore. I needed to be asleep so I could regroup. I just wanted the agony to stop. The mind and its thoughts were devouring my soul. There had to be something that would allow me not to feel, if only just for a while.

He tried handing me the bowl he already had in his hand. I pushed it away.

"I need something stronger Cameron."

He had to have some sort of commodity stronger than that. Drugs and animals were all he did, so surely he had some other substance to make this pain end for a moment.

"Skye, I really don't have anything stronger than some muscle relaxers."

"Ok, I'm going for a drive. I need some time to think."

"Skye...listen to you. You barely made it here."

I was shivering and shaking uncontrollably at this point. He placed his brown leather jacket around me while I pondered on his words. It didn't matter. I found what little strength I had left and walked towards my car. I think Cameron protested the whole way and maybe at one point tried to grab my keys to stop me. Who knew? But he was left in my rear view mirror with his hands in the air cursing my name.

I was heading to his main man James for a hookup. I knew his guy had stronger stuff than a dam pill. I sent a quick text to make sure James would be there. He offered just as eagerly at my request to come hang out. This guy always did like me, but he was never my type. Thankfully I only had to deal with him when Cameron was around. At his apartment we sat for a moment to converse on what exactly I was looking for. Once I conveyed what had happened, James responded.

"I have just the thing for you." He went into the other room while my phone lit up from texts from Cameron.

"Where are you?" He must have copied and pasted about ten of those to me.

I smiled and thought how funny he wouldn't know where I would be.

"Jimmy's house."

"Skye!! Please no! I'm on the way."

"Don't worry I'll be home soon."

"On the way…just stop please…don't do ANYTHING!"

I turned off the phone as Jimmy came back into the room, joining me back on the sofa. He had a mischievous smile towards me and took a deep breath. I didn't even care. I wanted to feel nothing, I wanted to be nothing.

He said to close my eyes and I did. There was a slight pinch and then a rush of pure elation. The feeling overtaking me felt like my purple robe after my showers. One huge warm liquid hug, only this one was ten billion more times comforting. Like a wonderland of winter bliss. I gagged as some sulfur taste crept in my mouth.

The sensation took back over, yanking me back to paradise. I was in the Garden of Eden just floating through. I cared about nothing, and that was exactly how I wanted it.

It might have been about twenty minutes or so when I heard the voice in the distance. "Skye…Come on. Snap out of it." I looked briefly and it was Cameron

I wasn't letting this feeling go. I was my Elysian Fields at the moment so he would have to wait for me to finish.

My eyes opened as if to convey the message, but then I felt the wetness from the rain again. This time it was piercing their way through the skin. There were all kinds of noise and commotion going on. OK I guess I better come back. I remember trying but then not. The waves came and went. I felt I was losing my grip for a minute. Turned out I lost it completely.

The sirens blaring in the background, and now I felt some tugging and pulling. It's off in the distance though; I can join them here shortly after I appreciate the non-feeling moment I was experiencing in this land of milk and honey. My eyes glued shut for the time being.

They called my name again. I really thought this time my eyes were open to greet them. I struggled haphazardly but to no avail. I had to try and make sense of all the loud noise.

Then came the blinding light, the red and white sirens, a haze caught some medics moving about. I was being whisked away in an ambulance it seemed. I heard that familiar voice in the background. It must have been Cameron trying to convince them to let him ride. Did I just hear him say I was his wife?

I didn't want to face him. In fact, I no longer wanted to face anyone. I closed my eyes, wanting it to be the last time. I could feel myself slipping into the dark. It was like I was getting caught in the undertow of a wave. I could fight but honestly, I just wanted to let go and wait until the wave released me and see where I would end up. Hopefully next to Robert.

Those words in the background, so distant and far away, came at me like a meteorite crashing into my gut. Cameron whispered in my ear.

"Please think of Little Karl, he needs you Skye."

"Oh little Karl, I had forgotten for a moment about that little guy. How beautiful his little soul was. "

It seemed so far to climb back to him right now. I didn't know if I even had the energy. Then it must have dawned on me. To not see what good came out of what we created would probably devastate me and wouldn't be what Robert would have wanted.

I tried shaking out of it, but at this point the darkness started embracing me. Struggling for a moment as the black sea swallowed me up, it seemed inevitable. Like my first encounter with Robert. I was fighting the need to succumb to the nothingness.

"Well I guess if I make it back from this, things would definitely have to change."